Tropic
OF

DECEIT

Tropic OF DECEIT

·

Christopher Larson

WILLIAM MORROW AND COMPANY, INC.
NEW YORK

It is the policy of William Morrow and Company, Inc., and its imprints and affiliates, recognizing the importance of preserving what has been written, to print the books we publish on acid-free paper, and we exert our best efforts to that end.

Library of Congress Cataloging-in-Publication Data

Larson, Christopher.
    Tropic of deceit / Christopher Larson.
        p.   cm.
    ISBN 0-688-12164-0
    I. Title.
PS3562.A75215T76   1993
813'.54—dc20   92-22214
                                                                          CIP

Printed in the United States of America

First Edition

1   2   3   4   5   6   7   8   9   10

BOOK DESIGN BY LISA STOKES

For Lyn

The island is beautiful and the people friendly, but an ambitious junior officer will find the chief attraction of the posting is the scope for initiative that a small embassy affords.

—Navidad Post Report, U.S. State Department

There is no occupation that fails a man more completely than that of a secret agent of police. It's like your horse suddenly falling dead under you in the midst of an uninhabited and thirsty plain.

—Joseph Conrad, *The Secret Agent*

The morgue smelled.

Captain Drabney gave an apologetic flutter of his hand. "It is the power cuts," he said. "I hope you haven't just eaten."

My friend Ben had seen me chatting with Drabney at the reception at the ambassador's and said we looked alike. Since I am not yet thirty and white, while Drabney is in his fifties and black, the remark took me by surprise. The police captain and I are both short, but otherwise there is not much resemblance. I am slightly overweight, while Drabney has an air of trimness achieved at great effort. His chest sticks out like a chicken in a children's cartoon show.

"Doesn't the hospital have its own generator?" I asked.

"Yes. It is not strong, though. I have spoken with the head of the hospital since the preservation of the corpse is important for forensic purposes. His position is that the living need the electricity more than the dead."

When I arrived on Navidad six months ago, I heard the power cuts were temporary. We still got them three or four times a week.

An attendant approached.

"We are here to see Richard Lee," Drabney announced with unnecessary forcefulness.

The attendant motioned us to a table. The body on it was covered by a sheet with a pattern of clowns climbing ladders, someone's charity tax deduction. Only Lee's head was visible.

"When will the doctor do the autopsy?" Drabney asked.

The attendant looked at a clock on the wall. "He was supposed to start twenty minutes ago."

Drabney sniffed. "The smell doesn't bother you?"

The man smiled. "I am used to it."

Richard Lee was a young black man in his late teens or early twenties. He had a stubble of beard. Whatever caused his death was not visible on his face. He had been good-looking.

I shook my head.

"You don't know him?" Drabney asked.

"No."

"You're sure?"

"Yes."

Drabney's eyebrows rose briefly, and he pursed his lips. "We might as well continue our conversation in more pleasant surroundings."

As we reached the door, a man in a white lab smock came through at a brisk pace.

"Are you conducting the autopsy on Mr. Lee?" Drabney asked.

"I'll be cutting up that poor bastard there," the man replied cheerily. "If that's Lee, then, yes, I'm conducting the autopsy on Mr. Lee. Who are you?"

"I am Captain Drabney, and this is Mr. Biggins, the American consul. What if he had been Lee's brother? . . . Would he have liked hearing him called a poor bastard?"

The doctor laughed. "I don't think he's Lee's brother. Not unless someone dropped him in a bucket of bleach."

I smiled, but Drabney took offense. "We have reason to believe that Lee was an American citizen. Mr. Biggins is professionally concerned. As am I. Please do your best."

"I always do," the doctor replied. He glanced at me. "I know Miss Garvey. Do you work with her?"

"No, she's in Yugoslavia now. I'm her successor."

"Oh . . . She was very good. Very efficient. I went to get a visa, and she gave me one after talking to me for thirty seconds. Thirty seconds!"

I nodded to acknowledge the compliment to a colleague.

"It was to go to a medical conference in Florida," the doctor continued. "Pathology. In the morning we learned about diseases, and in the afternoon we went to Disney World. It was very well organized."

His glance turned inward, recalling Disney World or diseases.

"Do you have any ideas about the cause of death?" Drabney asked.

"I have not yet started the autopsy," the doctor replied.

"But it was not a traffic accident——"

"So Dr. Lynch surmised. I have not yet looked at the body."

"Do you think——"

The doctor interrupted Drabney. "I will notify you as soon as my examination is completed. There is no point in idle speculation."

A man with no small sense of his own importance, Drabney could recognize the same quality in others. He turned to the attendant. "If anyone calls for me, I shall be in the cafeteria with Mr. Biggins."

We left the room. "We could take a stroll in the garden

before we have coffee," Drabney suggested. "A spot of fresh air would do us good."

The garden turned out to be a square of trees with a dry fountain in the middle. We stayed in the shaded areas, and neither of us spoke. Drabney made a production of inhaling lungfuls of air and blowing them out.

I was glad for the walk. I felt unsettled. The smell had not bothered me particularly, but I wasn't used to dead bodies.

After five minutes we went into the cafeteria and got coffee. The only dessert was rice pudding. I decided not to find out how fast it would go bad without proper refrigeration.

"Your not recognizing Lee . . ." Drabney said. "That is not unusual, is it? I mean, if he was an American tourist, you might not know him?"

"It's quite unlikely I would know him, unless he lost his passport or had some other problem that made him come to the consulate."

"I see." Drabney looked off into space. "Your countrymen do not come simply to pay a courtesy call?"

"Not usually. Is there a question about his identity?"

Drabney steepled his fingers. As on other occasions, I had the sense I might be watching an amateur production of a Noël Coward play.

"He was found on the side of Whalley Road at five this morning. He had no wallet and no papers on him. He was not even wearing underwear; just a pair of shorts and a T-shirt. Unidentified bodies are not common here, but we have a procedure. If the face is in recognizable condition, we take Polaroids and show them around. First we show them to our own men, of course. While we were doing that, one of the girls in the office recognized Lee. She had seen him last week at the Hi-Life Club."

Drabney sniffed, perhaps reproving the girl for going to the Hi-Life Club.

"She knew his name?"

"No. She thought he was good-looking, but she didn't talk with him. But the bartender remembered him; he had an American accent. We checked the Clairmont Hotel, which is nearby. The clerk told us his name. But he had checked out several days before and had not given a passport number when he registered. He paid in cash."

Drabney drummed his fingers briefly. "You understand, I did not learn of the case until past three. I called you as soon as I heard."

"I understand," I said. "I appreciate your promptness."

I don't know Drabney's exact title, but he is in charge of police liaison with foreign embassies. A month before I had been obliged to convey official displeasure at the failure of the Navidad authorities to report to me the death of one Albert King, a dual national. There was nothing mysterious about King's death—he had succumbed after falling from a ladder in his backyard at the age of ninety-one—but his Social Security checks had continued to be picked up from the consulate and cashed for eleven months after his demise.

"What was that you were saying to the doctor about a traffic accident?" I asked after a moment's silence.

Drabney had started to get up with his coffee cup in one hand. He sat back down.

"You only saw his face, yes?"

I nodded. "A car passed over his body," Drabney continued. "There was a bottle of rum next to him. The police officer who found him thought he had got drunk and fallen asleep on the road. It is not uncommon. But the doctor who looked at him when he was brought in said he must have been dead before he was run over. Dead for at least two or three hours."

Drabney went to get more coffee. At the other end of the

table some nurses were laughing. One glanced at me and smiled; I realized I had been smiling, too.

It was thanks to Richard Lee, poor bastard. His death, in circumstances that could with only slight exaggeration be described as mysterious, was the nearest thing to excitement since I started my tour of duty. It came at a good time. The first three months after reaching Navidad I had been buoyed up by the novelty of diplomatic life, but that had worn off. I had begun to see that I faced another eighteen months of granting visas and more frequently denying them, varied by the joy of writing performance evaluation reports for local employees who knew their jobs far better than I knew mine. Until now I had not even had the pleasure of assisting Americans in distress. The general Caribbean tourist boom had overlooked Navidad; not many Americans made it to the island, and those who did were annoyingly well behaved. But now things were looking up.

Drabney returned with a coffee cup in one hand and an envelope in the other. He handed me the envelope.

"U.S. Consuler, Morgue" was printed in hand on it. There was no return address.

Inside was a sheet of white paper. There were just two scrawled sentences: "Have a good time with the dead bodys. You will be one soon."

"Is something the matter?"

I felt short of breath.

It was interesting to find that simply reading something could make one feel ill. The only other time I had felt this way was during a blood drive in college; I had made the mistake of looking at a table covered with plastic bags of blood and broken into a cold sweat. This was just a piece of paper, but it was rather more personal.

I read the message over. From the viewpoint of excitement the day was coming along nicely.

"Is something the matter?" Drabney repeated.

I handed him the paper. He read it once and then carefully folded it and put it back in the envelope. He got a paper napkin and used that to grip the envelope.

"The morgue clerk gave this to me. Let's ask him how he got it."

I was sick to my stomach, but Drabney bounced out of his chair. I had to hurry to catch up.

The clerk said the envelope had been dropped off a minute after we left by a cleaning lady. We found her, and she said the secretary at the front reception desk had given it to her. The secretary told us she had found the envelope on her desk after returning from an errand.

Drabney posed a number of questions with the same point, but the secretary claimed to have no idea who might have left the envelope on her desk. She said she had been away from it for no more than five minutes. We asked other people who worked nearby, but nobody had seen anything.

"Did the people at the consulate know you were going to the morgue?" Drabney asked after finally giving up trying to extract information from a nurse's aide he had buttonholed.

"Ruby did," I said. "And Sammy."

"Well, we shall have to ask them if there were any inquiries," Drabney said. "Whoever wrote this moved fast."

"It would not have taken long to write," I said.

"No," he agreed. "Can you come with me to my office?"

"Why? Do I need to do that to make a complaint?"

"No, but I would like to take your fingerprints. We will check the envelope and paper, of course, but it would be easier if we knew which prints are yours."

I no longer felt scared. The bustling about and Drabney's businesslike attitude had made things seem normal. Even the questioning that got nowhere—somehow that struck a reassuring note.

The threat seemed more inconvenient than scary. But I could see no graceful way to refuse.

I had not visited Drabney's office before. It was in the Ministry of the Interior. The building was for senior officials and their staffs, not working police. He had to send out for fingerprinting equipment.

While we were waiting, I lapsed into silence. Perhaps Drabney thought I was afraid.

"I would not worry too much if I were you, Mr. Biggins," he said. "These threats—they always turn out to be the work of cranks. The people who do something do not write silly notes beforehand."

I grunted.

"I would tell your wife if I were you," he continued. "Otherwise she will find out and become hysterical. Tell her I said it is a crank. That will make her feel better."

"I'm not married."

He was silent for a minute. "It must be hard to come to a foreign country without someone to keep you company."

"Yes."

There was another silence. I admit I was unsociable, but he should have suggested that we go directly to a police station rather than to his office.

Finally the fingerprint kit arrived. The man who brought it pressed my hands to the paper while Drabney watched. It took only a minute.

As I got up to leave, Drabney alluded again to my marital status. "Do you have a young lady waiting for you back home?"

"No," I said. I felt more expansive now that I could leave. "There's no young lady waiting and, worse luck, no prospect of one. I am bereft of female companionship."

"That is sad," Drabney replied. "If I meet any suitable young ladies . . ."

His voice dropped off.

"Thanks," I said, wondering what sort of young lady Drabney would consider suitable.

I was supposed to meet Ben and Sarah at the American Club. I drove with the window down, and the breeze restored my mood. I looked forward to telling them about my adventures.

As I was going up the walk, one of the marine guards at the embassy stopped me and shook my hand. "Congratulations," he said.

It's odd. For half a second I thought he was congratulating me on my death threat.

"On what?"

"On what?" he mimicked. "Do you get engaged that often? Your fiancée's inside," he continued. "She's really cute. Lucky guy."

That was the first word I had of Bobbi Lyons's arrival.

"Friends—I said we were friends. Good friends," Bobbi said later that night when we were making up a bed for her in my spare room. "I never told him I was your fiancée. He made that up. Marines are pretty conservative, aren't they? Probably he thought if you had a girl visiting, she had to be your fiancée. Does this thing really work?"

Bobbi's question referred to the coil of mosquito repellent I had just lit with a match. She had asked for netting, but I didn't have any. A box of the coils had been included in the welcome package when I came to the island. A thin wisp of smoke rose from the burning tip.

"I don't know," I said. "I never use them. They're supposed to."

"Mosquitoes love me. They see my red hair and smack their lips and say, 'Lunch!' I swear they do."

I had never fixed up the second bedroom. It had just two pieces of furniture, a double bed and a chest of drawers on casters. On her inspection tour Bobbi rolled the chest back and forth a few times.

"Classy," she said.

She had not been impressed by the standard of taste achieved by the purchasers for the General Services Administration. "You'd think the government could do a deal with Leona Helmsley—give her a year off for some decorating advice."

Then the final condemnation: "This place makes Holiday Inn look ritzy."

Fortunately I had a set of clean sheets. It was hard to avoid thinking of things as we tucked them in. I wondered what she would look like lying on the bed with all her clothes off, except the green bow in her hair.

It's true, the best fantasies are the old ones.

Her appearance at the club had been a complete surprise. We had not spoken for over two years. I had not thought she knew I was in the Foreign Service, let alone where I was stationed. Of course, Bobbi had always been good at keeping track of friends who might be helpful.

I'd found her chatting with Ben and Sarah at the bar. She had landed on Navidad that afternoon. Apparently she had tried the consulate and then headed for the club as the second most likely spot. There she introduced herself to Sarah Jacoby, who confirmed that I was expected. It was lucky, but Bobbi was always lucky that way.

As we left the bar to have dinner, Sarah said tentatively, "Perhaps you'd like to be . . ."

"By yourselves" was left unvoiced. Bobbi quickly said, "Oh, no, join us."

Obviously she was feeling a little unsure of herself. Shyness was not normally part of her repertoire, but I suppose she did not normally drop in uninvited on old acquaintances expecting to be put up. And having been told I would soon be dead may have left me acting a little stiff. For some reason—shyness of my own, perhaps—I didn't mention the threat that evening.

She had, it turned out, been in Martinique for a shoot for a fashion magazine. Ben found his one moment of favor in her eyes when he asked if she had been modeling bathing suits. She laughed and said she was eight inches too short and eight years too old for modeling. The first part was probably true, although the second certainly wasn't.

It never was clear exactly what she had been doing. In response to a subsequent question of Ben's she called her work "editorial liaison and oversight." That was quintessential Bobbi talk; you didn't know whether she had been proofreading or managing the whole show. She also didn't say what was the nature of the dispute that had led to her departure.

After she quit—or was fired—a British millionaire invited her to take a cruise on his yacht.

"It seemed like a good idea at the time," she said.

She laughed ruefully. "I figured I could use a vacation from the Big Apple. Job prospects were not so good. All the places I'd be willing to work were enemy-held territory. These things change, but it takes time. Why not do the Caribbean thing? Also, I had a housing problem, and BFD was being unbearable."

The first time I heard Bobbi say "BFD" I assumed it stood for "Big Fucking Deal." I thought it was her way of cursing without actually pronouncing an obscenity. But I soon learned the initials stood for "Big Fake Daddy," her stepfather.

"I have this apartment on West Eighty-first, you know? . . . No? . . . Maybe I got it after your time. Anyway, BFD gave me the money to buy it. He gets very self-righteous about how generous he was, which is silly since obviously I'm going to inherit the money anyway, and this was just his way of avoiding paying my rent every month. He's so stingy; he makes me pay the maintenance. Fortunately it's not much. Anyway, a few months ago a lady I know asked me if I wanted to house-sit in her apartment, which is on Park Avenue and about ten times bigger and nicer than mine. Naturally I said yes. I rented my apartment—it's a condo, so no board approval or anything—and moved over to the East Side. My natural habitat really."

The candle threw a sketchy but warm glow on her. She looked extraordinarily pretty, a self-satisfied grin on her face.

"The lady swore she was going off to Paris forever," she continued after a second. "At least for a couple of years. But then, just before I head off to Martinique, I get this call from Charles de Gaulle Airport. It was all staticky and weird with those little dead blips of silence, you know? Anyway, she's coming back, and I have to move out. I was willing to be roommates, but no dice. I'm out on the street. Homelessness: *c'est moi.*"

"Couldn't you move back to your apartment?" Sarah asked.

"I'd given the guy a two-year lease. Besides, I need the rent he's paying. Otherwise Amex sends the leg breakers. So, anyway, I go to BFD to humbly ask for a little help, just a little allowance because I'm going to have this new outlay for rent, and he gets supernasty. I felt like Oliver."

We all looked blank. "In the musical," Bobbi said. "Remember? Oliver's eaten his gruel, and he asks for a little more because he's starving, and the cook or beadle or whoever goes, *'More???'* "

Bobbi picked up the sugar bowl and cupped it in her hands. Her face grew woeful: the suppliant waif in the workhouse. Sarah and I laughed.

Ben did not look amused. He was running his finger around the edge of his coffee cup, the way he does when he hears criticism of U.S. military interventions or praise for multicultural curriculum reform.

Bobbi put down the sugar bowl and resumed her tale.

"Anyway, there I was in Martinique with no job and no apartment to go back to and this English guy asks me if I want to go on a cruise. I'm so innocent. I figured he just wanted to have a friendly group of people on board, and maybe he was taking pity on me."

"So what did he do?" Ben asked. He was scowling.

"Well, he behaved abominably. In a word. Or two words. He was your typical despicable cad. It was basically either go to bed with him or walk the plank. I mean, I didn't do either, but I was going crazy keeping out of his clutches."

Ben's scowl deepened. He wears wire-rim glasses which give him a resemblance to the young Leon Trotsky. He took the glasses off and stared myopically at Bobbi.

"What did you expect when you went on board?"

"*Ben,*" Sarah said, rolling her eyes.

"I've never owned a yacht"—he plowed ahead—"but if I did and I offered someone a ride—excuse me, a cruise—I suppose I might expect something in return."

"Just one commodity for another?" Sarah inquired.

"It's not exactly that."

"Did you expect every girl you took out on a date to sleep with you?" Sarah spoke without vehemence, just her usual disbelief that she was hearing such unenlightened sentiments from her husband.

"Sure." Ben grinned. "If you don't expect women to go to bed with you, they never will. It's like selling encyclopedias," he continued. "I did that one summer. The least hint of insecurity is fatal. You have to project confidence."

Sarah slumped back in her chair and glanced wearily at Bobbi.

Perhaps it was just a case of two women presenting a common front against the obnoxious male world, but Bobbi and Sarah seemed to be getting along well. I was surprised. They had little

in common. Sarah was rather insecure, bookish, and quite intelligent. I could never make up my mind how smart Bobbi was, but
she was certainly not insecure or bookish, nor did she display
anything resembling Sarah's shy intellectual cosmopolitanism. Bobbi
relished every bit of folklore to do with the life she had led: the
prep schools she had attended, the clubs she had belonged to, the
parties she had gone to.

"What do you plan to do now?" Ben inquired.

"Find a job," Bobbi said.

"I thought you said the prospects were not so good," I said.

"I was talking about New York. I'll get a job here," she said
airily.

The silence lasted almost long enough to be uncomfortable.

"What's so strange about that?" Bobbi asked. "You all work
here."

"Not me," Sarah said.

"Well, you're married," Bobbi said. "You don't need to. But
I'm a single girl. I can't stay at Jim's house indefinitely."

Ben gave a short, sharp bark of laughter, and Sarah raised
her eyes quizzically. Bobbi turned to me. "You don't mind letting
me stay for a day or two?"

"I'd be delighted," I said.

"It's not that I don't want to work," Sarah said after a
moment. "The point is there aren't jobs. And the government is
sticky about giving foreigners work permits."

Bobbi frowned. "How about something at the embassy?" she
asked.

Ben smiled in my direction. Bobbi was my friend; I should
give her the bad news.

"It doesn't work that way."

"What do you mean?" Bobbi asked.

"Basically Americans don't get hired here to work at the

embassy. You join the State Department or some other agency, and then you're assigned to an embassy. Staffing decisions are made in Washington."

Bobbi looked into the candle. But she had never been the type to accept a no easily.

"But there have to be exceptions," she said. "Someone's really good and the embassy needs a job done. That kind of thing."

I shrugged. "Maybe if you were friends with the ambassador."

"Well, you should introduce me," she replied in a commanding tone.

Ben grinned. "We're giving the junior officers' dinner Friday week. Rollo is supposed to come. You could bring Bobbi."

Rollo was Roland Thomas, U.S. ambassador to Navidad. Even if he liked Bobbi, not impossible given his appreciation of young women, he would not create a job for her. Ben was just leading her on.

"Certainly I'll do that," I said. "But I think it would be wise to look for possibilities outside the embassy."

"Such as?" Ben asked.

There were embassy wives who taught at the school for expat children. I couldn't see Bobbi as a schoolmarm, though.

"Some Caribbean resorts have social directors," Sarah said. "There aren't a lot of resorts here, but maybe you could find something along those lines."

It was a good suggestion, but Bobbi did not appear taken with it. She tilted her head back and pondered the ceiling. "Who's the station chief here?" she asked.

It was pure luck she was turned to me and didn't see Ben gag.

"Station chief?" I echoed.

"Oh, come on," Bobbi said.

She was almost laughing. "The CIA honcho. Station chief is what *The New York Times* always calls them."

Ben's color returned to normal. "There aren't any CIA people here."

"I can't believe it," Bobbi said. Now she was laughing. "You people really say such things? Don't you feel awfully silly saying something everyone knows isn't true?"

"I wasn't saying that there's no such thing as the CIA," he announced pompously. "I merely meant that they don't have people here."

"Sure."

Bobbi smiled at Sarah: *See how silly the boys are.*

"Do you think the CIA has infinite resources?" Ben asked heatedly. "They have to concentrate where they're needed. What's there to spy on in Navidad?"

It was a question I wondered about whenever I tried to get Ben and he wasn't available.

"I have no idea," Bobbi said. "Pirates, white slavers, who knows? I'm sure there's something. Even if there isn't, I'm sure that wouldn't stop them. They'd just make something up."

Her smile acted on Ben like a red flag for a bull.

"I hate to disillusion you, but the CIA isn't nearly as ubiquitous as it's generally believed to be," he said.

The "ubiquitous" slowed Bobbi, but only for a second.

"Maybe you just don't know about it," she said mischievously. "They haven't told you."

"That's not the way they work," he said.

"Oh, really? How do you know?"

"Why do you want to know who the station chief is?" Sarah intervened calmly.

"So I could ask for a job. Obviously."

Ben looked away, trying to spot the waiter. "I've got some papers I should go over," he said. "Maybe we should be moving along."

"I think I'd make a good spy. An excellent spy. What do you think?"

She was looking at Ben. Later he told me this was the moment he realized she knew he was station chief and was intent on teasing him. He was wrong, but I didn't tell him that.

In any case he merely said, "I have no idea what it takes to be a spy, good or bad, so I can't say."

Bobbi didn't let the subject go. "It's simple. You have to be sexy," she said, lowering her voice to be sexy. "You have to know about wine and how to drive fast cars, and you have to be an expert shot. I can do all those things."

"You can shoot?" I asked.

"BFD is a gun nut. He made me take a class in pistol shooting. I was tops in the class." She pointed her finger at Ben and made a shooting sound.

It wasn't hard to see why he thought she was teasing him.

"I don't think those are the qualities people are looking for in spies anymore," I said. "Spies are supposed to be cynical middle-aged men with mortgages and unfaithful wives."

I could have spoken in Bengali for all the impact my words had.

"I think I would make a good Mata Hari," Bobbi went on. She struck a pose. " 'I regret that I have but one life to give for my country.' "

"Nathan Hale," Ben muttered.

"Pardon me?" Bobbi said.

"Nathan Hale said, 'I only regret that I have but one life to lose for my country.' "

"Oh." She turned to Sarah. "Have you noticed how it's always the man who gets credit? Mata Hari probably said it first, but this guy Hale gets the credit."

"She may have said the same thing," Ben said, "but not first unless she had a time machine. Nathan Hale was a Revolutionary War spy; Mata Hari was in World War I."

"Details," Bobbi said with a wave of her hand. "You do economics, didn't you say? You have to worry about facts and figures. The spy business is more people-oriented. That's why I would be good at it."

"HUMINT, not SIGINT," I said. Ben grimaced.

"Come again?" Bobbi wrinkled her nose in question.

"HUMINT is intelligence derived from human sources: *human intelligence.* SIGINT is data acquired from satellites and so on. It stands for 'signals intelligence.' "

"I see." She reflected briefly. "They sound like something from a show tune." She sang a few lines:

> *I'm SIGINT in the rain,*
> *Just SIGINT in the rain,*
> *What a glorious day,*
> *I'm HUMINT again.*

"That was very good," Ben said dryly. "Maybe you should go on the stage."

She shrugged. "It's too tough. A person's got to know her limitations. That was something Clint Eastwood said in one of his movies. He kept getting jumped by bad guys, and he'd beat them up or shoot them or throw them off a cliff, and while they were dying, he'd look at them and say, 'A man's got to know his limitations.' He was incredibly cool. Anyway, I know mine. Acting's not for me."

"Unlike espionage," I said for the hell of it.

"Oh, I don't say spying is a snap," Bobbi replied. "But if you get along with people, it's probably not too tough. If they like you, they'll talk to you, and you'll find out what you need to know. If you don't get along with people"—Bobbi looked at Ben, suggesting he might fall in that category—"then you probably wouldn't be a very good spy."

Sarah laughed a little more loudly than a good CIA wife should have.

"Most actors can't even get jobs in the field," Bobbi continued. "They have to wait tables to make a living. But when you're a spy, you're on the gravy train. If you want to go out to some trendy new restaurant, you just say you're meeting an agent there. Who's going to know?"

"You just have to watch out that the actor who's waiting on your table isn't studying up for a role as a spy catcher," Sarah said.

"Right," Bobbi agreed.

Ben's lips pressed tight together. For a second I thought he was going to request formal satisfaction. Pistols at dawn. No doubt I'd have to serve as second for both parties. I'd have to shoot myself if they didn't get each other.

Then Bobbi rose cheerily and excused herself to go to the bathroom. As she squeezed past Ben's chair, she gave him a pat—affectionate? condescending? threatening?—on the shoulder. She smiled at Sarah conspiratorially. We all watched her as she walked off.

"I like her," Sarah said.

Ben did a drumroll on the table with his fingers.

"What is it about her you don't like?" I asked.

Ben looked at me. "I don't want to criticize a friend of yours."

"I haven't seen her for years. We're not close."

After a few seconds' hesitation he spoke. "I told you, didn't I, that my dad was a Trotskyite?"

I nodded. That was what had made me realize the likeness between him and the photograph of Trotsky.

"A Trotskyist, my dad would say; 'Trotskyite' was the word the Stalinists used. . . . He died a month before I graduated college. He was a Trot to the last. . . . I never got along with him. He was a jerk. Always talking about the oppressed and always acting like a bastard to everybody, my mother and me especially. I can't remember a time I didn't think he was full of shit. Especially his politics."

"What does all this have to do with Bobbi?" Sarah asked.

"It's simple," Ben replied. "I hear her complaining about how Daddy won't give her an allowance and the apartment he bought her isn't very nice and her yachting boyfriend is too fresh, and it gives me a creepy feeling. Like maybe my father was right. Maybe we *should* expropriate the expropriators. I mean, I don't really think so. But if I'm going to destabilize Marxist governments and assassinate foreign leaders in good conscience, I'd like to think it's for the sake of a citizenry that believes in Emersonian self-reliance, not a Bloomingdale's charge account."

"I didn't think there were any Marxist governments left to destabilize," I noted.

"Yeah—I got all kinds of problems," Ben said forlornly.

No one was talking when Bobbi returned.

"Such silence," Bobbi commented. "Was I the topic of conversation?"

"Ben was telling us about his childhood. The psychosocial origins of neoconservatism," Sarah said.

The conversation shifted to other topics. We left not much later.

After making up the bed in the spare room, Bobbi and I went into the living room. I had a brandy; Bobbi drank club soda.

"Sarah seemed very nice," she said.

"Yes."

"Ben. . . ." She drew out the syllable and rolled her eyes.

Then she laughed. "But he's your friend," she added in the same tone Ben had used earlier.

"Yes."

"Do you see him often?"

"I guess he's my best friend here on the island."

Bobbi looked at me inquisitively.

"I enjoy his company."

I said it defensively. For someone whose opinion on any serious subject was laughable, Bobbi was very good at putting me off-balance.

She took a sip of her club soda. "I want to thank you for putting me up."

"It's no problem. As you see, I have plenty of space."

"It's very good of you. I should find a place of my own in a week or two. As soon as I get a job."

I shrugged. "There's no rush."

Right at the moment Bobbi didn't want to discuss her future. She reverted to Ben.

"Maybe it's because he's an economist."

"What?"

"Why I didn't get along with him."

"Oh." I stretched back on the couch. It had been a long day.

"The dismal science. That's what they call it, right?"

I was surprised she got it right. "Yes."

"Economists are not fun-loving types. But I'm a fun-loving girl."

I laughed.

"Don't you agree?" Bobbi asked.

"That you're a fun-loving girl, yes. That economists aren't fun-loving types, well, no. Some are; some aren't."

Grant brushed against my leg. I picked him up and put him on my lap. He's a neutered black cat that I was watching for the ambassador's secretary while she was on vacation.

Bobbi was staring at me.

That was when she guessed. What I said about economists could not have tipped her off; at least the words themselves couldn't have. Maybe my tone was a little off. Or maybe she just had a flash of telepathy.

"Ben is not an economist," Bobbi said.

"Of course he is," I said.

That was wrong. I should have said, "What do you mean?" I shouldn't have indicated that I understood she was calling him a spy. But it probably didn't make any difference.

"Is he the station chief?" she asked. "Oh, he's got to be. This place is small potatoes. He's probably the only person the CIA has here. I can't believe you didn't let me know." She sounded quite angry. "You could have kicked me under the table or something. You could have winked."

"Bobbi, this is ridiculous." I saw myself pointing at Ben and silently mouthing "CIA." It was hard not to laugh. I felt a small qualm of conscience at the poor job I was doing of maintaining his cover. I made one last attempt. "Ben is an economics officer."

She did not waste time rebutting me. "You just let me go on and on about how he would never be any good as a spy. How do you think he's going to feel about giving me a job now?"

Bobbi's arrival coupled with Drab-
ney's assurances put the death threat temporarily out of my mind,
but as the hours passed, I found my worries returning. "Crank"
was another word for "nutcase," and quite a number of people
had been killed by nutcases. What about Lennon's killer and John
Hinckley? Couldn't they have been described as cranks? I made
the mistake of saying this to Ben the next morning when I told
him about the threat. I got a heavily ironic silence in return. I
knew I wasn't as famous as Lennon or Reagan, but still, as U.S.
consul on Navidad I have a certain visibility.

But Ben did say I should tell Linda about it. Linda Wolf was
DCM, deputy chief of mission. She made sympathetic noises, but
obviously she shared Drabney's opinion. Similar threats had been
received every month at her first post, Manila. However, she sent
a cable to the regional security officer in Jamaica. The RSO cabled
back that I should cooperate with the local authorities and sug-

gested stationing a marine at the consulate for a month. There were not enough marines to do that and man the guard post at the embassy, so we got a guard from the company that provided security for the ambassador's residence.

Drabney called on Thursday afternoon, just after I had finished telling the guard about his duties. He had received my instructions—which were simply to keep an eye out for suspicious individuals—with such exaggerated seriousness that I ended up feeling ridiculous; consequently I did not press Drabney when he said the fingerprint inquiry had proved fruitless and reiterated his view that there was nothing to get excited about. I decided I had been worrying too much.

It emerged that the death threat was not Drabney's reason for calling. He had received the report on Richard Lee's autopsy.

"He died of an embolism, Mr. Biggins. Of stroke."

"Stroke? But he was quite young . . ."

"Yes. But the risk of stroke increases materially when you are scuba diving."

I was too surprised to reply.

"Apparently he was swimming at great depth and ascended too quickly. The nitrogen which had dissolved into his blood under pressure boiled out and caused the embolism. That, at least, is what I understood the autopsy report to say; I am not expert on this subject."

Neither of us spoke immediately.

"A couple of days ago you said something about his having been run over," I remarked.

"Yes," Drabney agreed. "The amount of bruising made it clear this took place some time after he died."

There was another silence.

"It's odd," I said.

"That he was run over after he was dead? Yes, it is odd."

"Do you think he was murdered?"

Drabney sighed. "The doctor—I called him after I read the autopsy report—said that this sort of death was a common accident for scuba divers. His body being on Whalley and the car passing over it—actually the marks indicate it was a light truck—those circumstances are, I agree, suspicious. It would be premature to speak of murder, but certainly the matter warrants further investigation."

I was surprised that Drabney conceded there were any grounds for suspicion. On the few occasions I had dealt with him in the past he had been extremely reluctant to admit that anything improper might happen on Navidad.

"The bartender at the Hi-Life—I told you Lee went there— saw Lee talking with a man. The bartender knew the man. His name is Winston Mannion. We have had dealings with him."

"We?"

"The police. Mannion is not a reputable fellow; he gets into fights and he is a thief. We talked to him this morning. He admitted driving Lee around to beaches to go scuba diving. That jibes with the autopsy report. Anyway, he said Saturday and Sunday they were at Jack's Creek. Do you know it?"

"No."

"It is quite a small place. It is near the Hook. Not in the Hook, but right where it starts."

The Hook is a large jut of land that early sailors thought resembled a fishhook. The terrain is too hilly and hard for farming, and in the old days it was a haven for slaves who escaped from the sugar plantations. It continued to maintain an unruly autonomy after emancipation and even after Navidad's independence. Thirty years ago most Navidadians, blacks maybe even more than whites, would have described the residents of the Hook as uncivilized savages. That language wasn't used anymore, but the attitude persisted. The inhabitants of the Hook had an equally unflattering opinion of their countrymen.

"Mannion said Lee rented a boat and went diving off the Hook. Sunday, he said, Lee never came back. I think he knows more than he is saying, but that is all we could get out of him. The lieutenant in Beverley is making inquiries. . . ."

"Yes?" I prompted.

"I must confess, I am not confident he will be successful. It is quite unlikely anyone will talk to him. It occurred to me, though, that you might have better luck."

"Me?"

"If you went to the Hook, Mr. Biggins. Of course, I realize you are quite busy, but since Lee was a fellow citizen . . ."

His voice trailed off.

"I'll be glad to, if you really think it might do some good," I said. None of the pending IV—immigrant visa—cases were urgent; I could certainly take an afternoon or two off.

"Oh, yes," he replied enthusiastically. "I think it might be quite helpful."

I told him I would go the following day, late in the afternoon. He was delighted.

That evening I told Ben of Drabney's call. After I finished, he gave me a pitying look. "You really don't see why Drabney agrees this is all very suspicious and wants you to go nosing around?"

I hate it when he gets superior like that. But I was curious.

He smiled. "Basic political geography. Something bad happens to a foreigner in Wellington, he just wants to sweep it under the rug, naturally. But if it's in the Hook, that's another story. If it turns out Lee was killed there, that's a weapon the PLA can use.

They can embarrass Cort and the other bosses. Hell, if they're lucky, they might even come up with some kind of criminal charge."

The PLA was the People's Labor Alliance. It was the ruling party, but it had virtually no support in the Hook. Cort, I dimly recalled, was the leader of a union in the Hook that was supposed to be more than commonly corrupt.

"Don't you think you might be overinterpreting?" I asked. "Couldn't Drabney simply be doing his job?"

"No, I don't think so." He snickered. "It's really a beautiful setup from the PLA point of view. They could smear Cort and make us look stupid at the same time, and we'd be doing the work for them. That is"—he paused and looked at me—"you'd be doing the work for them."

The PLA was far enough to the left to enjoy embarrassing the United States. But I still didn't follow Ben's reasoning.

"Why would we look stupid?"

His expression grew pained. "I know you haven't been here long, but you could read a little. We're the great defenders of the Hook—didn't you know that?" He took his glasses off and ran his fingers through his hair. "Rollo's predecessor had to explain a couple of years ago why we were cutting back on aid. The reason, of course, was that we wanted to keep the money ourselves, but he didn't say that. He talked about human rights and how the PLA didn't treat people in the Hook right. . . ." The snicker returned. "He even compared it with the Iraqi treatment of the Kurds. I doubt anyone in the PLA had ever heard of the Kurds—probably most of them don't know from Iraq—but they knew they weren't being complimented. Now if it turns out our poor defenseless friends in the Hook have been murdering Americans, well, I'd say we'd look kind of stupid."

I didn't speak for a while. "Well, I told Drabney I'd go," I finally said.

"Oh, you've got to go." Ben clapped me on the shoulder. "A consul's got to do what a consul's got to do. I wouldn't worry about looking stupid. . . ."

He looked at me. "Be careful, though. The Hook is a little rough. A stranger going around asking questions—the PLA is not necessarily the only thing those people there don't like."

4

Bobbi invited herself along the next day. I tried to dissuade her, but she said it sounded like fun, and besides, she had gone to the Apollo Theater in Harlem once, so what terrors could the Hook hold?

Actually I was glad to have the company. She slipped her sandals off as soon as we were in the car and propped her feet up on the dashboard. She slathered sunblock on her legs and hummed Springsteen tunes. Her knees were covered with big light freckles. She had painted her toenails bright pink. Gravity drew her thighs down in a soft and seductive line.

"Keep your eyes on the road, Jim," she said coolly.

It was a clear day, and the sun glinted brilliantly off the water.

"God, this place is beautiful," Bobbi said after a minute. "I can't believe the government pays you to work here. They should charge you. What a racket. Sarah says you get U.S. holidays *and* local ones. Is that true?"

"Yes."

"What a racket."

She sighed in ostentatious envy and leaned back against the side of the car. Neither of us spoke much. The roads of Navidad require constant attention if you want to survive. Bobbi was absorbed in the scenery.

I had met her four years ago, when she came to work at Hexter. It was some months after she started that someone pointed out her first day had been April Fool's.

I. J. Hexter is a small publishing house in New York City. It is best known for its textbooks and scientific journals, but Bobbi and I worked on a biweekly aimed at high school social studies teachers.

The work consisted of summarizing news developments, pointing out historical comparisons, and making suggestions for classroom discussion. It was, once you got the hang of it, quite an easy job. With its mildly educational aura it attracted people who liked a flavor of academia but were too dilettantish to pursue regular careers in it. The president of the company contributed to this atmosphere. Arthur Hexter was the son of the company's founder and had gone into publishing out of a sense of filial obligation. The company did not put out the sorts of books that become best sellers, but I think if it had, Arthur would gladly have traded away any such success for a term's dining privileges at an Oxford high table. He was an avid reader of journals of opinion and serious books, or at least reviews of serious books. Not having much to do in the way of work, he prowled around the office, looking for someone to talk to. The writers on *Events and Issues* were favorite targets. This became awkward on those occasions— the last day or two in each issue cycle—when we were actually busy. Generally, however, we had time to spare.

It was not a job for ambitious people. Most people, ambitious or not, left after a couple of years. I was one of the more treatment-resistant cases; I was there for six years.

Bobbi did not fit the pattern. Before she took the job, she had had interviews at *Time* and *Esquire* and other well-known magazines. Even though she didn't get a job at any of them, we were all impressed by the matter-of-factness with which she assumed she would eventually inhabit the upper echelons of the journalistic world. At the age of twenty-two she seemed to know scores of writers and editors.

How she acquired those contacts was something of a mystery. She had gone to a couple of decent but far from illustrious colleges. She spoke often of Harvard; you had to listen closely to discover she had attended one summer session. But however she managed it, she did know a good many people.

Looks undoubtedly helped. Bobbi was quite pretty. She was short—about five feet one—and slim. She had red shoulder-length hair and a redhead's coloring: pale, with abundant freckles. Her eyes were greenish blue. Her lips were broad and sensual. To judge by the way she looked in the pastel-shaded cashmere sweaters she wore, she had large breasts.

She liked to say, "Drugs, sex, and rock and roll," when the conversation flagged, but this always struck me as an advertisement that she was hip rather than an accurate description of her lifestyle. I doubt Bobbi ever even smoked marijuana; she was not the sort of person to relax conscious control. And her sex life, if it existed at all, she handled with great discretion. Most Mondays I got an earful of her activities over the weekend, and these usually included outings to clubs or galas with Wall Street lawyers or investment bankers. She spoke of her escorts as boorish moneybags whom she kept firmly at arm's length. Why she continued to go out with them was a paradox that was never explained. Or perhaps the explanation was self-evident: They had money.

Bobbi was one of those people who evoke a strong reaction.

Several of the writers took an instant and intense dislike to her. I liked her from the start, although I was never quite sure why.

I suppose the main reason was variety. I was used to people who were poor and intellectual and bashful about putting themselves forward. Bobbi was none of the above.

I saw a good deal of her because I had the job of training new writers. In most cases this was not complicated. It was largely a matter of creating an awareness that our subscribers were not interested in the latest advances in deconstructive interpretation or neo-Marxist feminism. With Bobbi, though, I had to start from scratch. She had glided through college on a combination of charm, bluff, and prompt completion of assignments. Not being slowed down by worries about spelling, subject-verb agreement, or logical coherence undoubtedly helped with the last.

The historical sidebars that accompanied the accounts of current affairs were an especial torture for her. "I was never that interested in dates and wars and stuff," she once confided, an attitude that could have indicated a preference for social or economic history but in her case did not.

Her ignorance of dates and wars and stuff was really quite impressive. She had a hunch that the French Revolution took place in France, but naming a specific century was beyond her. The incident that really did her in with Rhonda, the editor, was when she asked idly if Shakespeare was Victorian or Edwardian. Later Bobbi claimed she had been talking about the costuming for a particular production. Rhonda's response to this was a succinct "No way."

She lasted nine months. At Hexter there was no fast track even when it came to terminating hopeless cases. Still, I think Rhonda was ready to fire her considerably before she finally did, but she hesitated because Arthur seemed to be taking an interest in her.

They went out together three or four times in all. From

Bobbi's point of view, Arthur was too low-wattage to warrant a serious commitment. And Arthur, while not immune to Bobbi's charms, was too much of an intellectual snob to get serious about a girl who thought Rasputin was a new flavor of ice cream. Arthur was also thirty years older, but that was not a problem for either of them.

When Rhonda finally did give her notice, Bobbi interpreted it as a reaction to the dates with Arthur.

"She said something?" I was surprised; Rhonda's remarks about Bobbi had grown increasingly critical, but they referred only to her work.

"No, of course not. But I'm not blind. We're talking a serious green-eyed monster situation."

She was wildly off target. But even though the dismissal was amply warranted, I was sorry to see her go.

That feeling lasted a week. Then I got a phone call from her suggesting lunch. Just before she rang off, she mentioned she would be starting her new job at *Time* the following week. The contacts had come through.

It was not quite as outrageous as it first seemed: Her name never appeared on the masthead, and her job, which she never described in detail, was something modest in connection with a new project that might never see the light of publication. This was a minor consolation.

We continued to meet occasionally. I couldn't hold a grudge against her; she was too high-spirited and happy. I enjoyed walking down Madison Avenue with her, having her point out unattractive women and say, "There's your date for tonight." I admired the self-possession with which she would send her bran muffin back two or three times if it was not toasted precisely the way she wanted it, and I liked the way she would, as we were taking our separate ways, drop her voice an octave and say, "Good-bye, Mr. Bond," with exactly the intonations of Goldfinger or Dr. No.

One day I called her office and was told she no longer worked there. When I had seen her two weeks before, there had been no hint of a change in the offing. I tried her home, but the telephone had been disconnected. Maybe I called information; I don't remember. I did not expect ever to see her again.

Her appearance on Navidad was a complete surprise. But it was appropriate that she came back into view as a refugee from a yacht owned by a lecherous millionaire.

I looked at her. Her head was resting against the door, and her eyes were closed.

We entered the Hook; the road became even worse. We hit a bump, and her eyes fluttered open. She saw me looking at her.

"What's up, *kemo sabe?*"

"We'll reach Beverley pretty soon."

Beverley was the main town in the Hook.

"That's good." She yawned and stretched. "Don't worry. We'll make a great team. Holmes and Watson."

"Who's who?"

She smiled cryptically and closed her eyes.

When we got to Beverley, Bobbi went looking for a straw hat. We agreed to meet in an hour at a restaurant by the beach.

The police lieutenant was an athletic-looking man about my age. Working in the Hook had demoralized him. When I asked what inquiries he had made, he threw his hands into the air.

"I showed Lee's picture at the Ramble and Binneman's—those are drinking places where everyone goes—but no one had seen him. I asked the schoolteacher. She is from Wellington, of course—no one here knows how to read, let alone how to teach—but she did not know anything. I didn't want to ask questions about scuba divers."

He paused, looking at me. I nodded. The police were reserving the information about how Lee died. If a truck had been driven over Lee in an effort to disguise the cause of his death, there was no call to advertise the fact that the deception had failed.

"I did go to the pier, though, and show his picture." He laughed. "That was hopeless. Those fellows are all FL. They just spat at me."

"What is FL?"

The lieutenant's lip curled, and he laughed bitterly. "Fishermen's League. Cort's gang."

I should have recognized the initials; I had heard of the Fishermen's League. "That's the union he heads."

The lip curled again. "That's what Cort calls it. It is the gang that runs this town. All the stores—all the stores Cort doesn't own—have to pay FL money if they want to stay in business."

After talking to Ben, I had looked at the embassy file on Cort. The newspaper clippings were all from the *Bugle* and all savagely critical. Since the *Bugle*, besides being Navidad's sole regularly published paper, was also an organ of the PLA, that was to be expected.

The embassy bio observed the guarded tone the department uses for human rights reports on allies that are not above reproach. Cort was the subject of numerous unproven allegations, the writer observed. His first job had been as a janitor of a store in Beverley; when the owner fired him instead of giving the requested raise, it was said that Cort had knocked the man out, cut him, and then towed him through shark-infested water. It was perhaps not surprising that witnesses to his alleged crimes had been reluctant to come forward. In addition to the power he wielded as president of the FL, he was mayor of Beverley and an elected member of the Navidad Senate. He hadn't been seated because the PLA majority contested the legitimacy of his election. He was quite intelligent and articulate, the author of the bio said. He was around fifty now.

"If Lee was killed, I am sure the FL did it," the lieutenant said. "But you will never prove it."

The lieutenant clearly thought I was on a hopeless mission; I was beginning to feel the same way. But at least it made a break from routine.

Beverley is situated on a small bay. There are three streets running perpendicularly from the water's edge to a hill a few hundred yards away. It is not a picturesque place, not unless you find weathered storefronts with cleaning supplies in the windows picturesque.

I had a photograph of Lee I could show people, but first I wanted to try out an idea I had had. Why not see if I could enlist Cort's aid directly? The lieutenant had looked shocked when I proposed this, but he didn't offer any reasons to change my mind.

An attractive young black woman came to the door at the mayor's office. She couldn't have been more than eighteen.

"I was told I might find Mr. Cort here," I said.

She made no motion to open the door wider. "Who told you that?"

"A man at the police station."

"Griggs?"

"Yes."

She smiled. "You don't ask Griggs about Cort. He don't know anything. He's too busy being scared."

"I take it he's not here, then," I said.

As I spoke I remembered how Bobbi used to stick her tongue in her cheek whenever I said, "I take it . . ." I felt a flush creeping over my face.

"Who are you?" the girl asked eventually.

"My name is Jim Biggins. I'm the U.S. consul. I was hoping Mr. Cort could help me with an inquiry I'm making into the death of an American citizen."

She studied me a few more seconds, then nodded. "He's

down at Uncle Peter's. I'm going to meet him. You can come along."

We walked back toward the shore. The girl's name was Lucy. I told her about Richard Lee and showed her his photograph, but she didn't recognize him.

Along the way we passed a parked Volkswagen with diplomatic plates. The first two digits of the number were 51, which I was pretty sure signified that it was Cuban. All U.S. vehicles had numbers starting with 17.

"Brother Man," Lucy said with a soft laugh.

"Pardon me?"

"That car," she said, pointing at it. "That's Brother Man's."

This time I heard the capitals dropping into place.

"Who's that?" I asked. "Is he Cuban?"

"Yeah." Lucy smiled. "He's Cuban. He's friends with Cort. We call him Brother Man 'cause he's always talking about how whites and blacks are brothers. Brothers under . . . society?"

"Socialism?"

"Yeah. That's it."

The file had said nothing about Cubans befriending Cort. It was surprising since the Cubans had fairly good relations with the PLA.

If Cort himself said anything, I might have enough for a memcon. Having a memorandum of conversation in my file would help my chances if I applied to switch from the consular cone to the political. That was down the road, but I had spent enough time stagnating at Hexter not to want to repeat the experience in the State Department.

We walked down to the water's edge. "How much further is this Uncle . . . ?" I asked.

"Uncle Peter's? There it is."

She pointed to the restaurant where I had agreed to meet Bobbi.

Bobbi waved. She was holding a drink against her chest, laughing at something said by the man standing next to her. He was a very big black man wearing swim trunks and a "Virginia is for Lovers" T-shirt. When he turned to see whom Bobbi was waving at, I noticed a long scar running along the side of his neck.

"That's Cort," Lucy said. "The one with the pretty white girl."

Lucy and I sat down at the table. Cort shouted for a waiter and then settled into a chair. He was six feet three or four and must have weighed nearly three hundred pounds.

Cort turned to Bobbi. "This is the one you were talking about?" he asked, pointing to me. "This is the one who told you that story?"

Bobbi nodded.

"Mr. Biggins, you should know better than to tell foolish stories like that. An American like you, you shouldn't believe all that PLA propaganda."

"I'm afraid I don't—"

"About me killing my old boss. That shark stuff—that's just plain foolishness. I try to tell that to this pretty lady here, but she just laughed at me. And after what I did for her . . ." Cort shook his head in dismay.

"So how'd you end up getting the store?" Bobbi asked.

"I told you that. I told you that." Cort's voice was surprisingly high-pitched. He looked to me. "I told her, but she wouldn't listen."

He looked back at Bobbi. "After Mr. Shays died—that was my boss—after he died in a fishing accident, his widow asked me to run the store." He waved his hand to embrace the surroundings. "This is a pretty rough town for a woman by herself. Especially back then. Now we have a good mayor who keeps everything nice and peaceful. . . ." A big grin spread over his face.

"Anyway, Mrs. Shays knew I was big and strong and would do a good job. Then, when she died, she left the store to her son, but he was working in Port Royal and didn't want to come back. He sold it to me. That's all there is to it."

Bobbi raised her eyebrows but didn't say anything. Her eyes looked brighter than usual, and her cheeks were slightly flushed. I had seen her excited like that in New York when she struck up a conversation in an outdoor café with a man who owned a business magazine. The man didn't quite offer her a job on the spot, but he came close to it.

"Mr. Biggins wants to ask you about a dead man," Lucy said. "Some American. He's got a picture."

I said something about what a benefit it would be to get the aid of the mayor and then handed the photograph to Cort. He held it at arm's length.

"You get old, you can't see things close so good," he said with a smile. " 'Less they're real pretty, like Miss Lyons here."

Bobbi yawned for effect.

Cort studied the photograph. Then he handed it to a waiter and told him to put it in a safe place.

"I'm afraid I need the photo," I said, taken by surprise. "I want to see if anyone here recognizes it."

"Oh, you leave all that to me, Mr. Biggins. You go around asking people to look at a picture, they won't know what to think. People here, they don't much trust strangers. They sure as anything won't help you. If anyone's seen him, I'll find out."

Our eyes met for a couple of seconds. I had intended to ask for help, not leave the inquiry in his hands. My vision of myself as Philip Marlowe on a case was dying a quick death. But he was probably right.

Cort wanted to know why I was asking about Lee in the Hook if his body had been found elsewhere. I gave him the story

Drabney and I had agreed on, that Lee had said he planned to visit the Hook. Cort nodded impassively.

"I'm doing this for you," he said after a minute, "maybe you can do something for me."

"What's that?"

I was sure he would ask for a visa, either for himself or for a relative.

He smiled broadly. "Ask your friend to dance with me. I asked her, but she said no."

"It's too hot," Bobbi said. She leaned back and laughed.

"It's not hot anymore," Cort pleaded. "It's nice and cool." He turned to me. "You ask her—tell her it'd be a nice thing for our countries. It'd make for good relations."

Bobbi was sipping on the straw in her drink. She seemed to be enjoying the situation greatly.

"The thing is, Americans don't dance on government orders," I said. I was still a little annoyed at Cort's taking the photograph.

"No?" He looked despondent.

"There's no music," Bobbi said. "There's no place to dance."

"That's no problem," Cort answered. He waved at the waiter. "Move out those tables there. Make a space."

The waiter bustled off. The people at the tables got up quickly.

"Macho, give us a song," Cort shouted at a small man standing at the bar. "You like 'Lemon Tree'?" he asked Bobbi.

"Sure." She looked at me and shrugged her shoulders.

In a minute the waiter had cleared a small space. The man Cort had addressed as Macho stepped forward and started singing a cappella. Cort bowed toward Bobbi and offered his hand. They began dancing.

"Cort seems to have influence here," I said to Lucy after a minute.

"He owns this place."

"Oh."

"Everyone comes here if they got the money." Then she smiled. "Everyone except Griggs."

After a second I remembered the police lieutenant's name.

"I suppose he wouldn't come here," I said.

"He and Cort don't get along," Lucy added. "They're enemies. I mean, Griggs thinks they're enemies. Cort thinks Griggs is a little insect. A lizard."

"I don't think lizards are insects."

"They run around on the floor and you step on then. What's the difference?"

> Lemon tree,
> Very pretty,
> And the lemon flower is sweet . . .

The sun had dipped low. Its rays glinted off Bobbi's hair and a gold chain around Cort's neck. He looked awkward as he moved around, hunched far over to bring his head down to Bobbi's level. She was smiling as though he had said something quite funny. Or maybe she was just amused to be dancing with a Caribbean gangster.

The dancers came near our table. Cort leaned toward me. "Why don't you dance with Lucy there?" he asked. "She's a pretty girl."

Lucy was smiling lazily. She seemed remarkably self-possessed for such a young girl.

"Would you care to dance?" I asked.

She rose and took my hand. For a while we danced in silence. I thought about the memcon I was planning to write, wondering how much setting of the scene was customary. Presumably I could omit the pressure of Lucy's breast against my chest.

Macho started singing another song. "Is she your girl friend?" Lucy asked.

"What?"

"The lady Cort's dancing with—is she your girl friend?"

"Bobbi?" I glanced and saw her pull Cort's arm up onto her back. It had drifted lower. "No, she's just someone I know from New York."

"She must be a good friend, coming all this way to see you."

"She was visiting the islands."

We danced without talking for a while. Lucy kept an eye on Cort and Bobbi. "How long is she going to stay?"

"I don't think she's made up her mind."

"Oh," Lucy said. "Where's she staying?"

"Actually I'm putting her up. I have a spare bedroom."

Lucy gave a soft laugh.

The possible shark fisher glanced over. "Having a good time, Mr. Biggins?"

I smiled back awkwardly.

"What's the name of the Cuban who has that car?" I asked Lucy.

She puckered her mouth. "Caras? Carara? Something like that. It's a Cuban name."

"Has Cort known him long?"

"A month or two. No, maybe longer—I remember seeing him on my sister's birthday. He and Cort got some business they're working on. A hotel, I think."

Lucy didn't know any details. We sat down after the next song; Cort and Bobbi joined us a little later. Cort tried to keep an arm around Bobbi, but she disengaged herself in a friendly but efficient manner.

Bobbi informed me that we were staying for dinner at Cort's invitation. She and Cort did most of the talking, with Bobbi telling of clubs she had gone to in New York and Cort describing his early days. The self-portrait that emerged was of an unscrupulous but basically appealing go-getter. It was only when he spoke of the PLA that a tone of strident self-pity entered his voice.

"I tell you, Mr. Biggins, I am a black man and the prime minister is a black man. You know what that means? It means that whenever he gives a speech about how bad whites are, I just laugh. I laugh because I have never been treated as bad by a white man as by those PLA bastards."

I think he expected me to weigh in with a hearty condemnation of the PLA. I said something vapid and noncommittal.

Bobbi laughed. "Jim always sees the other side; that's why he's such a good diplomat. He'll let someone walk all over him rather than do something that looks selfish. He's more scared of looking selfish than of anything."

I thought of telling Bobbi that my ability to see other points of view was why I enjoyed her company. Instead I spoke to Cort.

"I hear you are discussing a venture with the Cubans. A hotel, is it?"

Annoyance came and went on his face.

"Yeah, something like that."

It was clear he didn't want to discuss the matter. Lucy saved me the need of making a direction question.

"We saw Brother Man's car on the street," she said. "What's his name? Caras?"

The annoyed look returned. Then he smiled, apparently deciding to make the best of it.

"Carreras." Cort laughed. "He keeps coming here to check out sites. I told him and I told him, the best place for a hotel—the best place in all Navidad—is right up there, next to the old mill." He waved his hand at a bluff overlooking the bay. "But that's FL property, and I guess he thinks I'm trying to cheat him or something."

I asked a few more questions, but Cort was not forthcoming.

He described the hotel as a sort of aid project for a depressed region. I didn't find out whether there had been anything more than talk or why the Cubans were prepared to channel aid to a region to which the government was not favorably disposed. Still, it seemed like enough for a brief memcon.

After dinner Cort prevailed upon Bobbi to dance again. Macho had disappeared, but a cassette player was unearthed and put into service. Lucy danced with someone she knew from one of the other tables.

I sat in my chair, feeling bloated. I had eaten too much. It was much better than the club food.

I didn't know what to make of Cort. He was very pleasant and, according to the file, a crook and a murderer. It was like something in a movie. Maybe for that reason I found it hard to credit. In my experience people were less colorful and less evil than their reputations. But then, perhaps the experience gained in a small-time publishing house was no longer relevant.

Cort, in any case, seemed completely absorbed by Bobbi at the moment. It was a slow song now, and he shuffled back and forth like some big, heavy piece of machinery running out of power.

It was purely by chance that I glanced at the bar when I did. The bartender moved his hand jerkily; he had been pointing at me. The man next to him was looking down at something; then he raised his eyes and looked at me.

We stared at each other for five seconds. Then he put down what he had been looking at and walked away. The bartender moved a few paces and started chopping viciously at ice.

I was sure the man had been looking at Lee's photograph. I wondered if he had been seeing the face for the first time. He certainly had seemed interested in it and in me.

Sometime later Bobbi decided she had had enough. She playfully pushed Cort away and refused to listen to any pleadings to stay longer.

On the drive back she told me how she had met him. She had been trying on straw hats at a tiny store. When she left without buying anything, the salesman ran out and grabbed her by the wrist. Maybe he was annoyed with her failure to buy; maybe he just wanted her to try on another hat. Bobbi didn't know.

"Anyway, there I was with this guy jabbering at me and I'm pulling one way and he's pulling another, and all of a sudden I hear someone shout, 'Let her go.' I mean, I heard it, but I don't think the guy heard it 'cause he keeps holding on to my wrist and yelling at me. Then all of a sudden he's lying on the ground. I hadn't even seen Cort, but there's this enormous black dude right next to me, rubbing his fist and saying how he's delighted to have been of service."

Bobbi smiled. "You should take lessons from him. That's the kind of diplomacy I like."

When Drabney called to find out how the expedition to the Hook went, I didn't mention delegating the investigation to Cort. I wasn't sure that would go over well. Drabney had no news regarding Lee.

A minute after he called a hubbub erupted in the waiting room, giving me an excuse to hang up. The disruption was caused by a man who had been rejected for a visa a few weeks before. He started shouting when Sammy said he should wait six months between applications. The security guard we had hired the week before was in the bathroom. The man started cursing as soon as I entered the room, but then Ruby bustled over, looking like a concerned grandmother, and persuaded him he would have a much better chance of obtaining a visa if he didn't call the consul a dirty bastard.

It was several days later that Ben dropped by. I hadn't spoken to him since our chat the day before I went to the Hook.

"You and Miz Scarlett making out all right?" he asked. "She don't miss Tara none?"

"Bobbi's from Massachusetts," I replied dryly.

"It's the mentality, Jim." The magnolia blossom accent was gone. "Pure southern belle."

I shrugged.

"She find a job yet?" Ben asked.

"Not yet. I think she's hoping you'll give her one."

He laughed harshly. Then he motioned for me to accompany him out to the patio.

"I can't imagine anyone would bother to bug your office, but there's no point taking chances. How would you like to be my backup at a secret rendezvous?"

At first I thought he was joking. Apart from a few coy allusions, Ben had never talked about his real work before. It turned out he was serious. The marine he normally called upon for such help was having an appendectomy. He didn't trust the others not to gossip about being spook for a day.

The rendezvous was for the purpose of firing Barry, an agent who hadn't been producing. I don't know if Barry was his real name or something Ben made up for my benefit. Ben thought it would be a good idea if the man, who was a hothead, saw Ben wasn't alone. My job would be to sit in a car and be present while the fellow got his walking papers.

"It doesn't sound complicated. What if something goes wrong?"

"You drive back to the embassy. In my desk is a cable form. It's addressed and marked 'flash' and everything. All you have to do is put down whatever happened and give it to the communicator. That's the end of your involvement. But nothing will go wrong."

Rather naïvely I imagined that during the drive out Ben might tell me about the agent. But he was more interested in discussing why girls scored lower than boys on math SATs. According to him, the women's movement was to blame.

It was a problem of attitudes. Feminists could be divided into two camps: the ones with a generalized left-wing distrust of science and the others who viewed it specifically as a conspiracy for enforcing patriarchal domination. Girls imbibed these attitudes and then, not surprisingly, failed to do well in science and math. This in turn reinforced the feminists' attitude toward those fields.

"And then, when they've screwed themselves, they blame us," Ben concluded, more in anger than sorrow.

"Do you think this guy we're going to see will be carrying a gun?" I asked.

"I doubt it," Ben replied shortly. "More likely a knife. What I don't understand," he continued in a tone of honest bafflement, "is how they can argue that the tests themselves are biased. I mean, where's the bias in a question about the maximum of a function, for chrissakes?"

"I guess it depends on the function, Ben. Look, if there is trouble, shouldn't I maybe drive a little ways off and then come back in a few minutes to see that you're OK?"

"No," he said, shaking his head decisively. "Look how well the Asians do. Is that because the Educational Testing Service is discriminating in their favor? Come on. It's because they study. Same with Jews, of course. But if you suggest that girls would do better if they studied more, you're a chauvinist——"

"Watch it!"

"I see him," Ben said calmly, swerving at the last moment to avoid a boy on a bike.

"It's so idiotic," he continued a minute later. "All these girls become doctors because they think that's more nurturing than being a mathematician or nuclear physicist. That's the buzzword, right? Nurturing. But there's not a lot of nurturing in being a radiologist or a brain surgeon."

I gave up. I'd find out about the rendezvous when it happened. "There are other specialties with more patient contact," I observed.

"Yeah, but you want to know something? Some of these deeply concerned ladies who go into OB-GYN would be better off being radiologists or mathematicians because when you get down to it, they're about as nurturing as Sheetrock. When we were in Washington, Sarah went through five or six gynecologists, all female, before she found one who was human." He shook his head heavily.

"Three o'clock and they're off to the low-impact aerobics class?" I asked.

"Damn straight."

I expected him, having settled women's hash, to move on to federal funding for the arts or set-asides for minority business, but instead he switched on the radio. For a minute we listened to the local station, which was listing appliances and construction materials that had arrived by freighter and were on sale in Wellington. Then he switched it off.

Ben had some gray at his temples, and the hair on his eyebrows seemed to stick out a couple of inches. But he had an eagerness about him that made me think of high school students. After we got out of Wellington, he stepped on the gas, and soon we were moving at a speed that was comfortably above what was safe. He hummed the theme from the old *Secret Agent* TV show.

As I looked at him, he took a handkerchief out and wiped off the sweat on his forehead.

He sensed my gaze. "Getting nervous?" he asked without taking his eyes off the road.

"Oh, no."

"That's good."

A little later we turned off the main road and drove for a

couple of minutes on a dirt road. We stopped near an abandoned building.

"I'll wait under the tree," he said. "We don't want the guy to get a good look at you."

He got out, and I moved to the driver's seat.

Ben went first to the front door of the building and tried to open it. It was padlocked. He peered in a window and then walked around the building. Then he walked over to a small shed, which was also locked. He peered in a window there, too. Then he gave a thumbs-up and walked over to the tree. He spread a newspaper over some cinder blocks and sat down on them. He started reading another part of the paper.

Half an hour later a man on a motorcycle finally appeared.

I had the window down, but I caught only every third word. The car was facing away, positioned for a quick getaway, so I had to twist in my seat to see. The first thing Ben did was point at me, I guess to remind Barry they were not alone.

Then Ben handed him an envelope. Barry opened it and counted bills and put them in his pocket.

He was a black man in his mid-twenties, perhaps an inch under six feet, and slim. He was wearing shorts and a T-shirt, and on his right forearm was a leather band with metal studs that reflected the sun.

Ben had told me what he was going to say. He wasn't going to say that Barry had been doing a lousy job and was a waste of time; he was going to explain that the funding had been cut so he couldn't afford to retain his services. If he got more money next year, he would put him back on the payroll. Ben had no intention of doing any such thing, but even if the guy only half believed him, it might keep him from doing something stupid. I was struck by how mundane it sounded. I had not thought spy personnel practices would mirror those of the ordinary world so closely.

Ben talked for quite a while, waving his arms. I couldn't hear what he said, but I had no trouble making out Barry's reply.

"This is shit," he said. "You hear me? You're treating me like shit."

"No, I'm treating you damn well," Ben said. "The stuff you've been giving me is shit."

Barry glowered at him. Then he turned and went to his bike. At first I thought he was going to leave, that the interview was over. Then I saw he was fiddling with a bag that was strapped to the seat.

I got nervous. The car's engine was already on; I put it in gear, with my left foot on the brake and my right ready to hit the accelerator.

But when Barry's hand emerged from the bag, it held a piece of paper, not a weapon. He went back to Ben and held it out.

"Look at this," he said.

Reluctantly Ben accepted the paper. He studied it for a while.

"That's what you're looking for," Barry said excitedly.

Ben shook his head and said something I couldn't hear.

"Yeah, that's it, that's it," Barry insisted. He was shouting. "You wanna meet the guy? You wanna meet him?"

Ben said something that again I couldn't hear.

"What the fuck you mean?" Barry shouted. "Why not? Why not? Where's my money? Why you keeping that and saying it doesn't mean anything? Why you keeping it then?"

He went on the same vein for a while. Then he kicked the cinder block. Maybe he did not realize what it was because it was covered with the newspaper. Or maybe he was just too mad to care. In any case, he kicked it very hard, and then he grabbed his foot and started screaming. I couldn't help smiling.

The tapping on the car's front window came as a complete surprise.

The sound was made by the hilt of a machete. They are

called cutlasses on Navidad, and when I arrived on the island, people were still talking about the cutlass-wielding thieves who had hacked to pieces a German émigré and his local boyfriend. The thieves were never caught.

The man with the cutlass peered in the window on the passenger side. "What are they fighting about?" he asked. I stared at him for a second, not saying anything.

"What are they fighting about?" he repeated.

I looked back. Ben and Barry were on the ground, Barry with his arms around Ben as though he had tackled him.

There was another sound. The man was trying to open the door, which I had locked.

But I hadn't rolled up the window. He reached in and tried to locate the lock. "How does this open?" he asked.

I took my foot off the brake and hit the gas. I had the car in reverse, and it jumped back toward Ben and Barry. I had to swerve to avoid hitting them.

They were rolling on the ground next to the car. The man with the cutlass was on the ground back where I had left him. He must have been knocked down when I went back.

I looked to see if there was anything heavy to hit Barry with. All I could see were two foam dice hanging from the rearview mirror. I got out to pull Barry loose.

Ben was pushing on Barry's chin with his right hand and with his left grasping Barry's right wrist, which held a switchblade. I hadn't seen that earlier. Just as I reached them, Barry freed his knife arm with a jerk and lunged at Ben. He didn't connect because Ben sprang away as soon as he lost his grip.

It was too late to back out. I jumped on Barry, grabbing the arm with the knife with both hands. He was off-balance, and I got a good grip.

My idea was that I would block off his other arm with my shoulder and back while I worked the knife free. That worked for about half a second. Then he twisted somehow and grabbed my left wrist. His hand felt like a vise. He was much stronger than I was. I could feel my left hand giving way, and after that happened, I knew I would not be able to control his knife hand with just my right. His arm was slippery with sweat. The knife itself was shiny and not too long and somehow unreal. I knew it could kill me, but the knowledge was abstract, unconnected with the grunting and shoving match we were engaged in.

Then Barry jerked. Ben had kicked him in the back. Ben kicked him again, this time in the head with the heel of his shoe. Barry let go of my left hand. Then Ben more or less sat on him, pinning his left side with his body and reaching over to pull the knife free.

"Get in the car," he grunted.

I got in and unlocked the passenger side. The man with the cutlass was sitting up now, but not moving. He watched me with a blurry expression.

Ben rose and kicked Barry in the groin. Then he jumped in the car, and we moved.

As we pulled away, he looked back. "Shit," he said softly. "He's sitting up. If I had got him good, he wouldn't be sitting."

We drove awhile in silence. Then Ben said, "You should have used your teeth."

"What?"

"You should have bit him when you had the knife hand. He wouldn't have liked that."

He reached over and patted my knee. "Thanks anyway."

Ben wiped the knife to remove fingerprints and tossed it out the window when there was no one in view. The sun was setting as we approached Wellington. At Ben's direction I pulled off the road by a store. He went inside and emerged a minute later with four bottles of beer. He gave one to me and took a swig of another.

"What a clown," he said.

"Barry?"

"Yeah."

He was leaning against the side of the car, looking at the sunset with a smile on his face.

"Why did he try to knife you?"

He took another swig. "Who knows? He wasn't in a very good mood to start with, and then he stubbed his toe. I guess that was it." A smile creased Ben's face. "We're not talking about Einstein here. This guy is to your average spy what Charles Bronson is to Laurence Olivier."

The debonair act was not very convincing, but if Ben wanted to pretend he was used to knife fights with crazy men, I wasn't going to argue. I wanted to eat something. I could still see the knife in Barry's hand, a few inches from my eyes.

We drove in silence. Bobbi wouldn't be at home; Cort had invited her to pay another visit to the Hook and had sent a car. I didn't expect her back until late.

Ben pulled up in front of my house and switched off the motor. "Don't get out," he said. "You want to know who Barry is, what he was supposed to be doing?"

He had leaned back and was looking up at the sky.

"Sure," I said, extremely surprised.

"You saved my life. Maybe. I guess I owe you something." He gave a weary laugh. "I'm afraid a major breach of security is the best I can offer."

He took another beer out of the paper bag and drank some. A breeze had picked up. The bugs hadn't come out yet, and it was really quite pleasant.

"On information received"—he looked over and flicked his eyelids—"what information I don't know, so don't bother asking—on information received, my boss thinks your new acquaintance Thomas Cort is smuggling drugs into the U.S. What makes it sexy is that the Cubans are supposed to be backing him. I'm supposed to nail all this down, and Barry was my chosen tool. What a joke."

I reached into the bag and took out the last beer. "Why is it a joke?"

"Why?" He drawled the word out. "Well, that's rather hard to say, Jim, because there are about a million excellent reasons. An effort of selection would be required."

I raised my eyebrows. He drew a breath and let it out. "Well, I'll do my best. But where to start. . . ."

He wrinkled his brow as though in deep thought. "Much as I love my job, I would have to admit if pressed that the profession of espionage as practiced on this island has an element of the ludicrous. Look at what happened today. A marine gets sick, and I have to draft you at the last minute. When I was doing training courses, it was assumed that a station would have five or six people, minimum. You'd never run a meet like this one. But I didn't have any choice. Do you know I'm supposed to have a subordinate, but the spot has been unfilled ever since I got here?"

He looked quite put out.

"No, I didn't know."

"Yeah, well, I never told you, did I?"

He did a drumroll on the dashboard with his fingers. "OK, leaving aside the staffing situation, which I confess has its bright side since it allows me to do more or less whatever I please, the operation itself was a joke."

"What's wrong with the operation?"

"Nothing or everything, depending on your point of view. What is it about? Drugs. Drugs in the third world. How nice and trendy. The cold war's over, so let's do a Gallup poll and find out what new target to go after. You have two choices: crazy Arabs or wicked drug dealers."

His voice dripped sarcasm.

"The only thing is, I'm not sure I buy it. The Russians still have a shitload of ICBMs, not to mention other goodies. And the outlook there is, shall we say, murky in the extreme. So maybe instead of Lenin they're going to do some bizarre ultranationalist anti-Semitic shtick. Does that mean we should settle down for a long winter's nap?"

Ben's worries about Russia I had heard before. In this context they seemed more than usually irrelevant.

"You're in the Caribbean, Ben," I said. "I would think you'd be delighted to go after the Cubans. They're about the only Communists left."

"Yeah . . . I have my doubts about that, too. There was some talk about Cubans and drugs a few years ago, but I find it hard to believe Castro's doing anything like that now. He's pretty much on the defensive." Ben chewed his mustache. "Shit, I said I would tell you the truth, I might as well. The biggest gripe I have against this operation is that it's my boss's idea. Anything that asshole comes up with has got to be garbage."

"Oh."

Ben looked at me questioningly. "You sound surprised."

"Well, it's just that you always come on like the true and faithful champion of the CIA."

Ben got out of the car. "The agency is fine," he said with heartfelt sincerity. "I love the agency. That doesn't mean I have to love every person in it. You ever see *Philadelphia Story?*"

I nodded, wondering what in God's name Ben was thinking of now.

"The guy Hepburn is engaged to, not Cary Grant but the other guy, the phony-baloney man of the people, that's my boss to a T. His father or his mother was a longshoreman, so he's convinced he's a paragon of working-class authenticity, on a mission to save the agency from the Ivy League douchebags who've been fucking it up. 'Douchebag' is one of his favorite words." Ben snorted. "As a Columbia grad I find his attitude offensive."

"So?"

"So now I'm going to have to report failure to Mr. Douchebag. He's going to chew me out, and the worst part is I deserve it. Hiring Barry was stupid."

He gave a bitter laugh. "You know what Barry was? A case of nepotism. I was lazy. His father's on my payroll, he's got a government job and gives me stuff every once in a while, not earth-shattering but useful stuff, and when I asked him if he knew anything about Cort, he said he didn't but his son knew people in the Hook."

"How could you know he didn't?"

Ben's mouth twisted into a grimace. "The first time I met Barry I could tell he was a loser. But hiring him gave me something to report, and then I could just say he was developing contacts. Only after a while you want some results, and he wasn't getting any." Ben looked up into the sky and then took off his glasses and polished them with a handkerchief. "So now you know the genesis of Barry, and I've compromised his dad as well. Two security breaches for the price of one."

I think Ben had decided it was time to quit talking, but I was still curious.

"Who was the other guy?"

"What other guy?"

"The one with the cutlass. He tried to get into the car when Barry and you were fighting."

"Oh, him." A car drove by, and Ben turned to look at it.

"I'm not sure," he continued after the car had passed. "Did you see the paper Barry gave me?"

"I saw that he gave you something, yeah."

"It was supposed to be a memo from the MFA." The MFA

was the Ministry of Foreign Affairs. "I think Barry cooked it up himself, although it was pretty sophisticated for him. Maybe he got help. Anyway, the memo said there's talk that the Cubans are planning to build a hotel in the Hook. The memo says inquiries should be made, like why the thing is not being discussed through normal channels and why, if there is money for such a project, it should not go for something more worthy. Barry said he could introduce me to the guy who got the memo. A clerk. Anyway, to answer your question, I guess that's who the other guy was: Barry's alleged contact in the MFA."

He licked a trace of blood off his forearm. Barry must have nicked him after all.

"Why didn't you agree to see him?"

"Because I had decided to fire Barry, if you recall, and also because the whole thing is ludicrous. We're looking for drugs, not Castro's plans for building a Best Western. Not that there's a chance in a million that the Cubans actually are doing anything like that."

I looked at Ben for a second before I spoke. "Have you read my memcon?"

"Your memcon?" He gave the word a sarcastic intonation.

"When I had that dinner with Cort, he was talking about the Cubans building a hotel there. It was all in my memcon."

Ben's mouth pursed in annoyance.

"Maybe you should go back and apologize to Barry," I said.

He rolled his eyes. "I find this very hard to believe. Was Cort just making things up for your benefit, do you think? I mean, maybe he's fantasizing about this because it makes him look good to the local citizenry."

"He didn't really want to talk about it. He said this guy Carreras—he's an econ officer, I looked him up—was checking out sites for the hotel."

"Oh, shit," Ben said.

"So you think they really are going to build a hotel?"

He looked at me with an unhappy smile. "I think I'm going to have to find someone to replace Barry."

He bent down and tied his shoelaces. When he straightened up, the smile was still there. "No, I don't think they're going to build a hotel. I think my boss unfortunately may actually be right about something. Carreras is head of Cuban intelligence here."

"Oh."

We said good-bye. I went inside and ate some ice cream. Later on I made grilled cheese sandwiches; I find it easier to sleep with a full stomach.

In the middle of the night I woke and remembered the fight, feeling Barry's hand start to twist from my grip. To take my mind off that, I tried to remember the actor who played Hepburn's fiancé in *The Philadephia Story*. I couldn't.

6

"**D**o you know someone named Man?"

"Man?"

"Or maybe his name is Demon," Rollo said, frowning in recollection.

"Demon," I repeated thoughtfully. Bobbi and I had just arrived at Ben and Sarah's party. The ambassador had beckoned as soon as he saw me. I had no idea what he was talking about.

"Paul Demon," he said, nodding affirmatively. "Ben was telling us about him before you got here. Apparently he's the worst thing to hit Western civilization since Genghis Khan, but unfortunately none of us has heard of him. As ambassador it would ill behoove me to confess ignorance. I had hoped Sharon"—he motioned to the pregnant lady with whom he was sharing the couch—"would sacrifice herself for the greater good, but she said not a word."

"Why me?" she asked, placidly rubbing her stomach. "I get plenty of Ben at work. It doesn't pay to encourage him."

Sharon was in the economics section. She kept Ben aware of what he should say he was doing for his cover job.

"Well," the ambassador continued, still curious, "can you shed some light? Do you have any idea who this fellow is?"

By now I had pieced it together. "Paul de Man," I said.

"Yes." The ambassador beamed. "That's how he pronounced it. Who was he? Hitler's second-in-command? Is he still alive? Hiding out in the Amazon perhaps? Or here on Navidad? I bet he's the chef at the American club; there's someone guilty of crimes against humanity."

"He's dead," I replied. "He was a professor at Yale."

"Oh." Rollo seemed taken aback. "Is that all? I know Ben thinks the universities have failed to inculcate proper values in the youth of America, but I didn't realize he felt as strongly about it as that. He virtually made this fellow out to be a war criminal."

"Yes, well, he was a sort of collaborator. He published anti-Semitic essays in a German-controlled paper during the war. Afterward he covered up. No one knew about it until after he died."

"I see. How do you know about it?"

"It became a tempest in an academic teapot. There were stories in the press."

"And no doubt Ben was busy firing off letters to editors. You know"—Rollo leaned forward, imparting a confidence—"sometimes I wonder if our gracious host might actually be a cultural affairs officer operating under cover as a spy."

He looked up at the ceiling, as though seeking divine guidance.

"Do you think Washington would do something like that without informing me?" he asked, apparently overcome by doubt. "It could be very embarrassing. Very embarrassing indeed. Here I am, blithely assuming he's stealing confidential documents and launching coups while in fact he may be secretly organizing poetry readings and modern dance performances."

Rollo rolled his eyes in mock anxiety. I laughed and glanced around. The one nonembassy person in earshot seemed not to be listening.

"This De Man business," the ambassador said slowly. "I am constantly amazed by the sheer fecundity with which people make trouble for themselves. Nature is a sluggard by comparison. As a doctor I can say that with certainty."

In earlier life Rollo had been a surgeon and hospital administrator. He was a political appointee, one of those rare black Republicans, and quite a good ambassador. While he had no particular connection to Navidad, he did have ties to the Caribbean, having been born in Jamaica and lived there until he was fifteen.

He settled back in the couch and flicked a bit of fluff off a shirt cuff. Then he continued his lament.

"What is cancer compared with the viciousness of a scholarly colloquium? What is a broken leg, a broken neck, next to the intolerance of the professional do-gooder? Even our own little suburb of Utopia, the State Department, occasionally features behavior reminiscent of Caligula in his salad days. Sometimes I think I should have stayed a simple surgeon. Cut and slice and never think a thought. It was like being a chef's helper, only better paid. Now I have to keep abreast of policy and make demarches and confer with undersecretaries and then, on top of all that, chuckle knowingly at professors' peccadilloes. It's really too much. Much too much. Eisenhower conquered Europe and read westerns every night. I don't know where he found the time. The last three issues of *Isaac Asimov's Science Fiction Magazine* rest on my desk completely unexamined. When I was a practicing doctor, I read it cover to cover the day it arrived in the mail. And these issues are packed with good stuff, judging from the illustrations on the covers. Extraterrestrial visitors, beauteous astronauts, things like that. But when will I have the time to read them? When?"

The speech was a typical Rollo performance. Bobbi had approached just as he began, and to judge from the attentiveness with which he looked her over, it was delivered at least partly for her benefit.

"Perhaps I may be introduced to this young lady?" Rollo said.

I did the honors. Rollo greeted Bobbi as "a pulchritudinous addition to our small but happy band." Bobbi giggled and said she was ecstatic to meet a real live ambassador. Then she asked Rollo if he was "plenipotentiary." I hadn't thought she knew the word.

I strolled off. I had a feeling the conversation would get around to jobs. That was fine, but I did not want to be in the position of having to testify to whatever competencies Bobbi invented for herself today.

Ben was in the backyard, sweating over a barbecue. Menati, the AID program director's wife, slipped away as I approached. Neither of us spoke for a while.

"Got your houseguest into bed yet?" Ben asked, looking up from the hamburgers with a pleasant smile.

I laughed.

" 'Subject giggled nervously when questioned directly,' " he said, as though dictating a cable. "That's a negative, I guess?"

"Bobbi's just a friend," I said.

"So you say. My impression is that you lust after her but are embarrassed to admit it. I can understand the lust, but I can't quite figure out the embarrassment."

He pressed the spatula down on the burgers, squeezing out juice. "I can think of two possible explanations," he continued in a detached tone. "One is that you don't think you'll succeed, which is probably the case, but you never can tell. The other is that if you did succeed, you'd face the prospect of a relationship with someone who probably thinks Winston Churchill is the backup drummer for the Stones."

"Bobbi isn't dumb. Just because she might not be able to write an article for *Commentary*——"

"I would say reading an article in *Seventeen* is more her speed——"

"There are other forms of intelligence."

Ben grunted.

"How goes the spy business?" I asked after a minute.

He grunted again. "At present we're experiencing a slight seasonal recession, but in the next quarter we look for a big spurt of activity in the bulge-bracket double- and triple-agent fields."

"You haven't had any further trouble with Barry?"

Ben looked down at the grill. He squeezed out more juice, which sizzled on the coals.

"He hasn't been lying in wait for me at the embassy, if that's what you mean," he said after a few seconds. "He hasn't bothered you, has he?"

"No," I replied. The idea that Barry would seek me out was an unpleasant thought. "He doesn't know who I am, does he?"

Ben smiled. "I didn't tell him. No, I don't think so, although you were certainly close enough for him to get a good look."

For a moment I didn't say anything. "You don't really think——"

"Relax," Ben said. "Barry's impetuous, but he's not the type to hang around nursing a grudge. I gave him pretty generous severance pay. He probably hasn't got over the hangover yet."

"That's good."

"Yeah. One of my real success stories."

"Have you found a successor?"

"A successor?" Ben's face was shiny with sweat. His glasses kept slipping down his nose, and he kept pushing them back up, smudging himself with the charcoal that was on his fingers.

"To Barry."

"Oh. Is this just a friendly inquiry or are you doing a little sideline business with the Cuban Embassy?"

I didn't say anything.

"It's so fucking hot," Ben growled after a few seconds. "That plate I put the cooked burgers on: That wasn't what the raw patties were on, was it?"

"I don't know."

"Shit." He looked at the plate with burgers on it. "Sarah read someplace you're not supposed to do that. Salmonella or something. I swear everyone did it when I was a kid and we all survived, but you can't argue with progress. I mean, I argue every once in a while, but I pick my spots."

He lifted a dish towel and found an empty plate. "This must be the verboten dish. We're OK."

He hummed briefly as he turned burgers over. "Sorry about that crack. It's my own damn fault. I tell you about an operation; naturally you're going to be curious. No, I haven't hired a successor yet. It's not so simple. You can't just run an ad in the paper, you know."

"I guess not."

"I suggested that once, actually. Ads in the paper. 'BORED? NEED MONEY? WANT A GREEN CARD? SPY FOR THE CIA— part-time work available.' "

"How did it go over?"

"The general feeling was that it did not suit our image. Too crass."

"Oh."

We chatted some more, but Ben did not volunteer any secrets. I did not want to appear overly curious. I had been lucky, if that was the word, to have one glimpse of the shadow world; there was no reason to think there would be any more.

I went back into the living room. Bobbi had taken Sharon's place on the couch; she and Rollo were deep in conversation. Bobbi's idea that she would be able to get him to give her a job still struck me as completely unrealistic, but she was certainly doing her best to charm him.

Before we sat down for dinner, Sarah got me aside and asked how I was bearing up. "Bearing up?" I repeated, wondering if she was talking about living in the same house with Bobbi. Then she said if she were in my position she'd be scared all the time. That confused me even more; the only thing I could think of was the incident with Barry. I was surprised Ben had told her about it. But it turned out she was referring to the death threat. I'm not sure she believed me when I said that I had forgotten about it and that it was a false alarm.

There were ten of us at the table, with a man from the Ministry of Economic Development the only non-American present. It didn't take long for Ben to find a topic of disagreement with him. This evening it was whether the slave trade had been essential to the economic development of the West or merely an accidental concomitant. Was capitalism evil in its genes, or did it merely have a slightly checkered past? It was no surprise that Ben took the latter view, but I was impressed by his managing to include a condemnation of New Yorker fiction in the argument. Rollo whispered in my ear: "See what I mean? I asked for James Bond and I got George Will."

Rollo left early. He always does, since no one leaves until the ambassador does. Not long after that Bobbi gave a polite yawn. It was the sort of signal a wife gives a husband, and for a second I was tempted to ignore it since Bobbi was certainly not treating me in other respects as a husband.

But I was ready to go. Bobbi went to the bathroom, and I went out to the car to wait for her. I looked up at the sky. There was no point in being annoyed; when I agreed to Bobbi's staying at my house, I knew what she was like. And as Ben had said, you never knew what might happen.

Ben joined me, a can of beer in his hand. "I told Sarah to keep Bobbi for a few minutes," he said. "We've got to talk."

I didn't respond.

"Bobbi went with you to the Hook," he said after a second.

"Yes."

"And then she went back a second time, to see Cort."

"Yeah."

"Why didn't you tell me?"

His tone was prosecutorial. I was annoyed enough to say nothing.

"Why didn't you tell me?" he repeated.

"It didn't seem important. I didn't know you were keeping tabs on her."

"You knew I was interested in Cort."

"Yeah, but——" I shrugged.

Neither of us spoke for a while. I killed a mosquito and thought that perhaps I should go in and roust Bobbi.

"Rollo asked me if I could find a job for her," Ben said, his voice studiously casual.

"*What?*"

"Not as a spy. I gather what he has in mind is that I might know someone who has a job opening for an out-of-work deb. He has this romantic notion that my work brings me into contact with all sorts of people."

"It doesn't?"

"Not if I can help it." He scowled. "I've got to hand it to her: She meets Rollo, and one hour later he's putting pressure on me to help out." He frowned. "Anyway, Rollo thinks it would be good if a job could be found quickly because otherwise she might take the existing offer."

"She has a job offer?" I felt a pang of annoyance that Bobbi would confide in Rollo, whom she had just met, instead of me.

"You didn't know?"

"No. I wonder . . ."

"What?"

"Nothing."

I had been about to say that I wondered if Bobbi was telling the truth. I was sure she would have no compunction about lying if she thought it would help. But I couldn't see what advantage she would gain. "What is it? The job, I mean."

"That's the fun part," Ben said.

"Yeah?"

He had a very odd expression.

"Cort wants her to be his private secretary. Mistress would probably be a more accurate description."

I felt a prickling on the back of my neck.

"Kind of makes her a plausible candidate for me to recruit, doesn't it?" he said eventually. His eyebrows rose provocatively.

"You're kidding."

"I am?" He took a swig of beer.

"You can't stand her."

I felt betrayed. I just wasn't sure whether it was Bobbi or Ben who was doing the betraying.

Ben leaned back and stretched. "This may come as a shock to you, Jim, but amiability is not the most highly prized quality in spies."

Bobbi appeared at the door. She was saying something to Sarah.

"You think she's dumb," I whispered urgently.

"She *is* dumb." He chuckled. "So what? Brains are overrated for spying. What matters is being in the right place. And it looks like good ol' Bobbi girl is gonna be that."

She walked briskly toward us. Ben's good-bye was effusive.

One could say he was laying groundwork for a recruitment bid, but I think mainly he wanted to annoy me.

Ben's capacity for alcohol was small. I told myself that he couldn't seriously be planning to hire Bobbi; he had simply had one too many. Even when he asked for information to run a security check on her, I figured it was just one of his top-heavy practical jokes.

A week passed. Bobbi visited Cort twice. Then she had lunch with Ben. It grew harder to maintain disbelief.

Then it became impossible. Ben called and said I needed some exercise. We walked together on the beach.

"I need your help," he said as soon as we were out of sight of anyone.

"I already told you everything I know. I only worked with her for nine months."

He shook his head. We walked awhile in silence. I felt at a disadvantage, knowing Ben was going to spring some request while I was worrying about jellyfish and lacerating shells.

"Bobbi's taking the job with Cort," he said eventually. "She'll move there in a few days, become his private secretary. I want you to take her reports and relay them to me."

His tone was so matter-of-fact that for a second or two his words didn't register. But then they did.

"*What?*"

"You'd just be a postman, Jim. That's all it amounts to. But it'd be a valuable contribution."

I didn't reply for a moment. Then I said, "You're crazy."

He grunted.

"A week or two ago you were telling me not to stick my nose into your business. This is ridiculous."

He grunted again. "Totally ridiculous," I said, wishing I could think of stronger language.

"Oh, goodness me," he falsettoed. "Is the big bad CIA man trying to make you do something you shouldn't? Oh, what a naughty, naughty man he is." His voice switched back to normal. "For chrissakes, all I'm asking is that you keep on seeing a friend. I'm sure you'd do it anyway."

"You're asking me to spy," I said coldly.

He shrugged. "Only a titch. You'd hardly notice."

We walked awhile. "I can't see why you even want me to do this."

When he spoke, his voice was uncharacteristically sanctimonious. "I'm asking this for Bobbi's sake. For her safety."

I didn't think he would sink that low. "Come on, Ben. You're the professional. She's bound to be safer——"

I saw his smile and stopped.

"I am, as you say, the professional. Respected by everyone. 'There goes Ben Jacoby of the CIA,' they all say. 'Chief of station,' they all say. Everyone knows who I am. That's why it would be safer for her to meet you."

"Yeah, but you'll meet her in some safe house——"

He cackled. "Didn't Rollo give you his 'Thou shalt not commit adultery' speech when you got here?"

I looked at him. "I don't know what you're talking about."

"What he told me was that he had nothing personally against adultery, but it was incumbent upon us as official representatives of the government to maintain an appearance of virtue, and on a small island like Navidad the appearance can only be sustained by the reality. 'If you pick your nose in your bedroom, they'll be discussing the texture of your snot over dinner that day.' Thus spaketh Rollo."

I was sure Rollo had never said anything like that, but Ben was nodding in approval. "He's right, Jim. It's a small town, and we're the best gossip they have. There's no such thing as a safe house here."

I skirted a brackish pool that Ben plowed through. When we were walking side by side again, I said quietly, "I won't do it, Ben."

"Of course you will," he replied cheerily. "You just have to get used to the idea. This is the best thing to come your way since you got here. You're bored. You go to the club and eat too much and you sit at home and pretend to read worthwhile books and you take naps. That meet you went on with me is the only time you've been alive since you——"

"Shove it, Ben."

We walked along without talking. After a while we came to a rocky area and turned around. A black man wearing only shorts rode a horse along the edge of the water, flashing a smile as he passed us.

"What does Bobbi think of this ludicrous idea?" I asked eventually. The silence was wearing on me; I was just making conversation.

"She's all for it."

"What?"

"She thinks it's a good idea," Ben said casually.

I was surprised. In New York Bobbi had been absurdly tight-lipped about whom she knew on various magazines; she was paranoid about others making use of her connections, however implausible it was that we would even try. It seemed odd that she would welcome a partner in espionage.

And then I understood. "She proposed it, didn't she?"

Ben didn't reply.

"Oh, that's got to be it," I continued. "All that stuff about her safety—she just doesn't like you, right?"

"Don't be silly." He frowned.

I laughed. "She wants to be a spy all right, but she doesn't want to work for you. She'd rather work for me."

I was amazed I hadn't seen it at once. It wasn't just that

Bobbi didn't like Ben; she probably figured it would be a disaster to work for him. She believed her failure at Hexter was due solely to the fact that Rhonda had been her boss. And whatever the differences between Ben and Rhonda, they shared a strain of intellectual puritanism that made both dislike Bobbi. Bobbi unquestionably realized that.

"I can't believe you gave me that crap about how much safer it would be for me to meet with her," I said after a minute. "You have other agents you meet with."

Ben smiled wanly. "It's not total crap. It probably would be more prudent for her to meet with you. You're a known associate." He cleared his throat. "She's your friend, after all. Spying on drug traffickers is not the most insurable occupation in the world. I would think her safety would matter to you."

"Sure. So I'll refuse to take part, she won't do it, and then she's safe."

We had stopped walking. After a moment he nodded. "Let's walk a little more."

The sun had dropped, and our shadows stretched yards ahead of us. The island was beautiful beyond words.

"You're right, Jim," Ben said in a mild voice. "It's all Bobbi's idea. I didn't want you—amateur case officers are not how we do things—but she insisted."

I started to speak, but he waved me into silence.

"Saying no is probably the wise thing to do, from your point of view," he continued. "Espionage isn't in your job description. I'm sure Rollo would be mighty pissed if he learned I'm asking you to do this."

"Yeah, I bet—"

Ben interrupted. "But don't kid yourself. If you opt out, Bobbi will still work for me. Being a spy is pretty sexy. She won't pass it up."

He gave a sour chuckle. "Here's what would happen. If you

tell me no, she'll make a personal appeal. She said she doesn't want to do that because it would be presuming on her friendship."

His eyebrows rose in irony. "I guess insisting that I make the appeal doesn't presume. Anyway, if you still refuse, she'll conquer her distaste for my company."

It stank. But I was sure Ben was right.

"So why bother asking me?"

He took his time replying. "Bobbi and I . . . lack rapport."

I snorted. "I already know that."

"Yeah, well, it's not good. It means she's more likely to lie to me. It also means she'd be in greater danger."

He paused for a moment. "Forget about the difficulty of meeting. I could work things out. The real problem is psychology. Spies start out scared and careful. When they're not caught, they get careless. You have to keep watching them. But Bobbi doesn't like me, and I don't think she'd follow my advice. Hell, I'd be afraid to give her advice. She'd probably do something stupid just because I told her not to."

We had reached the spot where Ben had parked his car. "Think about it," he said. "You don't have to decide this second."

That evening I called and said I would help him in the little matter we had discussed.

Cort sent a long black Cadillac
with an incongruous red racing stripe to pick up Bobbi. Macho,
the fellow who had sung at Uncle Peter's, was the driver. His
name was clearly ironic. He was in his mid-forties, small and mild-
looking. The years seemed to have worn away distinguishing marks
rather than added them. I tried to chat while Bobbi was getting
her stuff together, but it was hard work. Eventually he summoned
the courage to ask if Bobbi could grant visas. With some difficulty
I got him to understand she was not attached to the embassy. For
her sake, I hoped that was not a common impression.

Bobbi's good-bye kiss was emphatic. Afterward I wondered
what it meant. Should I have tried harder to get her into bed?
And what if I had? I was certainly not in love with her. Or did
the kiss simply testify to Bobbi's nervousness about what lay ahead?
I preferred these questions to the other that came to mind: What
the hell was I doing pretending to be a case officer?

Ben had suggested I not meet Bobbi for a week or two, to

give her time to establish herself. That seemed reasonable. Inactivity was within my powers. The first evening the house seemed very empty. The next three nights I went to the club. I tried not to eat too much. Things began to return to normal.

Then the consulate was bombed.

Most embassy offices are housed in the top two floors of a building in downtown Wellington. Until a year ago the consulate was located on the ground floor of the same building. The arrangement satisfied no one. The consulate was too cramped, and the other tenants did not like the way visa applicants spilled out into the hall.

Consequently the consulate moved to a house in the same suburb where embassy personnel lived. There were times when I felt isolated, but to balance that, I had a private bathroom and an office that was larger than the ambassador's. Afternoons I worked in my luxurious office; mornings I spent in a booth with bulletproof windows interviewing NIV—nonimmigrant visa—applicants. The booth occupied half of the short end of the L-shaped space that had been the house's living-dining area. The interviewee stood facing me, and behind him or her was a wicker partition which separated us from the long end of the L, which served as the waiting room.

On the day in question—a Thursday—I finished the NIVs at twelve-thirty. When Sammy came in, I was tallying approvals and rejections and how many of the rejections were 214(b). Almost all of them were, of course. The 214(b) refers to the paragraph of the Immigration and Nationality Act that mandates denial of a visa to any applicant who fails to rebut the presumption that he is an intending immigrant. In other words, if I'm not fairly sure he's going to come back home, he doesn't get in. On occasion the host government thinks the percentage of approval is dropping too low; it's good to be able to come back at them right away with the exact figures.

"There's something under the bench," Sammy said.

I didn't respond immediately. I didn't want to lose count.

"In the corner, where the benches come together," Sammy said after a few seconds.

I had granted eighteen visa applications and denied twenty-three. I looked up at Sammy.

"Very big?" I asked.

"No. Medium size. Lunch probably."

This was not an unfamiliar event. Every week or two someone forgot a parcel in the waiting room. It was always lunch or school-books or groceries. But it could be a bomb, so unless it was absolutely clear that it wasn't, the set procedure was to call the marine guard station. A marine came with a local cop. They brought a metal detector and a dog that could supposedly sniff explosives.

"I'll take a look," I said, and started to get up.

That was when it exploded.

It seemed as if I felt the explosion a millisecond before I heard it. The noise itself was stunning, like a firecracker, but louder than any firecracker I had ever heard and somewhat duller.

I found myself on the floor. The glass in the booth was covered with fracture lines, and it had torn loose from the frame. I could see the wicker partition lying on the floor, in pieces.

Sammy had been thrown against the wall. He was shaking his head but still standing.

He fingered the knot of his tie. "Was that——"

"A bomb." I smiled. I felt I had to make a joke of it. "Not a very big one, I guess, since we're still here."

Sammy shook his head again. "I'll see how Ruby is," he said. He spoke as though bombs were an everyday occurrence. Neither of us was acting sensibly.

He tried the door of the booth, but it didn't open.

"The lock?" I asked.

"It's locked," he said. He turned the lock, but the door still refused to open.

He looked at me. "Ruby was in the room." I got up and pushed with him.

Then we heard Ruby shout. "Mr. Biggins. Mr. Biggins."

I looked around to see if there was anything that could be used to pry open the door.

Then Ruby appeared, on the other side of the booth. She looked disheveled but uninjured.

"Are you all right?" I asked.

"We can't get out," Sammy said.

Ruby went to the door, the other side from us. I heard her stamping her feet. Then she pulled the door open.

"The floorboard was up," she said.

Her shin was cut and already starting to swell. The ring finger and little finger of her left hand were bent back in an unnatural position.

"You're hurt," I said.

"Dennis," she said. Dennis was the guard. "He poked it. With a broomstick. He was trying to look inside."

"How is he?" I asked.

"I think he's dead," Ruby said.

Dennis wasn't dead, but he was hurt badly. He was unconscious and breathing shallowly. There was blood all over him, and I could see the bone of his right arm. Three fingers were missing from his right hand. I had no idea about internal injuries.

The telephone was still working. Sammy called the hospital and the embassy and, a couple of minutes later, when we thought of it, the embassy doctor. I wrapped a towel around Dennis's arm. It seemed very hard to do that; to do anything, in fact. A reaction had set in. I felt as if I were moving under water; everything required vast effort and went slowly. After I finished with the towel, I stood up and wondered what to do next. Then I began to wonder if Dennis was already dead. I could see his chest moving, but in the dreamlike state of mind I was in then that did not seem convincing evidence. Corpses grew hair after they were dead, didn't they? Why couldn't a dead man continue to breathe? I was convinced that if I touched him, I would know if he was alive or dead, but that was the last thing in the world I wanted to do. Gingerly I moved a foot forward and pressed it against his side.

Ruby came into the room. I jerked my foot back, embarrassed. She must have seen me prodding him, but all she said was: "Don't move him. You shouldn't move an accident victim." After that we stood there and looked down at him, not saying anything.

Fortunately the embassy doctor arrived a minute or two later. His offices were in a house only a couple of blocks away.

The doctor replaced the towel with a proper bandage and stopped the bleeding from the other wounds. Dennis was in shock, he said. He told us to find something to use as blankets and asked if we had sent for an ambulance. Then he asked about police. Somehow we hadn't thought to make that call.

"There could be another bomb, you know," he said angrily. I went to call, glad to get away from Dennis but annoyed with the doctor. He hadn't just had a bomb explode under him.

The waiting room looked worse than it actually was. The windows were blown out, but the walls were still standing. Fortunately no one besides Dennis had been there. If the bomb had exploded an hour earlier, twenty people would have been hurt or killed.

I got an extra jacket I keep in the office, and the doctor put it on top of Dennis. He didn't seem to require our presence, so I had Ruby and Sammy come into my office while we waited for the ambulance.

"What happened?" I asked.

Ruby said Dennis had been the one to spot the bag. He had told her and Sammy. Then, on his own initiative, he had gotten a broom and said he thought he could insert it in the bag, widening the opening so he could see what was inside.

"I told him not to do it, Mr. Biggins—to wait for the marines. I told him that."

She was sitting at my desk. She shivered even though it was warm and she was wearing an old sweater of Sammy's. Ruby always took pains to look neat; the dirty sweater was like a flag of distress.

"I wasn't . . . I didn't say it *hard,* you know," she went on. "I just laughed and said, 'Don't do that, it's stupid.' And then, when I saw he was going to poke at the bag, I skipped out of the room. I knew it wasn't a bomb, you know, but I didn't want to stand there with him poking at it. But I should have shouted at him, I should have done something. . . ." Her voice trailed off.

"You did the right thing," I said. "It wouldn't have done any good for you to get blown up too."

The blast had thrown her to the floor. Her fingers must have got caught on a chair or desk, but she didn't remember. At that, she was lucky not to have been hurt worse.

Dennis was even luckier. By rights he should have been blown to pieces; the bench had channeled the explosion away from him. That was the first thing the police officer who showed up two hours later said. He wasn't the first policeman to arrive, of course, but he was the first who knew about bombs.

Dennis was long gone by then; I had also sent Sammy home, after the embassy doctor took a look at him and pronounced him OK. Ruby had gone to the hospital for X rays. The doctor told me to go home, too, or to the club if I preferred. Rollo came and virtually ordered me to leave; I think he would have escorted me himself if he hadn't been going to the hospital to see Ruby and

Dennis. But by then I was no longer feeling dazed. I hadn't been hurt; I wanted to stay and see what the investigation turned up.

Ben had shown up with the marines, a few minutes ahead of Rollo. I was standing in the demolished waiting room, momentarily alone.

"You OK?" he asked, taking off his glasses to clean them.

"Yes."

He looked at me quietly, moving his head slowly up and down. "The guard was hurt?"

"Yes."

"Is he going to make it?"

"I don't know." I felt tired but otherwise normal. "I guess so. The doctor seemed to think so, unless there was something he missed."

"That's good," Ben said, putting his glasses back on.

I didn't say anything.

"I came for two reasons," Ben said after a pause. "One was to see how you were. All I heard was there was a bomb at the consulate. I thought you might be dead."

"I'm not."

"No." He smiled. "You're OK. You're acting a little funny, but I guess that's to be expected in the circumstances."

I guess it was too much to expect that he should be an expert only on Paul de Man and SAT scores and capitalism. Of course, he had to know about bomb trauma, too.

He picked up a chair and leaned against the back of it.

"You're tampering with evidence," I said.

He shrugged, humoring me. He carefully put the chair back the way it had been.

"What was the other reason?"

He waited a few seconds before replying.

"As soon as I heard about the bomb, I asked myself if someone could have found out about our . . . arrangement with Miz Scarlett." He paused, then shook his head. "I can't believe it. She just got there. And if Cort did find out, this isn't what he would do. It just doesn't make sense. The only conclusion I can accept is that this is completely unrelated. Consequently it would be a mistake to mention our arrangement to the people investigating this. It would confuse the issue, and of course it would destroy the—the arrangement."

He looked at me with a bluffer's confident smile.

"All right," I said.

"What?"

"I agree."

My acquiescence took him by surprise. "I'm sure this has nothing to do with it," he said as if I had said the opposite of what I did. "She just got there a few days ago, and there's been no time, no time at all, for anyone to clue in to—"

I held up a hand. "Stop arguing, Ben. I agree. I won't say anything."

He didn't say anything for a while, just looked at me. "You're willing to go ahead with your part? We could forget about that—"

"No," I said. "It'd be better for Bobbi, right?"

"Yeah," he said. "I think so."

He seemed less sure of himself, standing in the middle of a bombed-out room. Then he smiled and said, "I'm sure it'd be better all around."

"OK, then, I'll do it." I couldn't resist adding, "As long as I'm alive."

He smiled wryly. "I don't ask for more than that."

The first police to arrive just secured the premises. After a while a lieutenant came and asked me what I knew, which was very little. Then he went through visa forms, getting names and addresses. They all would have to be talked to since one might have left the bomb or seen who did.

The explosives expert was a big man who had lived in Chicago for ten years and learned his job there. I went in to watch when he arrived, but after a minute I returned to my desk. He came in fifteen minutes later.

"It was dynamite," he said.

"Dynamite?"

"Yeah." He smiled broadly. "What's the matter? That not good enough for you? You want something fancy? X fifteen Triple Sec Terrorists' Delight?"

His thumbs hooked in his belt loops, and his body shook with silent laughter.

"No, but—"

"Dynamite's easy to get," he said. "They're building that road off by Gowey Hill. Use a shitload of dynamite for that. Blowing every day. Damn easy for someone to walk off with a little."

"You think it came from there?"

"Not necessarily. That's just an example. Stuff's all around. Easy to get." He shrugged. "I'm not sure yet how he detonated it."

I told him about Dennis probing the bag with the broom. His eyes widened in amazement.

"Man. That is stupid. Talk about a guy being too dumb to live, that is exactly what that guy is. That is pure grade A shit-for-brains." Then he walked out of the room, not saying another word. I sat at my desk, hot and tired and ashamed. The man had been vile, but I had thought what he had said.

I sat at my desk a little longer, but there was nothing to do. Sarah called as I was leaving and asked if I wanted to spend the night at their house. I declined. The ambassador had said there would be a guard at my house; I preferred to sleep in my own bed. It also seemed better, from the viewpoint of Bobbi's well-being, to downplay my friendship with Ben.

I went home. I was tired but not sleepy. I got a pizza out of the freezer and heated it. Then I listened to records, or rather I put them on, but I didn't really listen. I couldn't help thinking about Dennis, how utterly helpless he had looked on the floor. The blood and gore had turned my stomach. Wrapping the towel around him, I had had to look away to avoid being sick. Now, though, his wounds seemed terrible but not frightening. I was revolted at the way I had behaved. How could I have prodded him with my foot?

Images kept running through my mind. After three hours they were no more palatable than they had been at the start, but I was so worn out I thought I could sleep.

The doorbell sounded just when I decided to go to bed. It was the guard.

"Mr. Biggins, there is a man here who wants to see you. I didn't know . . ."

A rather short black man lingered halfway up the walk. When he saw me, he approached. A gold tooth reflected a gleam from the light over the front door.

"Hello," he said, taking a step forward. "You all right? I went by your other place. It's blown up pretty good."

He came up to the porch, smiling and waving back and forth. He looked seedy but cheery, a refugee from some Caribbean production of *Guys and Dolls*.

"What do you want?"

He looked at the guard and raised his eyebrows. "It is a matter of privacy, Mr. Biggers. It is better we talk in private."

I didn't really think he was the bomber come to finish the job, but I didn't want to be alone with him.

"Look, Mr.——"

I waited for him to supply a name, but he just smiled more intensely.

"It is better we talk in private," he repeated.

A grim suspicion took shape in my mind. "If you want a visa, I'm afraid you'll have to——"

He laughed. "No, no, Mr. Biggers. I'm not after a visa."

"My name is Biggins," I said, annoyed.

He didn't say anything, just continued to rock back and forth, smiling patiently.

"What is it then?"

He looked at the guard. I lost what patience I had. "I think it would be better if we took care of this during business hours," I said brusquely. I nodded and turned back to the door.

"It's about Ricky."

He spoke in a whisper, trying to keep the guard from hearing.

"Ricky?"

I couldn't think of any Ricky I knew.

"Yeah, Ricky." Then, seeing I was confused, he added a word: "Ricky Lee."

"Who's Ricky Lee?"

But as soon as I spoke, I realized. "Right," I said. "I know who Lee is. What do you know about him? And who are you?"

He inclined his head toward the door. "We can talk inside. Privately."

The persistence was impressive in a way, but this night in particular I didn't want a private meeting with someone I had never seen before.

"No," I said. "We're not going inside. You talk to me here, or you come to the consulate tomorrow."

I had forgotten that the consulate would not be open for business tomorrow.

He rocked back and forth. Suddenly an ankle folded beneath him, and he crumpled halfway to the ground. When he regained his balance, he spoke a little angrily.

"It's not what I want to tell," he said in an urgent whisper. "It's what you want to know."

Then he looked at the guard again, as if he had said more than he meant to. But after a moment he spoke again. "I'm not going to that consulate. Maybe someone knew I was going there today. I'm not going to get myself killed."

He was living in a fantasy world. I replied with the last shreds of my patience. "What do you know about Lee, Mr.— What is your name anyway?"

He gave me a card. The name Winston G. Mannion was printed in yellow and light blue lettering. Below that, in black script, it said "Private Automobile Excursions and Special Services."

I remembered Drabney's telling me about him. He had been with Lee the day he died, or maybe it was the day before, and he was a small-time crook.

"What do you know about Lee, Mr. Mannion?"

He looked at the guard, and belatedly I realized I had not been meant to pronounce his name. I didn't feel any regret.

"It's getting late," I said.

"I know what I know," he announced portentously. "What I don't know is how much you want to know what I know."

Now it's hard for me to see how I could ever have failed to understand him, but at the time it seemed like he was propounding a particularly inane brain teaser.

"About Lee's death? Of course I want to know about it. Very much."

"But how much?" His eyes seemed to get brighter. "How much do you want to know?"

"I'm not sure I understand," I said. In fact, I was beginning to.

"I just want to know how much you want to know about Lee getting killed," he said. Then he rubbed his thumb and forefinger together.

The weight of the day suddenly all pressed down. I reached back and opened my front door.

"I'm not giving you money, if that's what you're asking for,"

I said. "If you know anything about Mr. Lee's death, which I'm beginning to doubt, then I would like to hear it. You are, in any case, obligated to tell the authorities. But I'm not going to buy your story. That's not the kind of thing I do."

Then I went inside. I half expected Mannion to pound on the door or start shouting, but he just stood on the porch for half a minute. Then he walked away. A few seconds later I heard a motorcycle start up.

In retrospect, I would have to say those last words of mine were rather pompous. I don't normally ascribe my decisions to lofty considerations of principle. Nor do I now see what would have been so terrible about paying for information. All I can say is that I was extremely tired and not myself.

Still, it was unfortunate. If I had heard his story, I could have saved myself a lot of trouble.

Damn it, at least I could have found out what price he was asking.

8

My first operational meeting took place on the beach.

The maid at Cort's house must have given me wrong directions. The path I took was quite precipitous. I slipped a couple of times and scraped my hands before I thought of going down backward. Bobbi shimmered in the distance, an unreal vision under a red and white umbrella. Pebbles worked into my sandals, and I took them off, but I made a mistake in not putting them back on for the last bit. The sand was burning. I hopped across in a rush, making for the umbrella like a fugitive from East Germany trying to get past the wire in the good old days. Would a burst of bullets cut me down a few yards short of my goal? No.

Dark glasses hid Bobbi's eyes. She was smiling.

"Sand hot?" she asked innocently.

I brushed off the soles of my feet.

"Careful, careful," Bobbi said. "Don't brush that way. My nails aren't dry yet."

Her toenails were a bright pink, with white tissue paper between each toe.

"What's the paper for?"

"To keep from smudging. Macho did them. I'm teaching him a trade. He did a nice job, don't you think?"

I looked at Macho. He was sitting a few yards away, not in the shade. He smiled shyly.

"Very nice job," I said insincerely. "Where can I sit?"

"You didn't bring an umbrella? This is going to be *un peu intime*. Oh, well . . ."

She adjusted her chair, and I found a space at her side.

She was wearing a lime-colored swimsuit. She smelled of suntan lotion and looked pale and delicate. I wanted to eat her up before she melted.

"Oh, I forgot," she said. "Congratulations on not getting blown up. That would have been a real downer. Were you frightened?"

"Not exactly," I said. "It happened so fast. Afterward—"

"Yeah," Bobbi cut in. "It's different for me. If I were the kind of girl who gets frightened, I'd be frightened all the time here. I mean, it's like I'm the one white woman in darkest Navidad. Talk about major Mau Mau."

She sighed theatrically. "It's really primitive here." She waved a hand vaguely in the direction of Macho. "Everyone on the street looks like they're studying for a part in *Death Wish Three*." She rolled her eyes.

"So are you frightened?"

"No, not really," Bobbi said with a laugh. "Cort has put out the word that anyone who gives me trouble will be missing some major body parts. And he gave me . . . here, I'll show you. Macho, give me my purse."

Macho handed Bobbi her purse. She extracted a small pistol.

"He wanted to have my initials put on the handle, but I didn't want to wait. See that stick over there?"

She pointed to a piece of driftwood a little way off. The sound of the shot was sharp but not particularly loud. Sand jetted a foot from the stick. She fired three more times. One of the shots was closer than the first. None hit the stick.

"These short-barrel jobs aren't very accurate. But it would do the job if somebody was giving me trouble."

I didn't say anything for a few seconds. The idea of Bobbi's having a pistol ready to hand was not entirely reassuring.

"Is it legal?" I asked.

" 'Is it legal?' " Bobbi repeated in a mincing tone that wasn't at all what I had sounded like. "That's so you, Jim."

I grimaced. "Navidad has strict firearms laws. In the briefing manual we got it said that——"

"Oh, chill out," Bobbi interrupted. "Cort's the mayor, for goodness' sake. Of course it's legal. You're such a wuss. Macho, don't you think Mr. Biggins is a wuss?"

Macho's face was blank. "I don't know what that is, miss."

"That's easy." Bobbi laughed. "A wuss is like Jim here."

She gave a just-teasing smile. "Maybe you should go on up to the house, Macho, and tell them not to worry about those shots. We don't want the gendarmes to pay a call."

"Oh, they couldn't hear, miss. Not with the waves."

Bobbi lay back in her chair, grinning lazily. "You never know. Anyway, you run along. You might as well go and bring lunch down. Jim is probably starving. He has that lean and hungry look. Except with him it's more a plump and hungry look."

Macho got up reluctantly. He walked slowly off, turning to look back every now and then.

"Your shorts do look tighter than they used to, Jim. Is that a rip?"

There was a small tear in the seam by the crotch. It must have happened as I was climbing down to the beach.

"You should watch your diet more. You don't get enough exercise."

"Thanks for the advice."

"No charge. Speaking of which, did you bring any cash?"

I thought I had misheard. "Excuse me?"

"Did you bring any cash? A girl's got expenses, you know."

"Expenses? What do you mean, Bobbi?"

She raised her glasses and looked at me with exaggerated sincerity. "Just that if you have some cash on you, you could give it to me and Ben would reimburse you. Then you could talk with him so that I get a regular expense account."

I stared at her. "You're serious."

"*Mais oui, mon vieux.*"

She wiggled her toes. A twist of tissue fell out.

"I read somewhere that baseball players get fifty dollars a day, or maybe it's a hundred, whenever their team is on the road. Just as sort of walking-around money. That's in addition to the five million a year they get in salary. I tell you, I'm not getting paid anything like that. Nothing like that. And what I'm doing is a lot more . . ."

I had forgotten just how shameless she was.

"A lot more what, Bobbi?"

She shrugged. "A lot more everything, Jim. Dangerous. Important. Skilled. I mean, here I am risking my life to get vital information from a notorious drug dealer . . ."

"I was under the impression you were sitting on the beach looking at fashion magazines."

I was surprised how vehemently she objected. "You were the one who suggested we meet here. I thought you'd take me to—a what do you call it, a safe house. But no. We meet here, where I'm probably going to get skin cancer from lying out all day because I'm being a good agent and trying to look the part."

I almost felt cheap. "Safe houses are for big cities, Bobbi. Ben explained it to me. Navidad's like a small town——"

"Yeah, never mind," she interrupted cynically. "Ben's explanations I can live without." She picked up a magazine and flipped the pages.

"Next time we could go to a restaurant if you prefer," I said.

She went on reading.

"Where's Cort?" I asked after a while. Bobbi seemed absorbed in an article detailing the pros and cons of Retin-A as a means of removing wrinkles.

"The Bahamas. He left last night."

I watched a wave run up the beach and fall back. If Cort thought I had arranged to come when he was away, that might be bad. "Do you think, when he finds out I've been here, he'll——"

"I told him you might be dropping by," Bobbi interrupted.

"That was probably the right thing to do. Not hiding it, I mean."

"Yeah, I thought so."

"You don't think he's suspicious of me?"

Bobbi turned the page and kept reading.

"Do you think he's suspicious of me?" I asked again.

"Who?"

"Cort."

She looked up from the magazine finally. Her lips curved in a smile. "What's the matter? Nervous in the service?"

"No," I said, a little annoyed. "I was just asking."

The smile broadened. Her head leaned to one side, and one eye peeked from behind the glasses.

"No," she drawled, "I don't think Cort's suspicious. Niso——

that's Mr. Carreras to you—now, he's something else. He thinks you're CIA."

"*What?*"

She adjusted herself in the seat, getting comfortable before she spoke.

"The first time I met him, he asked me all these questions. Like what I had been doing and where I had been staying and so on. He was pretending it was just normal curiosity, but he really wanted to know. Then he said, 'Are you aware, Miss Lyons, that your friend Mr. Biggins is an employee of the Central Intelligence Agency?' That's how he talks."

She raised her eyebrows briefly, then returned to her magazine.

"Wait a minute, Bobbi. Did he really say that?"

"Yeah," she said. Then she bent forward and tapped me on the knee. "Relax. He was just saying that to get my goat. According to him, everyone at the American Embassy works for the CIA. He's like . . . he thinks he's suave and cool, a Cuban Marcello Mastroianni, but what he is mainly is a jerk. He's rude."

"Rude?"

"Yeah, rude," Bobbi repeated. "One night he was talking about Castro and he mentioned this guy Batista. I asked if he was a friend of Castro's. Well, apparently he wasn't, he was the guy Castro replaced, which since I wasn't even born when it happened I don't see why I should be expected to know, but he got real sarcastic about it."

Bobbi's face flushed with remembered anger.

"When he said I was in the CIA, what did you say?" I asked.

Bobbi shook her head, dismissing the memory of Niso's insult. "I believe I said the CIA might be feeble, but they couldn't be that feeble."

"Thanks," I said dryly.

She looked up, the picture of wounded innocence. "You should thank me. I was just doing my best to keep your cover in place. I told him you were real good at knowing where a comma should go and who won the French and Indian War, but you were much too nice to be a spy. You'd worry about offending the Russians or something."

She picked up her gun again and squeezed off a shot. The stick shattered. She gave a whoop. "How do you like that? Right in the middle. That guy is D-E-A-D dead. . . . Who did win, by the way? The French or the Indians?"

"Neither."

"It was like Lebanon?"

"Not exactly. Do you think Carreras believed you?"

"I don't know," she mused. "I told him you were gay, too," she added offhandedly.

"What?"

Bobbi looked up, startled. I had spoken loudly. "Hey, calm down, amigo," she said.

"Why'd you say I was gay?"

She patted me on the leg with the barrel of the pistol. "I did it for your own good," she said. "I know you're not gay. What do you care what Niso thinks?"

"But—"

I felt thirsty. There was a thermos at the edge of the blanket. "Is that water?"

"Lemonade. You want some?"

"Yes, please."

I had a cup of lemonade and wiped some of the sweat off my forehead.

"It just seems like a rather bizarre thing to say," I said after I had swallowed the last of the lemonade.

"Bizarre . . ." Bobbi pursed her lips. "No, I don't think it was bizarre, Jim. Your manner is . . . well, if someone doesn't know you very well, they might wonder . . ."

"Really."

She stretched and smiled. "It's the way you talk, Jim. You sort of dance around things, if you know what I mean. You insinuate. Nicely if you like someone, and snidely if you don't, but you never just say what's on your mind. I mean, I know it's just that you read too much Henry James in kindergarten or something, but someone who doesn't know you . . ." She stretched again. "Also, you're friends with women."

I waited, but there was nothing else.

"Oh, well, now I see it. Liking women is a telltale sign of homosexuality."

She glanced back up. "Well, it is. I mean, when you're friends with them without sleeping with them. Very faggy trait."

She smiled briskly and returned to her article.

"Bobbi, I wish you'd——I think it's best if you don't just go around volunteering lies."

"Oh, it's my lying that bothers you. I see." She laughed again. "Cort was there, too," she continued. "I said it partly for his benefit, so he wouldn't be jealous about my staying in your house. But as far as Niso goes, that was so he wouldn't think you were CIA."

"How does that figure?"

"Oh, come on," she said impatiently. "They don't have queers; they're a security risk."

"The same reasoning applies to the State Department."

"Does it? I thought for the State Department it'd be like a plus. I thought it was almost a prerequisite."

I looked back out to the waves. Bobbi must have seen a TV movie with a State Department character who was gay. Evidence like that admitted no rebuttal.

She closed her magazine. "Niso's been here three or four times since I came. He's slimy. I can't stand him. He doesn't trust me at all."

She sounded offended.

"Bobbi, you're spying on him. Why would he trust you?"

"Well, he doesn't know I'm spying on him; why shouldn't he trust me? But he doesn't. He's suspicious. That stupid Batista thing . . ." She frowned.

"I can see how that might make him . . . skeptical about the breadth of your historical knowledge," I said. "But why would it make him suspicious?"

"But he *is* suspicious, you see, and he tries to use silly stuff like that against me. I'm writing Cort's autobiography, you know?"

"No, I didn't know."

"Well, I am. Sort of *A Portrait of the Hoodlum as a Young Man.* Of course, he's too busy to write it himself, so it's a job for his private secretary. For me. That's OK, but Niso keeps making snide comments, like what kind of book will it be if I don't know stuff like who Batista was? I mean, really—who cares who he was? It's totally irrelevant, but he just uses anything he can to get at me."

Bobbi's cheeks were red with anger.

"Do you think . . . do you think Niso somehow has learned about you?"

She shook her head impatiently. "No, of course not. It's just the way he is. He's a jerk, and he's naturally suspicious, so he's suspicious of me." She leaned back and yawned delicately. "Actually it's not so dumb if you think about it. If I were smuggling drugs, I wouldn't like it if my partner suddenly introduced a girl friend from who knows where. It'd be one more thing to worry about."

Ben had said I should focus on how Bobbi was getting along with Cort. It was too early to worry about drug smuggling. But since she had raised the topic, I asked.

"Do you think they are smuggling drugs, Bobbi? If we can establish that . . ."

"If we can establish that, what?"

Actually I had no idea what the next step would be. "I just meant that it would be significant progress, Bobbi. So far all we really have is some suspicions."

She looked at me for a few seconds, pondering.

"Would Ben give me a raise, do you think?" she asked.

It was not what I had expected.

"Well, do you think he would?" Bobbi asked again.

"I have no idea, Bobbi."

"You know, it really doesn't make sense for him to be so cheap. If you want good work, you should pay well."

In New York Bobbi had lectured me on how she was being truly thrifty when she bought a dress for eight or nine hundred dollars. I spoke quickly to forestall another speech in the same vein.

"Look, Bobbi, your remuneration is a matter for you and Ben. I don't have anything to do with that. I do think, since you've been working for him only a couple of weeks, it might be a little early to—"

"What am I supposed to do, Jim? Wait for my five-year review? This isn't exactly a lifetime job."

"Well, no."

"So you'll ask Ben about a raise?" She touched my hand.

"Yeah, OK."

I knew Ben would explode if I suggested it. But agreeing was the only way to get Bobbi's mind off the topic. "Let's talk about drugs," I said. "Do you really think Cort and Niso are smuggling?"

Bobbi laughed.

"What's so funny?"

"Your expression, Jim. You're like—you're like a ten-year-old kid who's heard girls have boobs but doesn't quite believe it. 'You mean they really do? Wow!' That's what you sounded like."

I waited until she was done laughing. I spoke as matter-of-factly as I could. "Getting back to my question, do you think Cort and Niso are smuggling drugs?"

She had a lazy smile. "Yes, *mein Führer,* I do. No question about it."

Despite myself, I felt a chill of excitement.

"What have you seen?"

She looked up, as though asking the heavens for help. "It's not what I've seen, Jim. No one's leaving suitcases of cocaine lying around. It's just totally obvious; it's what they've got to be doing."

As quickly as it had come, the excitement disappeared. For Bobbi, the words "totally obvious" described anything she wanted to believe for which there was not a shred of objective evidence.

She noticed my expression. "No, Jim, it is. Why would Niso come here as often as he does if he's not doing something with Cort?"

"Maybe he is, Bobbi. Maybe he's talking with Cort about building a hotel. He's got an econ cover job; maybe he's just trying to solidify it."

Bobbi rolled her eyes in disbelief.

"Well, why not, Bobbi? Do they never talk about the hotel?"

"Oh, they talk about it all right. That's part of it. It's obvious it's a joke."

"Why is it a joke, Bobbi?"

She looked exasperated. "It just is, Jim. It just is."

"Why?"

She pursed her lips. For a second I thought she was going to dive back into her magazine. Then she gave a sort of weary smile. "Bathrooms," she said.

After a second she continued. "The first time I see Niso, he's there for dinner, right? So he talks a lot about the hotel project. It's all kind of phony-baloney nonsense mixed in with male chauvinism, all this 'don't you bother your pretty little head' stuff; well, he's Latin, of course, and they're all like that. Naturally I don't believe any of it, but it's not too ridiculous. I mean, it's just barely possible it could be for real. But then he starts going on about how this hotel is going to have the world's best bathrooms. Americans will go anywhere for a vacation if they know the hotel has good bathrooms, he says."

Bobbi smiled. She might despise Niso, but she enjoyed telling the story.

"Anyway, he starts describing the bathrooms. His and her toilets. Gigantic bathtubs. Jacuzzis. Everything marble. Bathrobes, of course. Towel racks will be heated." Bobbi rolled her eyes. "I don't think you need heated towel racks in the Caribbean, but that's what he said. Anyway, he kept going on and on, and I realized that he was making fun of me. Not just me, actually, but Americans. The idea is we're all superficial idiots who only care about bathrooms. And then he started getting really gross. He said he was thinking they would put in bidets, but he didn't know if American women liked bidets. Did I like bidets? Had I ever used a bidet? Did I know what a bidet was? I mean, he's asking this when we're having dinner, for heaven's sake. He really is a pig."

She snorted in disgust. Then her eyes lit up. "Then Cort, who's sort of been falling asleep through this and not saying anything, suddenly pipes up and says he doesn't know what a bidet is and will someone please explain."

Bobbi laughed briefly. "I mean, I didn't know whether to laugh or barf, but one thing I'm sure is that the whole thing was a joke for Niso. If you're really planning to build a hotel, you don't make fun of it like that."

I looked out at the waves. The sun had slipped behind a cloud, and for a moment the ocean wasn't dazzling. I wondered what to make of Bobbi's finding. At least I wouldn't have to be the one to write a cable about the meaning of bathroom fixtures. That was Ben's job.

"You see that, don't you, Jim?"

I looked back at Bobbi. "It's a point, certainly. It wouldn't hurt to have some more evidence."

"Jim, it's obvious."

The word "obvious" was beginning to wear on me. "It may be to you, but it still doesn't hurt to have some tangible indications. . . . If you want Ben to be in a position to argue for a raise for you . . ."

I felt a little bad saying that, since I couldn't imagine Ben would argue for a raise. But it was impossible to deal with Bobbi on a basis of strict honesty.

Bobbi thought for a while. "Well, how about all these trips here Niso has made?" she said.

"We already discussed that, Bobbi. It's not evidence by itself."

"No, you don't understand," she said. "The thing is, Cort doesn't want to see Niso. I mean, the hotel is supposed to be still undecided, right? Like maybe they'll do it, maybe they won't. So if it's a real possibility, Cort should be all over Niso, really eager to see him every time he comes. But he isn't. I can tell. He wishes Niso would stay the hell away."

"Well . . ."

"See, it makes sense if they're doing a drug deal," Bobbi continued eagerly. "Niso has set Cort up with the financing or the drugs, whichever it is, and Cort is going to do the rest. If that's the situation, then obviously Cort doesn't want Niso to keep sticking his nose in, and obviously Niso wants to keep track of what Cort's doing. He's got to watch his investment. It all makes sense."

With Bobbi so single-minded on one side of the argument,

I felt it was my job to play the skeptic. "Maybe Cort just doesn't like Niso."

"Oh, get real, Jim. People don't act like that when there's money at stake. If there's one thing I learned from going out with all those Wall Street creeps, it's that."

I looked at her. "Has it occurred to you that Cort's approach to life might differ from that of your friends at Goldman, Sachs or Salomon Brothers?"

Bobbi smiled. "Nicely put. But money is money."

For Bobbi, that settled the matter. She waved a foot at me. "Do you think it's a good color? The place I went to, the selection was pretty pathetic."

"Very nice toes, Bobbi."

She stretched and yawned. Suddenly her expression changed. "Oh, gosh," she said. "I forgot to tell you the biggest thing of all. This is proof positive."

"What is it, Bobbi?"

"Niso went out for a secret midnight rendezvous one time he was here."

Excitement and satisfaction lit up her face. She was terribly pleased with herself. If I used that tone of voice, I was accused of being a ten-year-old.

"Can you . . . expand that statement a little?" I asked.

"I'll tell you all about it," she said eagerly. "It was the second time Niso came. Or maybe the third, I forget. Anyway, we had dinner together, the three of us, and then I was told to excuse myself. I think they thought I was going to go to bed, but I didn't."

She leaned back and adjusted the straps of her bathing suit.

"What did you do, Bobbi?"

"I went out to the porch and sat in a wicker chair." Her voice became dreamy, reminiscent. "I was mad about having to make myself scarce, but I couldn't stay mad because it was such a gorgeous night. There were a million stars. No moon or anything, just stars. I wasn't tired, so I sat in the chair and thought about things. You know, about being a spy and how it was sort of a funny thing to be and you can never tell what life brings. Then I wondered what I'd do next, when I'm through here. I was just sort of letting my mind run. . . . Anyway, I sat there for a long time. Finally, just when I was about to go to bed, I heard George talking to the cook. It must have been eleven by then."

"Who's George?"

"One of Cort's men. Like Macho. Well, not like Macho—I wouldn't ask George to paint my nails. He'd probably pull them out to make me talk. He's heavy-duty. Like if someone needs to be killed, George is the one who kills him. Anyway, George told the cook he was going down to the boat to get things ready, but then he'd be back for Niso, and he needed some sandwiches." Bobbi lifted her chin triumphantly. "So, anyway, there's your proof."

"My proof?"

"For goodness' sake. Niso was going out on that boat at midnight. It has to be something connected with drugs, right?"

Bobbi's face held good-humored exasperation.

"I don't know, Bobbi. You said 'rendezvous' earlier. Do you know who he was meeting?"

"Oh, I just said that. I figure he had to be meeting someone. Some Colombian drug dealer, probably. Or maybe Castro."

"Or perhaps Batista?"

Bobbi looked briefly up to the heavens, but she didn't get mad. She was too pleased with her discovery.

"I'll tell Ben about it," I said. "We'll see what he thinks."

"Yeah, you tell Ben. Even that jerk will have to admit I've done something right."

"Ben's not a jerk, Bobbi."

"No, of course not. I'm a stupid, selfish little rich girl, and he's right to despise me."

"He doesn't think that."

"That's exactly what he thinks. But I don't care—I'm doing a good job, and to hell with him."

She picked up her gun and pointed it out to sea. The hammer clicked on an empty chamber. "Bang—GALLANT CIA ASSHOLE DIES IN THE LINE OF DUTY."

It was unusual of Bobbi to use such language. She really disliked Ben.

She was still looking at the waves when she spoke again. "The boat—that might be the key to everything. There's probably a lot of evidence on it."

"Do you know anything about it, Bobbi? How did Niso get it?"

"Oh, it's Cort's boat. His private yacht, don't y'know," she said in a *Masterpiece Theatre* drawl. "He's always trying to get me to go out on it."

"Cort?"

"Yeah. I guess he figures it's easier to seduce someone on water than on land."

I waited a few seconds.

"How are you getting along with him?"

It was the one thing Ben had stressed: that I should find out how Bobbi's relationship with Cort was progressing. "Who knows? One blow job, and he may turn state's evidence," he had said, sounding wistful.

"Getting along?" There was an edge to her voice.

"I just meant . . . I know you're friends—"

Bobbi's interruption saved me further floundering. "We're not lovers, if that's what you're asking. I'm not getting AIDS so Ben can win a promotion."

"Cort doesn't look like he has AIDS," I said mildly.

"Oh, great. You have X-ray medical vision now? That's reassuring."

When she spoke again, it was the more forceful of her quiet tones. "I'm patriotic all right, but I don't plan to turn hooker for the greater glory of the CIA. You can toss that idea right out."

"No one is suggesting that, Bobbi."

"Really? I bet Ben would go around scribbling my telephone number on bathroom walls if he thought it would help him."

"Look, Bobbi—"

"Never mind," Bobbi cut in. "He just gets on my nerves. I'm so glad I'm dealing with you."

"Well, that's good then," I said, patting her on the knee.

"But don't you feel a little weird about all this? I mean, I always thought you had the hots for me."

She smiled inquisitively.

"Well . . ."

"Aren't you jealous of Cort?"

"Jealous?" Anything to buy time.

"Yeah. It means you don't like someone 'cause they're getting something you're not."

"But he's not, right?"

"But if you really cared about me, you'd worry he might."

"I guess I would if I really cared about you," I said flippantly.

Bobbi laughed. "Touché. Anyway, you tell dear old Ben that it would be really dumb for me to sleep with Cort. If I did that, I'd just be one more chick he's had. As it is, I'm special."

I could see Macho up the hill. He was carrying a large wicker basket in one hand and a jug in the other.

"Looks like lunch is coming."

Bobbi twisted around to look, then settled back. She twirled a comb with her fingers.

"Do you know anyone named Malmierca, Jim?"

I thought for a while. "No," I finally said. "Who is he?"

Bobbi shrugged. "I don't know. Yesterday I overheard Cort when he was on the phone and didn't know I was there." A grin covered her face. "I love being a spy."

"What did he say?"

"I don't remember exactly. He had been looking for this Malmierca person, and he had finally found him. But he was—it was like he had to go slow; he had to be careful because he didn't want to get into things too deep."

"I see." It sounded pretty vague.

"Something like that. I couldn't hear too well."

"Was he talking to Niso?"

Bobbi looked exasperated. "How am I supposed to know? Maybe he was talking to his barber. I just figured I'd tell you 'cause it was something suspicious and I'm supposed to tell you when I hear something suspicious."

"OK, Bobbi. You did the right thing. Did you hear any more?"

"No," she said, slightly huffy. "The cook was coming, and I didn't want him to see me listening at keyholes. Or should I have tried to fade into the woodwork?"

"No, no. You did well. Laudable discretion."

She gave a sharp look but made no reply.

Macho arrived, and we stopped discussing business. After lunch Bobbi jogged along the beach and then swam for a while; I watched her. We walked up to the house together in the later afternoon, Macho trailing behind with the umbrella and other gear.

I was in the car when Bobbi told me to wait a minute. She disappeared into the house and then came out with a paper bag holding papers. It was, she said, a draft of the first chapter of Cort's autobiography.

"Just take a look at it, Jim," she said. "I did a pretty good job, I think, but you could check it over to make sure the spelling is right and everything. I want it to be in good shape before I show it to Cort. Kind of give you something intellectual to do instead of stamping visas all day long."

Macho was watching, but Bobbi showed no signs of embarrassment. She never had when she fobbed work off at Hexter either.

I told Ben about bathroom fixtures and Niso's midnight excursion and Bobbi's other discoveries. He did not appear greatly impressed. The only Malmierca in the CIA files who looked marginally relevant—simply because he was Cuban—was a rich Havana businessman who had disappeared with his yacht more than thirty years ago, just after Castro took power. Eduardo Malmierca's wife and infant son had got out earlier and lived in Miami now, but neither was suspected of anything to do with drugs.

I was depressed. At the end of the debriefing Ben had remarked casually that he was going to run along home to see if Sarah had been studying the special illustrated edition of the *Kama Sutra* he had given her. The world of conjugal ties—of any form of sex—seemed impossibly distant. I was on a desert island, and sex was somewhere else, across a big ocean. None of the airlines I knew went there.

I went home and cooked myself a hamburger. Then I read for a while and went to sleep.

The consulate reopened a week after I saw Bobbi. We now had two contract guards and a marine during working hours, as well as one guard keeping watch at night. It may have been a case of closing the barn door too late, but I was glad to see them there.

Captain Drabney called Friday morning and suggested we meet for lunch. I had lost my temper when he called the day after the bombing, but he refused to listen to an apology. "A terrible thing, Mr. Biggins, a terrible thing. You had every right to be upset." His voice was weary and civilized.

The restaurant was in the center of Wellington. It was crowded with bureaucrats from the government buildings nearby. Drabney sat in the corner, a cup of coffee in one hand although it was a hot day. He was reading a book bound in green library binding.

He rose rather formally and shook my hand. He was wearing a khaki shirt with epaulets.

"You are well, Mr. Biggins?" Drabney asked. "No ill effects from your shock?"

He had asked the same questions on the telephone. "I'm fine," I said. "I wasn't hurt at all."

"That is good to hear."

My eyes strayed to his book.

"Ah, you are curious about what I am reading. It is by your President. Your ex-President, I should say."

"Reagan?"

"No, before Mr. Reagan. President Carter. It is called *Why Not the Best?* Very good, too. You have read it, of course?"

I admitted I hadn't.

"I am surprised, Mr. Biggins. I would have thought that, as

a representative of your country . . . Of course, Carter is no longer President. You are a Bush man, no doubt."

On the wall over our table was a flyblown poster showing the late Harold Stokes, founder of the PLA and architect of Navidad's independence. Probably every official on the island had known Stokes personally, or at least knew his son, Charles, the current prime minister. It wasn't odd that Drabney would think I would be affiliated with the administration.

"You'd be surprised how little politics there is in my job," I said. "In any case, I'm afraid I've never been drawn to books by politicians. They're mostly written by ghosts, aren't they?"

"Ghosts?"

Drabney looked away nervously. Suddenly I was convinced he thought I was saying supernatural beings wrote the books.

"I just meant that since it is usually a hired writer who writes—"

"I know what a ghostwriter is, Mr. Biggins," he replied with a hint of asperity. After a moment he continued in a more friendly tone. "Have you ever been here before, Mr. Biggins? This place?"

"No."

"I come here often. Every day, just about."

"The food is good?"

"I like it," Drabney said, settling back in his chair.

He motioned to the waiter.

"Have you ever visited London, Mr. Biggins?"

The conversation certainly seemed to be jumping around.

"A couple of times."

"I was there some years ago," Drabney said, leaning forward and maneuvering a pair of sugar cubes. "In 1977. I went for a training course on police administration. At Scotland Yard."

He waited expectantly.

"I've certainly heard of Scotland Yard," I said, nodding sagely.

"Oh, yes," he agreed. "Everyone has. It is world famous. World famous. This course, the students were from various commonwealth countries. From Africa and here in the Caribbean and elsewhere. We—the students—stayed in a dormitory in Marylebone Street. It was quite nice. Do you know Marylebone Street?"

"No, I'm afraid not."

"Well, it is quite nice," he repeated, a little disappointed by my ignorance. "We took our meals there usually, but the man who taught the course, a senior British policeman, invited the students out to his home for dinner sometimes. Not all at once, but in small groups."

He paused again.

"That sounds pleasant," I said after a while.

"Yes. He was a good man. A strict grader, but a good man."

Drabney took off his glasses and polished them with a paper napkin. Then he put them carefully back on.

"He said he considered these dinners as a way of saving us from an awful fate, the fate of constantly eating institutional food." Drabney smiled. "When he said that, everyone laughed. Yes, we all agreed we would die if we had to eat any more institutional food. Until that moment, though, I don't think any of us knew that is what we had been eating."

I laughed. The waiter came over, but Drabney waved him away.

"Along with this discovery—that I had been eating institutional food without knowing it—I made another that same night. I discovered I liked institutional food. Certainly I liked it better than what the British officer gave us for dinner. It tasted better, but that was not all. I liked the place where we ate; it was friendly and bright and clean, but not—not too fussy. Simple. Like this place."

Drabney looked around. "We do not really have proper institutional food on Navidad, but this place does its best. When

I come here, I am reminded of my days on Marylebone Street."

"If we ever happen to be in Washington at the same time, I would be delighted to take you to the State Department cafeteria," I said. "You might like it there."

"That is very kind of you," Drabney replied. "I shall certainly remember the invitation."

"I can't promise it will equal the fare in Marylebone Street."

"No," Drabney agreed. "The English may be the masters when it comes to institutional food. But I would welcome the experience."

He ordered mulligatawny soup and a cheese sandwich, and I got an omelet.

"Have you found out anything about the bombing?" I asked when the waiter left.

"That is why I called you. To report our progress."

He picked up his coffee cup and cradled it in his hands. "We know where the dynamite came from. A Mr. Grissom, a rich Englishman, is building a house out on Graves's Point. He is laying pipes for sewage, and he uses dynamite. He reported a theft two days before the bombing. The shed where it was stored was broken into during the night."

Drabney looked up.

"Does that give you any leads?" I asked.

"We are following it up, but at this moment I am not optimistic. None of the workers seems to harbor a resentment against you or the United States." He smiled forlornly. "I should warn you, Mr. Biggins. It appears that more dynamite was taken than was used. I told your ambassador this morning, when I learned it."

"Oh." I felt short of breath.

"The bomb that exploded in your consulate contained only a small amount. As best as we can reckon, the attacker may have enough left for two or three more bombs."

"Oh, wonderful."

I looked around, wishing there were someone I could be angry at. Until that moment I had not really been scared. The increased guard presence at the consulate and my home seemed like a prudent measure, but in my heart I didn't really think it was necessary. I did not expect lightning to strike twice in the same place. Maybe people didn't like me, but I wasn't important enough to have enemies.

But the realization that there was more dynamite out there changed this feeling. It didn't make sense, of course. I should have assumed that someone with the will to do injury could easily acquire the means. But knowing the means were already there was upsetting, to say the least.

"We are pursuing other lines of inquiry, Mr. Biggins," Drabney said. He was trying to allay my concern.

"Yes?"

"We have talked to all the people who applied for visas that day."

"And?"

"Five of them remember an individual who cannot be accounted for. I mean, an individual who did not apply for a visa. We are certain of that. We have the passports of all the applicants, and we showed the passport photographs to these five, and none of them was the man they remember. Two of the five say the man sat on the bench in the corner, where the bomb was placed."

"That seems like something."

"Yes, I think it is quite promising. Unfortunately, none of the people who noticed the man knew who he was. We are endeavoring to arrange for a sketch of the suspect, however."

The waiter brought Drabney's soup. He blew on a spoonful and swallowed it deliberately.

I didn't quite understand Drabney's last statement. "What's the difficulty about getting a sketch?"

He dabbed at his lips with a napkin. "The artists here paint boats and market ladies with bananas on their head. Drawing a portrait from verbal descriptions is a special skill. We used to have a man who did it, but he left the island. I do not think he was very good, to tell the truth. He made everyone look too nice."

"So what are you doing?"

"There is a man in Trinidad who is very good. Quite first-rate. Normally we do not go to the expense of bringing him here, but a crime against a foreign diplomat, against a U.S. diplomat— that is another matter. Unfortunately, the fellow is on vacation, but we are trying to persuade him to come nevertheless."

The waiter returned with my omelet and Drabney's sandwich.

"If you do get a sketch, what will you do?"

"We show it to people and see if anyone can give us a name. We will show it to you, of course."

"But you said this man didn't apply for a visa."

"Not on that day, no." Drabney blew on another spoonful of soup. "But perhaps he had earlier. In any case, it seems that he had a grudge against you; maybe you know him."

It was irrational, but I did not want to look at the sketch. I wanted the man to be caught; I did not want to have anything to do with catching him.

"I'm not very good at recognizing people from pictures. Even from photographs—I don't have a very good visual memory."

It sounded thin as I said it. Drabney studied his soup for a moment before replying. When he did, all he said was, "No?"

"No," I repeated.

"Well, it is worth a try all the same," he said calmly.

For a while we ate without speaking. Drabney cut up his cheese sandwich with knife and fork and ate it carefully, bit by bit. After he swallowed the last bit, he looked up. "Did you learn anything about Lee last week? From Mannion, I mean."

For a second I was surprised. But it was obvious what had

happened. The guard at my house must have told a police patrol about Mannion's visit.

"No," I said. "He just came for a minute. He wanted money."

"Money?"

"For information," I explained.

"And you didn't give him any."

He sounded slightly disappointed.

"No, I didn't," I replied. "Why? Do you think I should have?" I was annoyed at the implied criticism.

He shrugged. "It would have been interesting to hear what he said. Of course, you probably would have wasted your money."

"Have you—have the police talked with him again?"

A frown replaced the smile. "We tried. He is no longer to be found at his address. His girl friend says he's worried for his safety. I suppose that is possible. He is—he is the sort of fellow who will eventually get himself killed, but only after he has run away a dozen times when no one was after him. The one time he should run away he won't."

Drabney heaved a sigh. Evidently Mannion was a depressing subject of thought. "He wants to be important, you see, but the only way for him to be important is to do something he shouldn't. It doesn't matter what, and it doesn't matter how stupid it is. We have a great deal of trouble from people like him."

"You know him?"

"No," Drabney said brusquely. "I have read his file. That is enough."

He motioned to the waiter. "Would you like coffee?" he asked.

"No."

"I cannot recommend the sweets here," he said as though forced to acknowledge an unpleasant truth. "They are not very good. They never have been."

He looked at me gravely.

"It's all right," I said.

"There is a store next door that has candy. Licorice, Bit-O-Honey, Tootsie rolls——"

"It's all right," I repeated.

"Shall we go then?"

We paid. Where had Drabney got the idea I always had to have something sweet to eat?

The captain and I walked a ways together. I had parked my car near his office. We went by a vacant lot with a big shade tree, with a weathered wooden chair hanging from a branch. Drabney gave it a push and stopped to watch.

"Your friend Miss Lyons is no longer here in Wellington," he said after giving the chair a second push.

"No, she found a job elsewhere."

"The Hook is——it is not a normal place for a young lady to find work."

Of course Drabney would know where she was. My effort at concealment had been pathetic.

"Bobbi is not exactly an ordinary young lady," I said.

Drabney pursed his lips. "Ah, I have not had the pleasure of meeting her. I have seen her. My wife's anniversary last Monday I took her to Chez Marlot for dinner." He smiled. "It is funny—I always call the anniversary of my wedding my wife's anniversary. I suppose it is because such occasions are for women."

Beams of sunlight passed through the branches, dappling the chair as it swung back and forth. Drabney's moment of reflection passed. "Cort was there. At the restaurant. He had a white girl with him. I had heard that Miss Lyons had taken a job with him, so I looked at this girl with particular interest. When we went home, my wife complained about it. I told her it was purely professional, but I am not sure she believed me." He shrugged.

"She talked a great deal," he continued. "I couldn't hear what she was saying, but I could see her talking."

"Cort couldn't get a word in edgewise, eh?"

Drabney smiled for half a second. Then he became serious. "Cort is not someone to make jokes about, Mr. Biggins. He is a hard man. He does not do the things he did when he was a young man. He has other people do them for him. He likes to pretend he never did anything bad, that he is a victim of prejudice. He is very clever at acting that part. Sometimes, I think, he convinces himself. But he is not someone to trifle with."

It was the first time I had heard the words "not someone to trifle with" used seriously in conversation. I wasn't quite sure how to reply.

"If she were my girl friend," he continued, "I would see if I could find her another job."

"Bobbi's not my girl friend."

"No?" Drabney raised his eyebrows. "Still, even if she were just a friend, I might wish her to be someplace else."

Drabney left me with that thought. It was nearly three when I got back to the consulate. One of the guards was eating a sandwich on the front porch while the other swept up in the waiting room. Jake, the marine, was doing pushups in a corner, a portable radio by his head.

I had barely sat down when Sammy hurried into my office. Bobbi had called three times in the last twenty minutes. He was handing me her telephone number when the phone rang again.

"You're there. Thank God," Bobbi said breathlessly.

"What is it?" I spoke curtly; I wanted to catch up on some work, and I was sure I was about to hear some grade A tripe.

"It's it, that's what it is. I'm hot on the trail, and I need you right now."

"Bobbi . . ."

"You've got to come right this second!"

I wanted to ask for details, but the line might be bugged.

"I'm at a place called Jocko's, in Selva. You've got to come now. Jocko's, in Selva. I need——"

The line went dead.

Sammy had a slip of paper in his hand. I grabbed it from him and dialed the telephone number on it. There was a busy signal.

Selva was somewhere on the north coast. I looked at the map of the island over the couch. There was a traced line from Wellington to Selva, indicating a direct secondary road, but the coast road did not look terribly much longer. It would certainly be faster.

I typed an account of Bobbi's telephone call and said I was going to meet her. I put the paper in an envelope and wrote Ben Jacoby's name on it.

"I have to go on an errand," I told Sammy. "If you haven't heard from me in a couple of hours, go to the embassy and give this envelope to Mr. Jacoby. Tell him that I will be in touch with him as soon as I can."

Sammy nodded as though it were an ordinary request, although it certainly wasn't. Everything felt absurd and melodramatic. But I could feel my skin prickling; at least this wasn't a typical afternoon at the consulate.

I went to the telephone again, thinking I was in for a big letdown if Bobbi answered and said she had had to rush off for a call of nature.

It was still busy. I left to drive to Jocko's.

10

The rendezvous was thirty-five miles from Wellington on the coast road. I made it in just under forty minutes, taking the dips on a diagonal and hitting my head against the roof on the bumps. I doubt Ben would have gone faster.

Selva means "jungle" in Spanish. Maybe there was a jungle there when the island loomed up as a Christmas present for a straying captain on Columbus's second expedition. There wasn't one now. There were just two streets of low buildings, with a few trees and a lot of empty space with scrubby grass and weeds.

Jocko's was a one-story wooden frame building with a couple of aisles of food goods on one side and some tables for eating on the other. By a cash register there was a rack holding out-of-date magazines. Two middle-aged men sat at one of the tables, one reading a newspaper and the other watching me.

Bobbi was nowhere to be seen. On a little table in the rear was a telephone with the mouthpiece not on the cradle.

"Dr. Watson?"

The words came from the man who had been reading the newspaper.

"You're Watson, aren't you?" he continued. "Your lady friend left a message."

"Yes?"

"She said you'd give a tip."

He looked at me expectantly. I took out my wallet and gave him five dollars.

He stuck the bill in his pocket. "She told me to keep the phone off the hook until you got here. She said you'd be here in ten minutes." He gave me an accusatory look.

"I was delayed."

"Why'd she want to keep the phone off the hook? Is it some kind of joke?"

"Yeah. She's quite a kidder."

"It's all right if I put it back now?"

"Yes. What was the message?"

"You should go to East Rock."

I asked a few questions, but there was nothing more. The turnoff to East Rock was on the other side of Selva, the man said, and then I had to go about two miles on.

The other fellow at the table had not spoken, but as I left, he said, "Have a good time."

The turnoff road was one lane wide. It rose at a sharp gradient, twisting frequently. Fortunately, I did not meet any cars coming the other way.

From a distance I could see a large house with an awning. I wondered if I would find Bobbi inside or another telephone off the hook and a message. But on the last switchback before the house she stepped out onto the road and waved me to stop.

She looked as if she had had a rough day. Her hair was tousled and her cheeks were windburned. She was wearing white culottes and a camisole top with little Mickey Mouses all over it.

"Do you have any seltzer?" she asked.

I was stunned. Not "They were after me, but I escaped." Not "Thanks for getting here so quickly." No, it was "Do you have any seltzer?"

I started laying into her. What had she been doing, calling me at the consulate? Why had she left the phone at Jocko's off the hook? And "Dr. Watson," for chrissakes.

She smiled wearily. "You're not making sense, Jim. First you're mad at me for talking on your phone, and then you're mad at me for fixing it so that we won't talk on it. Are you sure you don't have anything to drink?"

I went to the car and opened the trunk. I had visited the commissary in the morning and got beer. I gave her one and took one myself.

"Warm beer—just what I wanted," she said. But she opened it and drank.

"Sit down, Jim," she said, patting a rock. "You're getting overheated yelling at me. That's no good. Sit down, and I'll tell you everything. After that we can decide what to do."

She ran her hands over her legs. "I don't think they'll ever be the same. There's no skin left—just scratches."

Then she told her story. At breakfast she asked Macho to take her to a small island just offshore. He had refused, seeming nervous. From his manner Bobbi thought he was concealing something. At first she thought it might involve the island, but George was willing to take her there, so that did not seem to be it.

Macho said he had errands in Wellington. Bobbi cadged a ride with him and then, when she got out, gave him money and a list of shopping to do for her. She made him promise to go to Apley's Market first thing, to make sure the desired items hadn't sold out.

"I had decided to follow him, you see. As soon as he dropped me off, I rented a motorcycle." She nodded toward the hill, and I saw a motorcycle lying on its side, partly concealed behind a bush.

She caught up with him as he was leaving the market. The coast road made it difficult, but Bobbi was sure he hadn't realized he was being followed. She had rented a helmet along with the bike, and that helped. A lot of the time she lagged behind, out of sight, creeping up occasionally to check that he was still there. He never looked back to see if anyone was following.

He went through Selva and made the turnoff on the East Rock road. Bobbi continued on and then doubled back as soon as he was out of sight. She risked losing him, but she knew there couldn't be many possible destinations on this out-of-the-way lane. She was more worried about running into Macho around a sudden bend in the road.

But she didn't run into Macho, and soon she saw the big house, as I had. She went the last bit on foot. Near the house was a small clearing, where a number of cars were parked. Macho's, or rather the car of Cort's that Macho had driven, was one of them. From there she could read writing on the house awning. It said, 'Annette's.'

"I started to laugh. What a letdown. All the trouble I had gone to and scratches on my legs and everything, all so I could come to Annette's." She chuckled ruefully.

"What is Annette's?"

"Jim. I'm shocked. You really don't know? How long have you been here?"

"Longer than you, Bobbi, but I'm afraid I don't know every night spot on the island. If that's what it is."

"Annette's is a sporting house. A brothel," she added didactically.

"Cort's always making jokes about it. I gather it has some pretty hot merchandise, if you go for that sort of thing," she said after a few seconds.

She spread her arms and yawned. "Anyway, there I was, lurking behind a tree and feeling pretty foolish. I mean, of course, Macho's not going to tell me he's going to Annette's. I was really pissed. And then . . ." She smiled. "Then another car drove up."

She looked at me, her face blank.

"Well?" I prompted.

"Niso got out."

"Niso?"

"Yes. Mr. Carreras of the Cuban Embassy."

She scratched her leg. "This beer would be much better if it were cold," she said judiciously. "Anyway, I decided I hadn't been so dumb after all. Obviously they're like meeting for a secret rendezvous. You know what I think? I think maybe this is where they transfer the drugs. Like maybe Niso gets them through the diplomatic pouch and he brings them to Annette's and they do the trade here. You know, I bet they're making the transfer right this second."

The final sentence came out in an inspired rush. She looked inordinately satisfied with herself. She picked up her beer and drank a little. Then she made a face and put the can down. She looked at me again. After a while she got impatient. "Well, what do you think?"

It was hot, and my shirt was sticking to me with sweat. Also, I had just realized that I was missing a talk on the new guidelines for promotion to the Senior Foreign Service. What I said came out ruder than I meant to be.

"Did you figure this out all by yourself, or did you have an old *Miami Vice* episode in mind to help you out?"

Her face went red. It was nearly a minute before she replied. "Look, Jim, I'm terribly sorry I am the way I am. So stupid and obvious, I mean. Yeah, of course, all my ideas are straight out of the boob tube. Where else would a dumb person like me get an idea? But I don't know if you've noticed one thing: At least I'm trying. At least I have an idea or two. I haven't heard anything from you except cracks and complaints."

She kicked her beer can. It went sailing off end over end, pale beer spattering the air. Then she walked over to her motorcycle and bent over it. I don't know what she had in mind. Perhaps she didn't either; she fiddled with it but didn't attempt to set it upright.

I wasn't in a mood to offer an apology, but when I spoke, I tried to imply the disagreement was behind us. "When you called me, Bobbi, what did you want me to do?"

"Oh, that doesn't matter, does it? It was bound to be idiotic."

I took a breath. "I think, Bobbi, you've made a worthwhile discovery. Finding out about this meeting, I mean. I'll tell Ben."

"Oh, my goodness, you'll tell Ben I've done something worthwhile. Oh, joy. Oh, rapture unconfined."

"Look, Bobbi. If I offended you, I regret it. I didn't mean to. I just want to know if you had some particular reason for wanting me to be here. When we spoke on the phone, you sounded urgent."

"Can I have another beer?"

It was a peace offering. "Sure," I said.

She got the beer but just studied it without opening it. Then she looked up warily.

"After I saw Niso, I just thought it would be a good idea to let you know. But when I was calling, I realized I shouldn't really say anything, so . . ." She shrugged cheerily.

"Didn't you think disconnecting in the middle of a sentence was a little melodramatic?"

"It got you here, didn't it?" She smiled. "Since there are two of them, I just thought it would be more fair if there were two of us. I don't know—maybe you could tail Niso when they leave, and I could tail Macho. Or vice versa, I don't care. Anyway, we should probably get our act together; they may be coming along any moment."

I wondered if she could possibly be serious. But obviously she was. Various rejoinders came to mind, but I quelled them.

"I think, Bobbi, we should be happy with what we've got, and let the rest go. You found out Macho was here to meet Niso— that's the key thing. They'll probably just go home from here."

A mocking smile appeared on her lips. "Cold feet?"

"Yes," I replied. "I'm driving a red Chevy with U.S. diplomatic plates. I'm not going to tail anyone. And you shouldn't press your luck anymore either."

She wiped away a speck of dirt on her knee with a moistened finger. "OK," she said tiredly. "If that's what you think best."

I wrestled her bike into the trunk so we could go back together. By the time I got it stowed I had made up my mind that the real reason she called me was to have someone she could boast to.

But I may have been wrong.

"You know, I did have one thing sort of in mind," she said lightly. She hesitated. "I mean, as something you could do. I don't know, maybe it wasn't too realistic."

This was not like Bobbi. "Why don't you just say it?"

"Well, I was thinking maybe you could go into Annette's. You know, as a customer. You could find out where they are and sneak in and overhear them. That'd be really major."

I just looked at her.

She giggled. "Well, maybe it wasn't such a great idea at that. But look, suppose they have girls with them? You could go in and then, when they leave, you could go with one of the girls and find out what they were saying."

I didn't say anything. After a while she smiled. "I didn't think you would do it," she said. "But I thought it was worth suggesting."

I wiped the grime of the motorbike off my hands with a handkerchief. "I'm flattered, Bobbi. I thought to you I was just a wuss."

"Sometimes you act wussy, Jim, but that's not how I think of you. You just don't have enough self-confidence. You know, you can be whatever you want to be."

Bobbi had missed her calling. She should have been a recruiter for the armed forces.

We got in the car. I turned the key in the ignition. Bobbi reached over and turned it off. "I just thought of something else," she said.

"Oh, no."

"Come on, Jim, we're supposed to be having fun. Try to get into the spirit of it."

"What did you think of?" I kept my voice level and my hand on the key.

"Nothing risky. I just remembered that the car Niso came in, it wasn't his usual car. We should go get the license number. Maybe Ben could put it into a computer or something."

"Can it be seen from the house?"

"No," Bobbi answered eagerly. "It's off to the side. There's a garden between the parking lot and the house; if we see anyone coming, we just hightail it back here."

I don't know if by that point I merely wanted to be agreeable or if I was so off-balance that I was actually worried about being a wuss; at any event, I agreed. So I can't really blame Bobbi for what happened.

No, that's wrong. I certainly can blame her.

We walked along the road a little ways. Just before we crested the hill, we took to the trees. We came to a gully, and Bobbi said it led to the parking lot. She had shed her fatigue; she was practically skipping along.

There was a breeze, and the trees lent some shade. I was

nervous, but it would be a lie to say that I wasn't also excited. Bobbi's mood had infected me. A bright green lizard regarded me from the leaf of a plant. I could see the pulse in its throat, the only movement there was. What was I doing? it seemed to ask.

"God knows," I said under my breath.

"What?"

"Nothing."

There were five cars in the clearing. Bobbi pointed to a white sedan. "That's Niso's. When he comes to Cort's, he always drives a Volkswagen."

The car was an old Toyota, with nothing unusual about it. The license plate was not visible from our vantage point.

We stood for a minute, watching and listening. Bobbi had lied; the parking area was visible from the house. Still, at the moment there seemed to be no danger. The only sounds were the wind and the muted splash of water in a fountain.

"I'll go check the license plate," Bobbi said. "You keep watch."

She walked calmly to Niso's car. I lingered behind the tree for a second, then went to a van and looked around. The house was forty or fifty yards distant. A curtain shifted slightly in a window, but it was only the wind. In the garden a bird descended upon the arm of a bench, pecked twice, and flew off.

Bobbi was staring in the window of the car. Then she turned toward me. She sucked in her lip and raised her eyebrows.

She ran over. "There's a letter in there. Stuck down between the front seats."

"Let's go, Bobbi."

"I said there's a letter there." She grabbed my arm. "We've got to get it. You don't have a wire hanger, do you?"

"Jesus Christ," I said in disbelief. "No, I don't. Let's go."

"You keep watch here," she said brusquely. "I'm going back to look around."

She walked off, her eyes on the ground.

I growled her name again, but she paid no attention. I thought of running after her and dragging her back, but it didn't seem a good way of avoiding attention.

I turned to look at the house. The door was opening.

It was only the screen door, moved by the wind. It closed. The sound was barely audible. Bobbi's eyes were fastened on the ground.

The tops of the trees were moving in the wind. Clouds scudded across the sky. We might be in for a shower.

There was a noise, and I looked back at the house. The screen door had slammed again, this time louder. No one was visible.

I wondered if afternoons were a slow time for the brothel trade. It wouldn't be convenient to have someone drive up now.

Two birds landed in the garden and disputed a crumb.

There was a crunching noise nearby. Bobbi was standing by the driver's window of Niso's car, a rock in her hand. She had her Windbreaker wrapped around the arm holding the rock.

Half the window was gone. Bobbi pulled her arm back and struck again. More glass broke. She reached inside, careful to avoid cutting herself, and opened the door.

She got the letter and waved it, a trophy. Then she seemed to be gingerly positioning herself to reach for the glove compartment. She moved carefully; there must have been a good deal of glass on the seat.

"Hey there," a voice shouted. "Who're you? What're you doing there?"

A black man in workman's clothes half walked, half ran up to Niso's car. He had a slight limp.

"What you doing?" he shouted. "You stealing? You stealing something?"

He looked around forty, muscular and fit. His clothes were

very dirty, and he had a spade in his hand. He must have come from behind a hedge on the far side of the cars. I had been looking in the other direction.

Bobbi said something I couldn't hear. The gardener shook his head vigorously. "No, it's not your car. Why you break the window if it's your car? You broke the window; I saw you break the window."

Bobbi replied inaudibly.

The man shook his head again, waving the spade for emphasis. "You lose keys, you get someone to open the car for you, you don't break the window. I think you're stealing."

He reached in to grab Bobbi's foot. "We'll go see Mr. Tompkins. We'll go see him."

I heard Bobbi then. "Stop," she shouted. "You're hurting me."

I glanced at the house. There was no sign of activity. The gardener had been speaking loudly, but not enough to carry to the house.

The gardener released Bobbi and stepped back a pace. "You get out," he said. He sounded less excited but no less determined. "We'll go and see Mr. Tompkins. You tell him what you're doing. You tell him."

"I'm not getting out," Bobbi said.

The gardener stared at her.

"You get out," he said after a second.

"No," Bobbi snarled. "Go away."

The resistance seemed to surprise him. For a couple of seconds he had a perplexed expression. Then he grinned.

"OK, you stay there. Stay right there. I'll honk the horn, and Mr. Tompkins will come here. He'll see you right in there, stealing."

He reached in toward the horn. I had to do something.

"You," I whispered.

The gardener jerked as if he were on a string. "Who's that?" he said. He spoke in a whisper, too, imitating me.

I had ducked behind the van as soon as I spoke. I couldn't see him, and he couldn't see me. I could see his shadow, though. For a second or two it remained motionless. Then he took a step toward the van.

"Stop," I hissed.

The shadow stopped.

"Sit on the ground."

The shadow was motionless.

"Sit on the ground," I repeated. "I have a gun."

After a second the shadow shortened. He had sat down.

"Shit," he said in a low voice.

I heard some noise from the car. Presumably Bobbi was extricating herself.

"What's your name?" I asked.

The shadow wavered slightly, as if the gardener was twisting his head.

"What's your name?" I repeated.

"His name's David," Bobbi said. "He has a name chain."

"OK," I said. I took a breath. "David, the lady and I are going to leave. If you come after us, I'll shoot you. If you tell anybody what you've seen—if you describe the lady to the police or anyone else—I'll shoot you. Or someone else will. I can do that. It's easy—you work here, your name is David, there's no trouble finding you. You're dead if you tell anyone."

I spoke as calmly as I could. Bobbi appeared around the edge of the van. She gave a big smile, which almost undid me.

I took another breath. David wasn't making a sound.

"You sit there," I said. "Don't do anything for an hour. Then you can go up to the house and tell them the car has a broken window. But that's all you've seen. You understand, David? That's all you've seen."

Bobbi had taken a few steps toward the trees. She motioned for me to follow.

"You understand, David?" I repeated.

"Yeah," I heard, very quiet and breathy.

"If you talk to the police, I'll know," I said. "I don't want to kill you, but I will."

I paused, but the gardener said nothing. "You keep quiet, there'll be a letter for David the gardener next month. With cash in it. You understand?"

This time the "yeah" was even quieter.

Bobbi was in the trees, walking away. I followed her briskly. No sound came from the parking lot. After a little while we started running.

At the gully we slowed a little. It was uphill, but we kept up a fairly good pace. By the time we reached the car my lungs were on fire.

I drove as fast as I could. Bobbi was twisted around, looking to our rear.

By the time we got to the coast road I had got my breath back. Bobbi took one last look up the lane, then bent over and kissed me.

Then she let out a stage sigh. "Jesus Christ, Jim, the way you go on. I thought you were going to give that guy your life history."

11

I am not fatalistic by temperament.
I can't help asking myself what was the point at which I truly
abandoned all good sense.

The day of that visit to Annette's seems like a strong candidate
for the honor. There are other possibilities, certainly, but that day
is what stands out in my memory.

I'm not speaking of the time we spent in the parking lot.
I'm referring to what happened a few hours later.

Bobbi was manic on the drive back. Every moment of the
last thirty minutes had to be relived a dozen times. It reminded
me of summer camp when other kids insisted on rehashing the
daily softball game for hours on end. I did not enjoy those sessions.
Even if I had performed adequately, I always knew I could have
done badly. It was worse with Bobbi spouting off beside me. Missing
a routine fly ball is, after all, no tragedy. But what if the gardener
had decided to see whether or not I had a gun? That would have

meant the end of my diplomatic career, if not jail. I had been a fool. A lucky fool certainly, but a fool.

And it was still far from clear that we were safe. What if the gardener ignored my threats? All he had to do was furnish a description of Bobbi. Certainly Niso and Macho would know who was being described, and the police would not have much trouble either. Navidad was simply too small, with too few white people, for there to be difficulty identifying her. The gardener hadn't seen me, thank God, but those men at Jocko's had. If Bobbi were arrested, how long would it be before they took their tale of plump Dr. Watson to the police?

At the coast road I turned right. Left would have taken me back the way I had come. I had a half-baked idea of throwing off the pursuit if there was any; also, I wanted to make a phone call and I didn't want to do it in Jocko's. Twenty miles up the road was Smithtown, the biggest habitation on the north coast. I stopped at a restaurant there.

Ben sounded surprisingly calm when I got him. He thanked me for the card, so I knew Sammy had delivered my note.

I said Bobbi and I were fine, but we'd have to cancel out on the drinks invitation. For once I was glad his line was probably bugged. A direct order to come over was not possible. As it was, he did his best to change my mind, but he had to play it as a social event.

I knew I was doing the wrong thing. It seemed clear the operation would have to be aborted. If the gardener talked, as he could at any time, Bobbi would be in trouble and the embassy would face substantial embarrassment. Clearly, the first thing to do was consult with Ben and then see about getting Bobbi off the island. If she weren't around, things would probably blow over.

But I was too drained to see him now. I just couldn't face it.

Bobbi had made a beeline to the bar when we came in. She

downed her second margarita as I hung up. "Put it on Herr Jacoby's tab." She grinned. I steered her to the car.

From Smithtown we took an interior road, cutting through the spine of hills in the middle of the island. The road was narrow and probably had not been resurfaced since it was built. I had to go slowly.

After a while Bobbi's flow of talk began to flag. Suddenly she drew a breath.

"Oh, gosh. I forgot. The letter."

She reached in a pocket and drew it out.

"Turn on the light," she said.

I turned on the interior light. She studied the envelope.

"Spanish stamps. Addressed to Henry Wood," she said. "You think Wood is Niso? It'd be funny if we went to all that trouble and he's not. Maybe it's a rented car, and Wood is just some guy who had it before and left his mail lying around."

Bobbi chuckled. I reflected sourly that it must be nice to be so comfortable that you could treat anything and everything as a game.

She unfolded the letter—it was one of those overseas letters, on which you write on the paper and then fold it to form the envelope—and started to look at it.

"Oh, damn. Curses. Fuzzballs."

I grimaced. I had let a woman who used "fuzzballs" as an expletive put my career at risk. I needed psychiatric help.

"It's in Spanish," she said disconsolately. Then she brightened. "Do you read Spanish?"

"A little."

She tried to hand me the letter. "Let's wait until we get back," I said.

"I could drive while you read," she offered eagerly.

"I can't read Spanish very well, Bobbi. I'd rather not try to do it in a bouncing car."

"We could stop."

"Let's wait," I said. "I have a Spanish-English dictionary at home; I'll probably need it."

She folded the letter and put it in her pocket with an amused smile. "Oh, Jim. You never cut loose, do you? You're always deferring . . . what is it you defer?"

"Gratification?"

"Right. You're big on deferred gratification."

"When I don't forgo it altogether."

She smiled again but didn't say anything. She stretched and yawned. "I feel wonderful," she said. "Won-der-ful. I can't think when's the last time I had two margaritas. It must be years. Probably when I graduated college." She giggled. "That was another miraculous escape. Graduating college."

She stretched again. Her head was lolling on the back of the seat. She leaned over toward me.

"You were terrific, Jim. It was like you turned into someone else. It was like *Plain It Again, Sam,* when Woody Allen turns into Humphrey Bogart."

"He does?"

She yawned. Her shoulder brushed mine.

"Yeah," she said. "More or less. He has this thing with Diane Keaton, who's married to his best friend, but then he gives her up, like in *Casablanca* Bogart gives up Ingrid Bergman."

"I see," I said dryly.

She smiled. "You're making fun of me," she said. "But I don't mind. You were good today. Very good."

"Thank you." I nodded minutely.

"I mean it," she said. She touched my arm.

"Well, thank you again," I said.

I felt awkward. I was accepting her compliments under false pretenses.

"I'm glad you think I handled myself well, Bobbi. But I'm

afraid—I think that may have been our last foray together. I think you should leave Navidad. You can spend the night at my—"

She stiffened. "What are you saying?"

"I'm saying that we'll have to talk to Ben, but I guess he'll agree with me that it wouldn't be safe—"

She bent forward and turned off the interior light. "I can't stand that glare," she said sharply. "It was in my eyes."

She took a breath. "I don't know what you mean, Jim. We're doing great. We found out about that meeting—I found out about the meeting—and we bamboozled that guy in the parking lot and we got this letter and it's probably full of vital secrets. I mean, everything's going great. Why should I leave now? That's crazy."

I told her my thinking. She managed to keep from interrupting until I started talking about diplomatic embarrassments and police pursuit. Then she exploded.

"Well, you can forget about that," she said in a tone of complete dismissal. "That's ridiculous. Totally ridiculous. Niso's smuggling drugs and he's a Cuban spy and he's at a secret rendezvous at a brothel and the car is probably hot—I mean, there isn't a chance in a million he'd go to the police. That's the silliest thing I ever heard."

I had been too worried about my own vulnerabilities to think of Niso's. I had a bizarre feeling that what Bobbi was saying might actually make sense. But there was another factor.

"It may not be in Niso's hands. Suppose the owner of Annette's—"

"Right," she broke in contemptuously. "Jim, for a smart guy, you can say some pretty dumb things. You really think the owner's gonna do something a customer doesn't want him to? When he's running an illegal business himself? Let's get real."

She was right. The incident would not be reported to the police.

There was still the matter of Niso and Macho's learning about her. I could sense Bobbi holding her breath, waiting for me to bring it up. I didn't, though. I was too tired. It would be easier to make her see sense when I didn't have to concentrate on driving.

Eventually her shoulders dropped their rigid set.

For a while neither of us spoke. It turned completely dark, except for the slight radiance cast by a new moon. We descended from a big hill, and buildings rose up darkly to our left. I had driven by once before. It was an abandoned nineteenth-century sugar plantation. Even by day the ruins looked old and mysterious; at night they were beautiful.

A half mile on there were a few houses by the road. They were shacks really, but in the dark they promised an idyllic island simplicity. Music leaked out through the windows. I couldn't see any people, but a goat tethered to a stunted tree loomed up gray in the headlights.

I was acutely conscious of Bobbi's physical presence. She had moved close when she was comparing me with Woody Allen and Humphrey Bogart; she hadn't moved away when we argued. I couldn't help thinking how pleasant it would be to be taking this drive if we had nothing to worry about. Of course, if those were the circumstances, we wouldn't be taking the drive.

We must have been traveling in silence for fifteen minutes or so before she spoke. Her voice was low, with that intimacy darkness gives. "We're going to your house?"

"Yes," I said. "I thought you should spend the night. I think it would be safer, until we know how things stand. . . ."

I sounded awkward to myself. I figured this would signal the end of the truce. She'd insist on going back to Cort's.

But she didn't. "OK." She whistled one long note. "It'll be nice to sleep somewhere civilized for a change."

"Your room there isn't——"

I felt as if I were talking for the sake of making noise. Bobbi laughed lazily. "The room is fine. All modern conveniences. I was talking about the human conveniences."

We lapsed into silence again. Soon the outskirts of Wellington appeared. Our route went by the American Club. People were sitting down to dinner now or having a last drink at the bar. They'd be talking about the new rules for the Senior Foreign Service, how they would affect their chances. Those who had got videocassettes mailed from home would be inviting others over to see them. No doubt the Casino Night Committee would be holding another meeting, with the usual inexplicable riotous laughter. It wasn't a terrible way to spend an evening. In the time I had been on Navidad I had spent many evenings in exactly that fashion.

At the moment it seemed quite remote.

There weren't any police at my house. I hadn't really been expecting them, but still, I was relieved. The guard who had been keeping watch since the bombings gave a friendly wave, not looking at Bobbi.

"Jim, I've just absolutely got to have a shower," Bobbi said. "Can you give me a towel and a robe?"

I fetched the required articles. "If you have some champagne, hero, you could pop it in the freezer. I've already had my month's quota of alcohol, but we deserve it, don't you think?"

I found a bottle of Mumm's Cordon Rouge left over from the surprise birthday party for Ben's wife and put it in the freezer. Then I took a shower myself.

Bobbi's shower was still running when I got out. I dressed and put out champagne flutes. Then I tried to read a magazine article about Sylvester Stallone. What would Rambo do in my place? Wiping out Niso and Cort would pose no problem, but wouldn't Bobbi be a little troublesome, even for him?

Finally she appeared, her pale face framed by damp hair. She was lost in my robe, and its shade did not suit her coloring.

Somehow that didn't matter, or rather it contributed to the impression she made. That was of someone softer and more vulnerable than her usual self. The effect no doubt was largely due to the fact that she wasn't wearing makeup, but at the time it seemed as though a layer of assurance had been removed. Her eyes were wide and seemed slightly confused.

"I took out my contacts," she said with a smile. She made an effort to focus. "You're looking elegant. What is it—are we dressing for dinner?"

I had risen. "Oh, no," I said. "This was all I had."

"Really."

She seemed amused. I got the champagne from the refrigerator and carefully essayed the cork.

The silence grew burdensome. "About dinner," I said. "I don't think it would be smart to go to a restaurant. Until we know more, I mean. There's some frozen pizza we could heat up—"

"Jim."

I looked up.

"I don't want pizza."

Evidently something was very funny.

"I want you."

I had trouble finding someplace to put the bottle, but I managed.

We did eventually eat the pizza, but that was two and a half hours later. Before that we made love and Bobbi called Cort and we made love again.

The picture that stays in my mind is of her dialing the telephone. She was lying on her stomach, propped up on her forearms, slantwise across the bed. Her tongue was in her cheek and her brow furrowed in concentration as she dialed. That expression was familiar from dozens of occasions at Hexter. What I hadn't seen then, though, was the long bow of her naked back and the soft rise of her buttocks.

I suppose it was the combination of old and new that fixed the sight in my memory.

"I don't know," she replied when I asked what she was going to say. "I'll think of something."

It wasn't Cort who answered the phone. Bobbi told the person to find him. As she waited, I started wondering what she possibly would say. I began to get tense. It seemed an incredibly difficult problem.

Of course, it wasn't. She told him that she was watching a movie at my house, that it wouldn't be over until late and she was going to stay because she wanted to do some shopping in Wellington in the morning. He entered a mild protest, but she told him not to be silly.

"Don't you think I'm a natural as a secret agent?" she asked as she put down the phone.

Sex was a surprise. That is, it was certainly a surprise to find myself in bed with Bobbi, but it was also a surprise how good it was. Insofar as I had thought about it, I had figured that sleeping with her was bound to be a disappointment. That seemed a more or less inevitable consequence of the fact that reality does not stand comparison with fantasies. Also, Bobbi had a streak of prudishness—"fuzzballs" and so on—that didn't augur well for relaxed carnality.

But she was soft and delicious. I was the one who was tense. Eventually, though, I relaxed.

Afterward, while the pizza was warming up, I puzzled over the letter. Some expressions defeated me, but I was able to get the drift. The writer had been traveling in Spain and described places she had been. She paid particular attention to real estate values in Madrid and Barcelona.

It wasn't very exciting stuff, and my translation proceeded slowly. Bobbi got bored. At the end, though, there was a positive note. The writer said how much she missed Niso and that she hoped he was exercising sufficient caution. At least we hadn't stolen the letter of some poor innocent.

When we went back to bed, Bobbi gave me a massage. She talked about New York, about how women were not attracted by superficial things like looks (no doubt calculated to be reassuring), and about where she would live if she had all the money she could want. Apparently it would be a couple of months each in London, Paris, and New York, with summers on a Norwegian fjord and winters in the South Pacific. I grunted a response once in a while.

She also talked about being a spy. She knew she wasn't perfect, but she was doing her best, and she thought she was doing a pretty fair job actually. She was earnest and uncharacteristically modest.

She did my back first. Then I turned over, and she worked down from the head and up from the feet. That left her in the middle, and when she got there, she began doing something else, something that she was very good at.

Bobbi can be devious, but she's not subtle. I knew what was going on. By allowing what happened to happen, I was promising she could continue in the job. And that meant I was promising to lie to Ben.

As I said, she was very good at what she did.

12

New things are unreal. When I
joined the Foreign Service, the first few weeks seemed make-
believe. I woke up in the morning expecting to find myself back
in New York, going in to work at Hexter. And when I started
serving as Bobbi's case officer, it was like a game we were playing
for an audience that wasn't there.

But no longer. The balance had tipped. The fright in Annette's
parking lot and what had passed between Bobbi and me the night
before made it real. Knowing I was about to lie to Ben just
confirmed it.

At breakfast Bobbi called Macho and arranged for him to
pick her up at the consulate at noon. The idea was that she and
I would see him and decide whether the gardener had talked. If
Macho behaved oddly in any way, then everything was off,
and we'd concentrate on getting her off the island. I had insisted
on that.

As we left the house in the morning, we saw Rollo. The

ambassador was out for his morning jog, moving slowly but springily, wearing an overpoweringly bright yellow and green outfit that made him look like some bizarre Caribbean parrot. He gave a wave and shouted a greeting I couldn't hear. Lewis, a tall, thin marine, was weaving from side to side so that his faster pace would not take him away from Rollo. Before the consulate was bombed, Rollo had jogged by himself.

I dropped Bobbi off in town and went to see Ben.

He was in his office. As soon as I started to speak, he put a finger to his lips, then guided me to the conference room that is supposedly impervious to electronic eavesdropping.

He smiled thinly. "I knew Bobbi was a loose cannon; I didn't figure you for one, too. What the fuck happened?"

I told him. When I got to the part about Bobbi breaking into the car, he intoned, "Holy shit," quietly. Those were his only words during my report.

I left out the gardener's seeing Bobbi. Otherwise I gave a faithful account.

He frowned. "Why did Bobbi spend the night at your house? She should have gone right back to Cort's."

I shrugged. "She gets tired of it there."

He exploded. He had been waiting for an opportunity, and that was it.

"She gets tired of it? What the fuck does she think she's doing, taking a rest cure? She's supposed to be getting Cort to trust her—"

The way he was going, the Cubans wouldn't need electronics; they'd hear him fine in Havana with a favoring wind.

"I heard her talking to him on the phone," I interrupted. "She's got him dangling on a string. She knows what she's doing."

He muttered, but there wasn't much he could say. He couldn't debate the ways Bobbi chose to exercise her appeal, since for him it was nonexistent.

Macho and Niso's rendezvous sounded like a standard fallback arrangement, he said. "You know, Cort needs to get a message to Niso, but it's awkward to meet in person. So someone calls the Cuban Embassy and says the rain falls mainly on the plain. That means Niso goes to Annette's. It's corny, but it works."

But even if that was what had happened, we still had no idea what the meeting was about. When I tentatively mentioned Bobbi's notion that Niso might be bringing drugs to Macho, Ben's left eyebrow shot up improbably high.

"Niso's crude, but he's not as crude as that. He won't get near the drugs himself."

We had been talking for a while when I realized that I was no longer tense. Lying was not as hard as I had thought it would be.

Complacency is a mistake. Ben smiled slyly. "Get any action last night? In training they always said the best time to get someone into bed was right after they got back from a mission. . . ."

I was glad to leave.

Bobbi breezed into the consulate a minute before noon, shopping bag in hand. "Ze selection of feelthy underwear in this burg is *vraiment pathétique,*" she said.

She perched on my desk, her legs coming to rest on my chair. She bent forward and whispered, "Everything go OK with the bad spy man?"

"Everything's fine."

She smiled. Then she lifted her eyes to the ceiling as if a thought had just struck her. She took a pen and a piece of paper and wrote on it. In the morning I had cautioned Bobbi about talking in my office. Naturally she was making a game of it.

Two words were on the paper. "Expenses? Raise?"

I shrugged. Annoyance crossed her face for a second. When she spoke, though, her voice was normal. "You know, Jim, I'm sure you're a great diplomat, but you've got to remember that the Foreign Service is like anything else: You've got to stick up for yourself. That's very important. You've got to stick up for yourself *and for your friends*. If you don't, who will?"

There was a knock at the door, so I was spared having to reply. Sammy ushered Macho in.

I was nervous. What if he had a poker face? We were betting Bobbi's life on our ability to tell if he knew something, yet I hardly knew him at all.

The meeting proved to be an anticlimax. Bobbi was very good. She was never anything but natural, but mixed in with her complaints over the heat and the bugs and the shopping possibilities of Wellington she managed to elicit from Macho a full account of his previous day's activities. Of course, we knew he was lying; the thing was to see if he suspected that we knew.

I'm willing to believe I can be fooled, but not by Macho in those circumstances. It was clear he had no idea what Bobbi had been up to. After twenty minutes she turned to me and smiled.

"We'd better get going," she said. "Cort's cook is a prima donna. If we're not there by two, we don't eat. Ta-ta," she said, blowing a kiss.

After she left, I had a letdown. That was natural, I suppose, but I hadn't foreseen it. I walked around the room, then stood in front of the map and retraced yesterday's journey. Sammy looked in while I was doing that. I got embarrassed and went back to my chair. I didn't love Bobbi, certainly, but there was no denying she had an impact.

I pushed papers for a while, but it was pointless. I couldn't focus. I left for the club.

Rollo was leaving as I arrived. He asked if I had a moment to spare. We sat on a bench by the swimming pool.

I had no idea what he was going to talk about. If anything crossed my mind, it was the rather dreamlike notion that having seen Bobbi and me together that morning, he might inquire whether my intentions were strictly honorable. Of course, that wasn't it, although it took me a while to see what his subject was. Finally, though, I got it. He wanted to tell me that I had better take care or people—ignorant people, but no less important for that—might think I was a spy.

It was one thing to socialize a good deal with Ben Jacoby—indeed, that was admirable, helping lay to rest old agency rivalries—but having subordinates call him with urgent memos and running off to the quiet room for chats were another matter. Tongues started wagging, and the one thing Rollo's brief career in the State Department had taught him was that gossip once started never stopped. It was deplorable, but then people had so little to talk about they would talk about whatever they had, wouldn't they? You couldn't really blame them. And somehow—servants and local employees and sheer thoughtlessness—the talk never stopped at the embassy door. The fact that there was nothing behind it actually contributed to its diffusion, since no one was as careful as he would be if a true secret were at stake.

Rollo didn't actually say "a word to the wise." That, however, was the message. It would behoove me to watch my step.

Once he was on the verge of asking what Ben and I had been discussing. He didn't, though. I was grateful for that.

At lunch I recalled how Bobbi had looked at five that morning, when I had woken briefly and watched her sleeping beside me. It was, perhaps, worth an ambassadorial warning.

13

When Bobbi and I met for lunch
a week later, Ben was in Washington. It was a relief knowing the
school monitor couldn't disturb us.

She looked beautiful. She wore a green silk blouse and a gold
bracelet I hadn't seen before. She was nibbling her straw hat as I
entered the restaurant.

"A bit more comfortable than last time," she said, glancing
around.

"I was happy with our last meeting." I sounded besotted
even to myself.

She smiled. "My legs are still a disaster."

I bent to look at them, but she grabbed me. "Don't be silly.
Did you talk to Big Bad Benjamin about my raise?"

I hesitated. "I mentioned it."

"And?"

A foot, the shoe off, caressed my calf.

"It's under consideration. Ben is in Washington. For consultations."

The foot probed under my knee, drew a line on my thigh, then retreated. A waiter brought our salads.

"You told him about the boat?" she asked when the waiter left.

During the night at my house Bobbi had said she thought Cort's boat bore investigation. She had mentioned it before, at our first meeting.

"Yeah. It'll be one of the topics in Washington."

Bobbi was more than ever convinced Cort was engaged in nefarious projects, but she hadn't discovered anything concrete. His mood fluctuated without any visible reason. Therefore, there had to be a hidden one.

I gave a skeptical smile.

"No, Jim, you've got to trust me on this. It's not like he just didn't sleep or something. He's doing something at night, and sometimes it goes well and sometimes it goes badly."

"How are you getting along with him?" I asked after a pause.

"Not like I got along with you."

Her eyes narrowed. Then she leaned back and laughed. "We're getting along fine. He'd like to have me handcuffed in bed, and I'd like to have him handcuffed in prison, so we split the difference and go out to fancy places for dinner."

She looked away at something not visible. "If he weren't such a terrible person, he'd actually be interesting in a scary sort of way. He's very smart. He started out with nothing, you know. He's obviously made something of himself—"

"Murderer, drug dealer, extortionist," I agreed.

She chuckled. We looked into each other's eyes. The restaurant was part of a hotel; I was about to say something about getting a room for the afternoon, but some impulse toward neatness, a desire to finish with business before going on to pleasure, made me ask a question that had been troubling me. "Do you think . . ." I let the sentence trail off.

"What?"

"The whole premise of this operation seems to be that at some point Cort will decide he's known you long enough and he'll say, 'By the way, I just want you to know I'm smuggling drugs for the Cubans and my next shipment is coming in tonight at the old vacant lot by the drugstore.' But do you really think he's ever going to say that?"

She laughed deliciously. "Sure. He'll say exactly that. Then he'll try to cop a feel and I'll slap him, hard."

"No, Bobbi, seriously . . ."

Her foot returned, sneaking underneath my pants leg. "You're such a silly, Jim. Of course he won't say it like that, but it'll come out. It always does."

I wondered how many Caribbean drug lords she had dealt with, to speak so authoritatively.

While we ate, we talked about a variety of things, but drug smuggling was not one of them. One subject we discussed was Richard Lee. Cort had asked Bobbi to tell me that he had discovered how Lee died.

According to Cort, Lee had gone to a bar in Beverley and drunk himself into a near stupor. About one in the morning he left. He had passed out on the road, and an hour or two later the owner of the bar had run over him on his way home.

The barkeeper was convinced that if he reported the accident, the police would put him in jail. He was not at fault, but he was a friend of Cort's, and the police welcomed any chance to attack Cort or his followers. He was also afraid that if he simply drove away, the accident might be traced to him, so he put Lee's body in his car and transported him to a vacant stretch of road outside Wellington. He did not tell anyone, of course, and at first he didn't tell Cort. But Cort knew about Lee's visiting the bar—something Griggs, the police lieutenant, had never learned—and eventually he learned the rest.

Bobbi said Cort shared his friend's opinion of the police. It was only because he trusted the discretion of the U.S. consul that he was telling me what he had learned.

I had not told her that the autopsy showed the vehicle injuries occurred after Lee was dead. "Do you think Cort's telling the truth?" I asked.

She shrugged. "Anything's possible."

Bobbi wasn't interested in Lee's death. I was, but I didn't want to burden her with more secrets, so I let the conversation drift to other topics. I told her I had nearly finished the chapter of Cort's "autobiography" and would send it to her in a few days.

When the check came, Bobbi looked at her watch and said she should be getting back.

That was an unpleasant shock. I had hoped for a tryst after lunch.

"I thought we might—"

"What?" she asked, eyeing a table with a man and two women.

"I thought we might get a room here."

"What for?"

She wasn't teasing; she just wasn't paying attention.

"For purposes of sexual intercourse," I said heavily. The restaurant was air-conditioned, but I felt hot.

She turned back to me, a wide, apologetic smile on her face. "Oh, Jim, I'd love to spend the afternoon with you. But I can't. I told Cort I'd be back by three, and it's practically that now. He's going to tell me more about his poor, deprived childhood or something equally boring."

She glanced around. "Anyway, we couldn't do it here. That was the one thing Barfy Ben said that made sense. This whole island is like gossip central. If we got a room here for the afternoon, it would get back to Cort in a flash. I don't know what he'd do, but I don't want to find out."

It made sense. It was strange, though, to think of myself as the less prudent of the two of us.

The sun was blazing when we went outside. I felt bloated and fat.

But when I put her in her car, she pulled my face down and kissed me passionately. Then, as our lips parted, she tapped me lightly in the crotch. "Remember, big boy, all things come to him who waits."

She drove off. I watched her, thinking a great deal must be coming to me.

Ben had given me instructions for how to reach him, but that was for emergencies. The collapse of my plans for a quiet orgy did not qualify. I spent the evening by myself, restless and out of sorts.

After the bombing I had finagled a temporary assignment in Washington for Ruby, as a kind of therapeutic break. When I went in to work the next morning, there was a cable from her. She had recognized the police sketch of the bombing suspect.

The police had brought the sketch by a couple of days ago. It showed a thirtyish black man with a full beard, wearing plastic frame glasses. His lips may have been a little thinner than average, and his ears bigger, but he did not have any striking features. The sketch was, I guess, a fairly professional job, but somehow with its somnolent forward-looking stare it reminded me much more of police sketches I had seen on TV than of any real person.

Neither Sammy nor I recognized the man, but as a matter of routine we faxed a copy to Ruby. In her cable she said that the man had applied for a visa repeatedly over the past three years. He had been refused every time. He hadn't had a beard, Ruby said, but she was sure it was the same man. The last time he came he had kicked up a fuss because Sammy had told him to leave without taking his application.

Unfortunately Ruby did not remember the man's name. It would be in our files, but it would be a hell of a job to find it. The files are not organized with a view to identifying homicidal rejects.

Captain Drabney was delighted when I called him. "Wonderful news, Mr. Biggins. This is wonderful."

His voice grew confidential. "There was some resistance, I must confess, to bringing in the artist. The expense. But I argued that the protection of foreign envoys is a matter of national honor. I am happy that the effort has been crowned with success."

I wondered if Drabney talked this way with his wife or if the high style was reserved for foreign envoys.

"If this man applied for a visa, you will know his name, I presume," he continued.

I explained about the files.

"I understand, Mr. Biggins. Still, since it is your own safety—and that of your colleagues and workers—I would hope that—"

"Oh, yes," I broke in. "We'll get you the name as soon as possible. But there's only Sammy and me, and we can't completely stop everything else—"

"What about this lady who recognized the sketch? Can't she help?"

I explained that Ruby was in Washington and the files were here. Drabney observed that it might be good if she returned, both to assist in the identification effort and as a possible witness.

"She'll come back," I replied, "but . . ." I paused briefly.

"There are health considerations," I resumed. "She was injured in the bombing. She had to go to the hospital. We thought a break from normal duties would be in her best interest. Ruby is a very old and valued employee," I concluded awkwardly.

"She went to the hospital?" Drabney asked.

"Yes."

Drabney said nothing for so long that I began to fear we had been disconnected.

"I am sorry, Mr. Biggins. A thought occurred to me. It is probably nothing, but I would like to look into it."

He sounded abstracted. "Well, I will not keep you any longer. I wish you luck with your search. Please call me as soon as you learn anything."

I put Sammy to work on the files. He gave a pained grin. The boredom of the task was evident, and the bombing, although it had occurred only a few weeks ago, had already begun to recede into the unbelievable past. I didn't have much sympathy, though. Obviously we had to find out who the man was as fast as we could.

A couple of hours later I finished my NIV interviews. I was wondering whether to go out to lunch or put in an hour on the files. My efforts wouldn't amount to much, but it might be good for Sammy's morale. Then the phone rang. It was Drabney.

"We've started," I said, "but I'm afraid we haven't got far yet. It's a big job."

"The suspect's name is Charles Tinsley," Drabney replied. "Perhaps that will help you find his file."

At first I was too surprised to speak.

"How did you learn his name?" I asked eventually.

"Something I should have thought of much sooner. You recall the death threat at the hospital?"

"Of course."

"I assumed at the time that you had been followed to the hospital. If I had thought about it, I would have realized that was not possible. The person would have had to move quite fast, and in any case, why not simply send the threat to the consulate? No, what I should have seen from the start was that the most likely course of events was that you were recognized at the hospital by someone who wished to threaten you."

He paused. After a moment he resumed speaking. "I had a man take the police sketch to the hospital. He had to ask only two people to get the name. Charles Tinsley worked as a handyman there until one week ago. We sent people to his home address, but unfortunately he has not been there for a week."

He stopped. I said, "Oh."

"I must confess that I did not originally take the threat very seriously." His voice was husky with apology. "If I had, I would have thought about it more and come to see how it happened. But as it was . . . And then the consulate was bombed."

"That made it serious, I would think," I said.

"Oh, yes," Drabney agreed. "Very serious. But you see . . ." His voice grew tight. "With a major crime such as the bombing, my role becomes circumscribed. I am not, you understand, in the investigation section. I am responsible for relations with foreign embassies. The offices who actually conduct the investigation do not welcome my assistance. If it is something trivial, I may make suggestions, but in a serious affair, such as this bombing . . ."

With an effort, he spoke again. "In general I have found it best—for the sake of minimizing friction—to confine myself to relaying the results of the investigation. That is easier to do, I find, if I avoid thinking too much about the case itself."

Drabney had always struck me as a contented, if slightly comical, figure. This sudden cry from the heart took me by surprise. I was embarrassed enough to want to switch the conversation back on course. "Do you think you'll be able to find this man? Charles Tinsley?"

"Oh, I should think so," he replied energetically. The confessional mood departed as quickly as it had come. "Now that we know who he is, we will be able to talk to his friends, learn his habits, determine where he would be likely to go. That is, the investigators will," he concluded awkwardly.

"They didn't do such a good job identifying him," I said.

"No," he said quietly. "I believe, though, you would find that even in the United States people sometimes do not do their jobs perfectly."

I didn't feel like arguing the point.

"Are you sure this guy—Tinsley, is that his name?—are you sure he's the guy? I mean, granted he's the one in the sketch, are you sure he planted the bomb?"

Drabney gave a soft laugh. His self-confidence had returned. "Oh, yes, I would say we're fairly positive about that. A nurse he took lunch with sometimes was quite helpful. One thing she told us was that Tinsley had conceived a vehement hatred for you, Mr. Biggins."

"Me?"

Given what had happened, I shouldn't have been surprised, but I was.

"Yes. Apparently Tinsley has wanted to visit the United States for a number of years. He applied for a visa several times."

"Ruby said that in her cable."

"Yes," Drabney agreed. "Your predecessor did not give him one, but apparently he told Tinsley—"

"She," I interrupted.

"Pardon me?"

"My predecessor was a woman."

"Oh, yes. Miss Garvey. Well, I doubt that matters, although I suppose it may have affected Tinsley's state of mind. In any case, your predecessor gave Tinsley the idea that he was—he was improving his chances with each application and would soon be eligible. At least that is what Tinsley told the nurse. Then you came, and I gather rejected him summarily. The nurse said—"

"What?" I asked after Drabney stopped short.

"Oh, she simply said that Tinsley was quite mad after his rejection."

For some reason I wanted very much to know exactly what the nurse had said. I pressed Drabney. He kept refusing, but finally he heaved a sigh. "What she said, Mr. Biggins, was that for two weeks Tinsley went around complaining that—I quote—'that fat little bastard made up his mind two seconds after he saw me.' "

I laughed as best I could.

"So that's why he bombed the consulate?"

"Not entirely. Tinsley was enamored of a young lady. Not the nurse; someone else. A few months ago this girl went to New York and found a job there, looking after someone's children."

Drabney made a kind of meditative clicking sound with his tongue. "I suppose you gave her a visa," he said after a few seconds. "In any case, Tinsley received a letter from her—he showed it to the nurse—saying that she was marrying a man, a U.S. citizen, she had met in New York. It was, the nurse said, not a very nice letter. After that Tinsley became quite obsessed with his wrongs. And then he returned to the consulate but was not even permitted to apply for a visa. At least that is what the nurse said. Could it be true?"

"Well, we have certain rules, and one of them is that you have to wait at least six months——"

"It doesn't matter," Drabney interrupted. "I gather that was the last straw. The nurse said he became quite depressed. She stopped having lunch with him since all he would talk about was his troubles. At least that is what she said; maybe she thought it was better to tell us that."

Neither of us spoke for a while.

"Why did he quit last week?" I asked.

"He was on the verge of being fired. His work had become very bad."

"And you think you'll find him soon?"

"I think so. Until we do, of course, you must not relax your vigilance."

"You think he'll try again?"

"I have no idea, Mr. Biggins. But there is no harm in being careful."

I looked out the window. Just before Drabney called, I had done a count. I had denied visas to seventeen people today. I wondered if any of them harbored homicidal inclinations. How many people would I reject tomorrow, and the next day and all the remaining days of my tour of duty here? And then there would, in all likelihood, be another consular post waiting for me after this one.

It was odd. Since the bombing took place so soon after I became Bobbi's case officer, I had worried that it might be connected. Ben said that it wasn't, and I had accepted his arguments, but a layer of doubt remained. It had been something to worry about. It hadn't occurred to me that my daily routine was what I should have been worried about.

"Mr. Biggins?"

"Yes."

"I have told you all I know, for the moment. I will keep you informed."

My eye fell on a memo I had written for the record, giving Bobbi's account of Richard Lee's death. "There's one other thing."

"Yes?"

"It's about Lee."

"Who?"

"The man—American—whose body we saw that day in the hospital when I got the threat."

"Oh, yes."

Drabney sounded impatient.

"I just wondered . . . how definite were those autopsy findings? Is it possible that Lee did actually die in a traffic accident?"

Drabney laughed. "Has that woman got at you?"

"Woman?" My chest tightened. How could Drabney have learned of my talk with Bobbi?

"Was it Mannion himself then?" he asked. "I hope you didn't give him any money."

"I don't think I know what you're talking about."

I breathed deeply. Drabney launched with gusto into a story, his impatience forgotten.

"A week or two ago Miss—what is her name?—Leeds, yes, Jossie Leeds, went to the Royalton substation and said she had information about the murder of an American. Richard Lee. She said Lee had been killed in the Hook, driven over by a truck on purpose, and why weren't the police doing anything about it? She said her boyfriend, Winnie Mannion, had seen the murder. The lieutenant told her to go fetch him in. She left and didn't come back. Neither did Mannion. After a while the lieutenant stopped by her house. She told him then she had been teasing, there wasn't any murder, she doesn't know anything about Lee. The neighbors said Mannion had been living there, but he left an hour earlier, after a big fight."

Drabney spoke momentarily to someone in his office, then resumed. "The lieutenant got the file on Lee. He was too excited to read the autopsy results, but he saw my name and called me up. I told him about the autopsy, but he was determined Lee had been murdered. He made me call the doctor to check. There was no mistake. Lee was dead two or three hours before the truck went over him."

Drabney's voice betrayed a prim satisfaction.

"You don't think the doctor could have made a mistake?"

"No. He is a first-rate man. Besides, you may recall, there

was another doctor who saw Lee's body before the autopsy. He was also of the opinion that the vehicle injuries occurred after death."

Drabney gave a tolerant chuckle. "I can understand why the lieutenant was excited. It would be quite a thrill to arrest Cort."

"Cort?" I echoed foolishly.

"Didn't I say that?" Of course, he knew he hadn't, and was relishing the revelation. "There were several men who were in the truck or hanging about when Lee was run over, according to Miss Leeds, but Cort was the one in charge."

We exchanged good-byes. I told Sammy to find the file of Charles Tinsley and left for lunch at the club.

14

Ben leaned toward me. His mustache quivered with excitement.

"Well, consider this," he said. His voice had that lightness people use for a particularly devastating argument. "Let's say I get myself a nice blue six-pointed star, a Jewish star, and I smear it with shit. Is that a work of art? I think most people would agree, the deficit being what it is, there are better things to spend tax money on than that. But how is it esthetically less worthy than a crucifix in a jar full of urine? If it's cool for the NEA to give money for one, why not for the other? Maybe I should send in a grant proposal."

He settled back in his chair, eyebrows rising to solicit approval of his artistic ambitions.

He had got back that day and called up to suggest dinner. The first thing I discovered was that on the airplane down he had read an article on federal funding for controversial art exhibitions. He was against it.

"It's not exactly the same thing," I said after a few seconds.

"Why not? Why not?"

"Well, I doubt Senator Helms would complain about a Jewish star smeared with shit."

Ben looked up from the tablecloth, which he had covered with stars and crosses drawn in mustard. "I'm discussing a philosophical issue, Jim." He adopted a wounded expression. "Helms happens to be right in this case. Should we have avoided fighting fascism because it put us on the same side as Stalin?"

One dinner I tried to count the number of times Ben referred to World War II. I stopped when I got to seven.

"Well," I said, and paused. I looked at my plate for inspiration. It was empty. "Wouldn't you agree that anti-Semitic displays are more dangerous than anti-Christian ones, inasmuch as Jews are a minority and consequently more likely targets of discrimination?"

It did not seem the most brilliant observation a Gentile could make to a Jew.

"So? Catholics are a minority, too, aren't they?" He put down the spoon he had been spreading mustard with and ran his finger around the rim of his wineglass. "Anyway, it sounds to me like you're saying it's wrong to provide public funds for art that makes a minority unhappy, but it's OK if it makes the majority unhappy. What's the name of this grand theory? Reverse utilitarianism? Art consists in the greatest offense to the greatest number? So if I want funding for my shitty star, I should go to where Jews are the majority—like Israel? I'm sure they'd love it. What?"

His last question was addressed to the waiter.

"Would you like another bottle of wine, sir?"

"No," he snapped. The waiter retreated.

He turned back to me. "Where was I?"

"Reverse utilitarianism."

"Right." He smiled. He was happy, and I wasn't unhappy. I preferred Ben's rants to hearing for the fifteenth time how Foreign Service compensation compared with what German diplomats got or any of the other conversational staples at the club.

"The thing that gets me," he continued, "is that the liberal culture Mafia is so fucking predictable. You read an op-ed piece by any one of them and you know that sooner or later—generally sooner—they're going to trot out the old standby: that great art is always controversial. That's the party line. It doesn't matter that it's totally false. I mean, how controversial was Chartres Cathedral? How controversial was Virgil or Shakespeare or Mozart?"

He looked around, but Mozart and company were not seated nearby.

"Perhaps they're talking about art in the modern era."

"Yeah. If you're an artist now, you have to be controversial. That's the rule. No exceptions allowed." He looked grimly off toward the bar. "And you know what they say next? After they say art is always controversial? Then they tell you how the Paris crowd rioted when the *Rite of Spring* was first performed. It's obligatory. You've got to talk about the rioting at the *Rite of Spring*. It's a rite. The rite of citing the *Rite of Spring* riot. It's like a Fourth of July speech: You got to have Washington telling his mom he chopped down the cherry tree. It's the same thing."

I looked at him. He was serious.

He picked up his wineglass and held it with two fingers so that it reflected the light.

"Y'all see Miz Scarlett while I was away?"

I glanced around.

"Speak quietly, it's OK," Ben said.

I told him about my lunch with Bobbi. He nodded, asking questions occasionally.

"Did you learn anything in Washington?"

"Yeah, I learned something." He smiled. "My boss showed me what got him suspicious of Cort in the first place. A telephone intercept."

He gave a sour chuckle. "I think we're on a wild-goose chase."

"Bobbi thinks they're smuggling drugs," I said after a few seconds. "She doesn't think it's a wild-goose chase."

He belched. "Yeah, well, she wouldn't be the first agent to lie to justify her paycheck. Anyway, she hasn't really said anything. Just that Cort is behaving suspiciously. I'd be surprised if he weren't."

The waiter brought our desserts. I took a few bites of cheesecake.

"So what's going to happen?" I asked eventually. "Does this mean it's over?"

I wasn't sure how I felt about that. I'd be glad if Bobbi weren't around Cort anymore. But if it meant she would leave Navidad, then I was opposed.

Ben ended his slow inspection of the other customers. "Oh, no. We don't work that way. She's due for a bonus, in fact."

A sardonic smile appeared on his face. "The bonus is for if she checks out Cort's boat. Bobbi says it's suspicious, and my boss can't think of anything smart to do, so I guess he figures doing something dumb is the next best thing. Anyway, you can tell Ms. Lyons she gets a thou for looking over the boat and another ten thou if she finds something."

"Like what?"

"Good question," Ben said. He frowned. "A couple hundred pounds of coke would be suggestive, I suppose. Apart from that, I don't know: hidden compartments, mysterious maps with X on them, computer disks with names and addresses for the distribution network . . ."

I'd heard Ben being cynical before, but never so outright contemptuous of the job he was doing. It was a little unnerving.

He raised his eyebrows. "I said it was stupid. That's one reason why. They don't know what they're after. Bobbi thinks the boat is being used by Cort, well, OK, she should go aboard and find something to confirm that." He shook his head in disgust.

"I'm low man on the totem pole," he continued after a few seconds. "I wasn't invited to the planning sessions. I got the impression that at one time the idea was floated that Bobbi should try to stow away to observe one of Niso's secret outings. It's crude, but it might work. I mean, if something's going on, which I sincerely doubt, then Bobbi might find out. But apparently people decided it was too risky."

"You don't agree?"

Ben laughed. "Oh, it's risky. Personally I don't think Bobbi would be any great loss, but . . ." He shrugged. "No, it's perfectly sensible to decide against her trying to stow away. But why bother with the boat then? If she's going out there with Cort's knowledge, she won't see zip. And why give her a bonus? I think Fearless Leader is hoping the money will encourage her to do something reckless, like stowing away, but then it'll be on her own initiative, so he won't be blamed. That's stupid, too, because if it blows up in our face, he *will* be blamed, but . . ." He shrugged.

"I'll tell her to be careful," I said.

He grinned.

"No, I'll really emphasize it. Or . . . I could just not tell her about the bonus."

Ben shook his head. "You can't do that. Somewhere along the line she may get debriefed by someone from Langley. I sincerely hope not, but it could happen. But she doesn't need the money, does she? Tell her to take the thousand, since they're giving it away, but forget about the ten."

I finished the cheesecake. Ben's advice was sensible, but it wouldn't work.

"What's the matter?" he asked, seeing my expression. "You can say that, can't you?"

"I can say it, sure. But Bobbi likes money."

His face hardened. For a moment I thought I'd hear another tirade. But he just let out a slow sigh. "You know, Jim, I've tried, I really have, but I can't see why you like her."

"Well, she's . . ."

I stopped. I didn't know the answer to Ben's question. There was the sex, of course, but I could hardly mention that. I wondered if the CIA had rules against case officers sleeping with agents, like professors and students. Perhaps I should be worried about an ethics board review as well as Cort and Niso and that crazy visa rejectee.

Anyway, sex wasn't it, or not all of it. I had been attracted to Bobbi even when I thought I would never sleep with her. Maybe it was simply that she was different, ignorant where I was knowledgeable and knowledgeable where I was ignorant and always so damn self-confident. It didn't seem like a good basis for a relationship, but it worked pretty well for an obsession.

Ben broke into my reverie. "She's anti-Semitic, you know."

"Bobbi?"

"We weren't discussing Eichmann."

"Why do you say that?"

Ben took a sip of coffee. "Ed ran into her the other night. At the Hungry Capon."

Ed was Ed Steib, Ben's nominal superior in the econ section. The Hungry Capon was a dance hall with a picture of a scrawny chicken by the door.

"Was Cort with her?"

"Yeah. Ed said it was crowded, but when they came in, it was like the Red Sea parting before Moses. Anyway, she introduced him to Cort and then asked a question: Which of his colleagues does the Hungry Capon look like?"

Ben looked as though he had swallowed something he didn't like.

"And?"

"Ed did his usual imitation of a brain-dead virus. Bobbi gave hints, but they didn't help because he forgot that for public consumption I'm an economist. Finally she told him. Ben Jacoby *is,* as the movie ad says, the Hungry Capon. Ed naturally got a real kick out of telling me."

I looked away. "I can see you might not like it, but how does it imply anti-Semitism?"

"What do you think was supposed to be the resemblance between me and the picture?" he asked icily. "I don't have feathers. I'm not yellow. I'm not, thank you, a eunuch, and ten will get you one Bobbi doesn't know what 'capon' means anyway. But I am Jewish, and the bird in the sign has a prominent beak."

"Oh, come on, Ben—"

"Come on yourself," he said. "Jews have big noses. That's what she was thinking. It's about as sophisticated a thought as her mind can hold."

I took a sip of water. Bobbi was inclined to think in stereotypes, but I didn't believe she was anti-Semitic, not on any deep level.

On the other hand, I didn't know if she was anything on any deep level.

"I doubt that was what she was thinking—"

Ben looked up at the ceiling. "I'm sure it was. But you know what? I don't give a fuck. I couldn't care less what she thinks about Jews. Or blacks or Serbo-Croatians or Islamic fundamentalism or any goddamn thing. But it was unprofessional. Cort's got to know I'm chief of station. And now he knows that she knows me."

"She made a joke, that's all. It shows she has nothing to hide."

Ben snorted. "She does have something to hide: that she knows me." He shook his head in disgust. "That 'we know that he knows that we know' stuff is crap. If something isn't suspicious because it's freely admitted, well, maybe it *is* suspicious because it was calculated that freely admitting it wouldn't be suspicious. It's an infinite regress. The thing to do is avoid raising questions in the first place. Your friend failed to do that."

I examined my plate. Not a trace of cheesecake remained.

"What did you learn in Washington?" I asked.

Ben grimaced but abandoned the topic of Bobbi's sins. "Several months ago Niso Carreras called a house in Panama from a hotel there. There was a bug on the Panama phone because of a tip that a big drug dealer lived there. A woman answered—maybe the lady who sent that letter Bobbi so brilliantly obtained. At least, Niso seemed to be on good terms with her, and the letter suggests a romantic liaison."

After a sip of wine he continued. "The lady asked Niso how his knee was. That fits, by the way; he had an accident several years ago, and his knee still bothers him. Then she asked, 'How goes the affair?' Niso replied, 'Well, I hope. I have talked with him.' Then the woman said something that could, possibly, have been 'Cort?' It's hard to make out on the tape. Anyway, that's the big revelation."

Ben looked away briefly.

"Cort's name wasn't mentioned again. Anyway, Niso said the man—Cort, we presume—had complained about the great difficulties he would face but was eager to pursue the quest."

"Quest?"

Ben rolled his eyes. "The translator is some idiot grad student doing a thesis on Borges, earning a little spare change working for us. Anyway, near the end of the conversation the lady asks, 'Will you know when he has it?' Presumably they're talking about Cort again. Niso says, 'I'll know.' She says, 'You're sure?' and Niso says, 'Yes.' Then she asks, 'Will he deliver?' Niso laughs and says, 'That is the question, yes. It is a matter of convincing him of the necessity of honoring his obligations.' Then there's static on the line, but it seems like Niso is saying he knows something that will give him some leverage. The number seventy-eight is audible. This supposedly is more proof that Cort is involved because in the file there are rumors he was linked to the murder of some crazy cult figure in 1978."

"I don't remember that," I said.

He grinned. "Not your file. Our file. Nothing was ever proved, but conceivably Niso has something on him. Anyway, that's it."

Ben took his glasses off and gnawed on an earpiece.

"Well, it seems like something," I said after it was clear he wasn't going to volunteer a comment.

"Oh, it's proof that Niso and Cort are cooperating on some illegal enterprise, and since the call was made to a drug dealer's house, it's narcotics." He smiled ironically.

"So what's the matter? Why don't you believe it?"

The waiter served coffee. Ben waited until he left.

"Sarah stayed in Tulsa with her folks. One night I was strolling in Georgetown and I ran into an old girl friend. Pre-Sarah. She's DEA. We met when I was doing a two-week familiarization at the FBI."

His face lit momentarily in remembrance of flings past. "We had dinner together. I told her about the Cort investigation."

He rolled his eyes as though amazed at his own turpitude. "Strictly against the rules, of course. But, then, my using you is against the rules. Anyway, I was pissed at my boss and pissed at the operation, plus she is DEA. Almost a colleague. And telling her felt like an acceptable infidelity. An intimacy that wouldn't threaten my marriage." He laughed. "Anyway, I told her."

"So?" I asked after a few seconds. "What happened?"

"Nothing that evening. But two days later, the day I was leaving Washington, she called me at my hotel."

"Yes?"

"She had checked the file on the Panama tip. It was a DEA operation all along; my boss got that one transcript because Carreras was identified as the caller. But that wasn't why she was calling. The tip that initiated the surveillance was a phony. The house was not being used by a drug dealer. A neighbor had a grudge against the guy who owned the house. That's all."

Ben settled back in his chair. He had sprung his surprise.

I felt queasy. It was as though I had committed some enormous social gaffe, some supremely embarrassing faux pas. I could feel sweat springing out of my temples and forehead.

Ben leaned forward. "Are you OK? You're all red."

I drank some water, but my forehead still burned.

Until then I had not realized how much I enjoyed thinking of myself as a spy, privy to secret information. To have Ben banish my pretensions without even realizing he was doing it was devastating.

"I could call a doctor?" he said interrogatively.

I shook my head. "I'm fine."

I took another drink of water. When I put the glass down, I felt more or less normal. I then asked a stupid question. "What did your boss say when you told him?"

"Tell him? Tell him I had talked out of school to an old girl friend?"

Ben waved to the waiter and made check-writing motions.

"Actually, I did drop by his office. I asked if he had any more on the Panama end—any leads I could follow up. I thought if I could prod him into checking into it, he would learn about the phony tip and we could quietly and ingloriously call it a day."

The waiter brought the check. I offered money, but Ben waved me off. Apparently it was a business dinner.

"Fearless told me that side had been handed over to the DEA—a little lie there, since it was DEA from the start. There was some tut-tutting about DEA security not being all it should be and a lecture about their tendency to poach on the least provocation." Ben snorted. "Of course, what it boils down to is he wants to claim sole credit if and when the investigation produces something."

He shrugged. "I did what I can do. From here on in we go through the motions. Eventually he'll write it off as a loss."

He got up. Dinner was over.

"Don't say that about going through the motions to Bobbi. In fact, don't tell her any of this. I've still got to send in reports, and she's getting paid to do a job. Who knows? Maybe she'll find something out."

He cracked a smile. The heavens would fall before Bobbi found anything out, the smile said.

That night I decided Ben was wrong. Wrong, at least, to think that what his DEA friend said removed all grounds for suspicion. Even if the telephone call had been intercepted because of a bogus tip, it still indicated that Niso was up to something with Cort. And what Bobbi had observed supported that. Ben had allowed himself to be swayed by his dislike for Bobbi and his boss.

I felt better after reaching that conclusion. Not long afterward I went to sleep.

Two weeks later the consulate bomber had still not been caught, and I had not slept with Bobbi again, but I had been invited for a cruise on Cort's yacht. Bobbi had insisted on my presence. "I told him I wanted a chaperon, Jim. You're it."

Bobbi was resting in her cabin when I boarded. Macho showed me where to stow my gear and said Cort wanted to see me.

I had forgotten how big he was. He filled up the eating compartment. He had been drinking and didn't seem happy I was aboard.

"Tell the cook not to put butter on Miss Bobbi's fish," he told Macho in an irritated tone. "She doesn't like it that way. He does it again, I'll kill him. You tell him that."

Macho nodded and left. Cort studied me.

"He puts butter on fish usually. You want it left off yours?"

"No, no. Butter's fine."

Cort smiled grimly. "Bobbi, she can't stand it. Butter, cream, lots of things. Things I like. And she gives me hell when her food isn't cooked just right. How am I supposed to know? Why doesn't she like it? Some fad they have in New York City?"

I got a Coke from the bar. "I think she's watching her weight."

"She's thin. You—you're fat. If you said no butter, I'd understand."

Considering Cort's own girth the comment seemed unfair.

"It's very kind of you to invite me for this cruise," I said after a while.

Cort looked at me closely.

"How long you and Bobbi know each other?"

It was so abrupt it was almost rude.

"About three years," I said. "No, nearly four, I guess."

"Is she a virgin?"

I was too surprised to reply.

"You think she's a virgin?" Cort persisted.

I coughed. "Actually we've never discussed that topic."

"Can't believe anyone's a virgin these days," Cort said with a pained smile. "Grown woman like her, I mean. But Bobbi . . . I'll tell you one thing: I haven't got any."

I raised my eyebrows. I had no idea what to say.

"I asked if she didn't like black men, if that's why she wouldn't go to bed with me."

He looked at me with a fixed stare.

"I very much doubt that that's—"

"You know what she said?"

"No." I didn't try to offer a further defense of Bobbi's dating civil rights record.

"She said a college boy tried that on her and it hadn't worked then and it wouldn't work now. Said he was a lot better looking than me, too."

Cort stared briefly before cracking a smile. "She slapped me in the face a few nights ago."

"What?"

He grinned. "I was feeling her behind. Got away with it for a while, but then she whacked me. 'Keep your dirty hands off me.'" His voice fluted upward momentarily in imitation.

Cort seemed amused by the memory.

"Felt good. Her ass," he added. "You have any idea what I should do?"

"Pardon me?"

"If I want to feel her some more."

I pondered. "I'm afraid the issue wasn't covered in my training."

I wondered briefly how the instructional module would have been titled. "Facilitating Foreign Exploration of Amcit Bottoms"?

Cort stared out at sea. A burp rumbled briefly and died out, overwhelmed by his massive torso. He put down his beer.

"You sleep with her?"

A wave of fear swept over me. "Me?"

"Yeah." A more audible burp escaped Cort. "Did you sleep with her?"

I should have simply said no. There are times when a straightforward lie is best. But that would have been a lesson in Ben's orientation, not mine. What I said was actually true. "Bobbi is . . . basically not the sort of woman I go out with."

Cort eyed me suspiciously over his beer bottle.

"You think she's pretty?"

"Oh, yes."

"Why don't you like her then?"

I shrugged. "I like her. It's just . . ."

"Bobbi said you like boys."

I let my breath out slowly. "She can be wrong occasionally, you know."

He laughed. It was an obnoxious laugh. I decided it had been a mistake to come on the cruise.

"You know what?" he said. "I'm jealous. I've never been jealous. I've had a lot of girl friends, but I've never been jealous. But Bobbi is—she's not like the others. Most of them I fucked the first day I met 'em."

We stared at each other. It had definitely been a mistake to come on the cruise.

"You look sweaty," he said after a while. "Maybe you should go lie down. We won't eat till seven."

"That sounds like a good idea," I said.

As I was walking away, he spoke again. "I'm glad you didn't sleep with her. I might have tossed you overboard."

I didn't say anything.

I opened the porthole in my cabin, but it was still stifling.

Bobbi came to my cabin a couple of hours later. We had to plan our course of action, she said. I raised my eyebrows interrogatively, and she said brusquely, "We've got to search the boat, remember?"

She was seasick, and her eyes were puffy from a cold. I think the discomfort gave her a short temper. When I said Ben was sure Cort would not have left anything compromising aboard, she practically snarled. "There damn well *is* stuff here. I already know that. Haven't you found out anything?"

"Found out . . ."

"Have you looked around at all?"

I had assumed Bobbi wanted me along for moral support. The idea that I should sneak around myself had never occurred to me.

She regarded me with a look of disgust. She had made Macho give her a tour of the boat. One room—he called it the engine room—was locked, and he wouldn't let her in. That was where they must keep the stuff.

I said mildly that there were probably a million legitimate reasons for keeping the door locked.

"Jim." Her voice suddenly lost its edge; she was pleading. "I know you think I'm just some ditzy girl who doesn't know anything about history or literature or anything." She waved a hand, quelling my protest. "But you know, I'm not *stupid*. I'm *not*."

"Bobbi, I never—"

She interrupted. "I thought we were, after that night we spent together, I thought maybe you . . . well, I guess sex doesn't mean much to some people. It does to me, though—that's why I don't sleep around, because for me it's special and I wouldn't sleep with someone if I didn't respect them."

"Bobbi, that night was special for me, too. Very special."

I could feel my cheeks growing warm. What cliché would I have to spit out next?

I drew a breath. "Actually, Bobbi, I've been hoping we could repeat that night."

Her mouth quirked up. "Saying you want to fuck me again isn't exactly what I meant by respect. What I meant was if I say there's something inside a room, you might give me credit for not making it up. I was *there,* Jim. I saw how Macho looked. He was shaking in his shoes. I'm sure there's stuff in that room."

She said some other things as well; I don't recall it all. After another ten minutes, though, I had agreed to help her get into the engine room.

Bobbi slipped into my cabin a little past one. Everyone else, we hoped, was asleep.

Her robe opened as she sat down on my bunk. I ran my hand up her leg. "Cort said he'd kill me if we were sleeping together," I said casually. At least I tried to sound casual.

"Really." She was amused. The ill humor of the afternoon had passed. "Did he say what he'd do to me?"

"No."

"I guess if he comes in now, I'd have to tell him this isn't what it looks like, that we're really just spies."

I moved my hand to the inside of her thigh. Her legs opened infinitesimally. I moved my hand higher. After a minute she gave me a nudge on the shoulder. I ignored it. There was another nudge, and then she whispered, "Jim, please." I ignored that, too.

"I hear him," she said, quietly but distinctly. I stopped instantly.

"Just fooling," she said.

My heart had gone on overtime. I could feel sweat on the back of my neck.

Bobbi chuckled. I should have hated her, but she was simply too desirable for that.

"What would you do if I had a heart attack right here?" I asked.

"Go back to my cabin," she said cheerfully. "You'd be discovered in the morning, and there'd be a burial at sea. No problem."

She gave a shiver of anticipation and drew her robe more tightly around herself.

"OK, I've been thinking. Here's what we do," she said with a hint of smugness. "Macho has a ring of keys. One is for the liquor cabinet. I'm going to go to his cabin and say I can't sleep, I need a drink, and will he please give me the keys?"

"What if he just gives you the one key?"

"I've been browbeating him for the last month. He'll do what I tell him." Her face showed confident scorn. "The liquor's where we had dinner. Put on some clothes and wait there, like you're reading a book. If Macho comes with me, we'll work out some diversion, so one of us can get down and unlock the engine room."

It sounded sketchy, but not immediately fatal.

"What if the key to the engine room isn't on the ring?"

"Then we try something else," she said with a shrug. "But it will be."

She leaned over and kissed me. "You're a good friend, Jim." She wiggled her hips on the way out.

Twenty minutes later Bobbi appeared in the main compartment, holding a key ring aloft like a trophy.

"Now we're cooking." She grinned. She got vodka out of the liquor cabinet and poured a glass. "Roll over, Goldfinger," she intoned, taking a sip and offering me the glass.

"What took so long?"

"Macho's drunk," she said. "It took him forever to answer the door and even longer to understand what I was asking for. Then he did try to give me just the key to the liquor cabinet, but he couldn't get it off the ring. I grabbed it out of his hands and told him I'd bring it back. He's so blotto he probably would have given me the wrong key. Pretty good, huh?"

I finished the vodka and put the glass on the bar. Someone had straightened up; the dirty glass stood out like a sore thumb. Of course, that didn't matter; Bobbi had told Macho she wanted a drink. But I was beginning to get nervous.

"What do we do now?"

She replied in a fake German accent that got on my nerves. "Ve go oonder und check out ze engine room. Ve find ze drugs und I become big-time famous spy. Now getten ze uppen."

The stairway down to the engine room was so steep it was almost a ladder. At the bottom, on one side, was a larder. Bobbi had inspected that in her previous tour. On the other side was our target: a solid-looking locked door.

On the last step Bobbi gave a muffled shriek. "God damn it," she said, not loudly but intensely.

"What is it?"

"A splinter."

"Oh."

"It's excruciating."

She sat down and tried to look at her foot. It was too dark to see. I waited on the step above her.

"Are you just going to stand there?" she said bitterly.

She was blocking the way; there was nothing for me to do. She kept uttering low groans.

"Bobbi, look . . ." I said after a while.

"It's not your foot, is it?" But she rose gingerly and took the last few steps to the locked door, favoring her right foot.

She gave me a box of matches. "Light one."

I lit a match. Bobbi started trying keys.

The seventh key worked. The door creaked, but it could not have been audible on the deck.

My last match guttered out before she opened the door. I was about to light another when I remembered reading that fuel vapor explosions were a shipboard risk.

"Light a match," Bobbi said.

I explained why I didn't want to do that.

"Oh, great," she said, but she didn't urge me to light another match.

We both peered into the gloomy room.

"I wish we'd brought a flashlight," Bobbi said. For the first time that night she did not sound sure of herself.

"Our eyes will adjust," I said doubtfully. Still, there was a moon that might send some light through portholes. Since we were here, I wanted to get it over with.

"You go in and start checking it out," Bobbi said after we had looked in fruitlessly for a few more seconds. "I'll take the keys back to Macho."

"What?"

"I told him I'd bring the keys back. Or would you rather he came looking for them?"

She started climbing back up the stairs. After a few steps she turned toward me. "You might as well get going. The sooner we're done, the sooner we can leave."

Then she continued on up.

I was furious. It was clear why Bobbi had invited me on the cruise: Let the poor sucker cop a feel and then send him off to the wars. A few yards away slept a man who had admitted he would welcome an excuse to murder me. And in front of me was a pitch-black room I was supposed to explore. The joke was, even if it were a well-lit and fully equipped drug factory, I probably wouldn't know it. It wasn't the sort of information one needed for determining visa eligibility.

I stood for a minute, reviewing my grievances. I even got to the point of regretting the lies I had told for Bobbi years ago, when she was fired from Hexter and potential employers called for recommendations. It wasn't one of my finer moments.

Her footsteps died out. There was only silence.

I went in. It wasn't quite pitch-black. The boat's rocking, which usually had a calming effect on me, made me nervous. In the dark, as I moved slowly, it was hard to keep my balance.

I found the diving gear first, the wreckage second.

It was a nylon net bag that I came across first. Despite my caution, I almost tripped. The bag was lying on the floor, and I slid a foot into it. Fortunately I didn't fall.

The bag was big and empty. My eyes had begun to adjust, but I figured out what it was by touch as much as by sight.

A few steps on I found a scuba air tank. A couple more were right by it. A pair of regulators were in raised open boxes next to the hull. In another box I found face masks and fins and other equipment.

Ben had tried to get me to go diving with him a number of times. I had always refused. From what he had said I thought the usual thing was for divers to rent air tanks, not own them.

I didn't think of that there in the room. What I did think of was that Cort had explicitly denied any interest in scuba diving. At dinner I had asked if it was one of the things he used his boat for. I had just been making conversation. His negative had been categorical.

There was a creak. I turned toward the door and said, "Bobbi?" softly, but there was no answer. It was just a boat noise.

I continued along the wall. I decided I would circle the room and leave. If Bobbi hadn't come by the time I was done, I wouldn't wait for her.

I found rubber raincoats lying on the floor and a chest with tools in it. There was another, smaller chest next to it that was locked. I lifted it. It was heavy, and I heard something clank inside. Another toolbox, probably.

I had one moment of sheer panic. I had stifled a sneeze and was taking a look around. A shaft of moonlight illuminated two men facing me. Neither had a head.

They were wet suits, hung up on a line. I went over and felt them. They were dry.

In the corner was a tarp covering something. Lines of cord attached to hooks held it in place. It wasn't hard to pull a line loose. By that time I was convinced I wouldn't find evidence of drug trafficking—either it wasn't there or I wouldn't recognize it—but the tarp seemed to constitute an effort toward concealment, so I investigated.

The first thing I found was a rusted piece of metal, with a corroded bolt sticking out of one end. Then I got a small box. It was empty and also corroded. There was an encrusted object that might have been a cup. A knife. A broken hairbrush. A section of pipe. Something which might have been bone. I was lucky I didn't cut myself. Everything seemed to have been underwater for a long time, except for a diving face mask that was neither corroded nor old.

On impulse I held the mask up to a porthole. There was writing on the strap. It took me a while to make it out in the bad light.

I decided to leave. It seemed like I had been in the room a long time. Maybe Bobbi had been detained, or maybe she had just decided to leave the dirty work to me, but I didn't think she was going to come. I had searched the room. Maybe I hadn't done a great job, but it would take hours to look in every nook and cranny, and even then I would miss a lot.

I put everything back under the tarp except for the mask. I had decided to take that with me. Then I tied the tarp back down.

At the door I was undecided. If Bobbi had simply been delayed and did want to search the room herself, it would be a mistake to pull the door shut so that it locked. On the other hand, it wouldn't do for Cort or George to find it open the next day. I stood in the doorway for a couple of minutes, trying to make up my mind. With every second I got edgier and more annoyed. Finally I decided to leave the door open, make a brief reconnaissance, and, if I didn't see Bobbi, come back and close the door.

My head was just barely above the level of the deck when I heard the voices. I retreated a step and listened.

It was Bobbi and Cort. I risked a peek. They were sitting in the compartment where we had had dinner; George was there, too, leaning against the bar and staring out a window. I couldn't hear what they were saying.

I shifted my weight from one leg to the other, the balls of my feet getting warm under me. There was absolutely nothing to see, except a few stars in the sky. As I watched, a cloud smothered them.

I know how long I waited. It was only seventeen minutes. But it seemed forever. Finally I heard a chair scrape. I looked again. Bobbi had risen, and I made out the words "beauty sleep."

She headed toward her cabin. After a second Cort followed her. George watched them go.

He stood there a minute, motionless. Then he turned and walked toward me.

I almost didn't make it. As it was, I got down the stairs, pulled the door to the engine room shut, and ducked into the larder just as the light came on.

The moment I have done something the regrets start. As soon as I stepped into the larder, I realized I had been thinking with a guilty conscience, that it was far more likely George was coming for a snack than to check the engine room. I was trapped.

But my first instinct had been right. I heard him trying the engine room door, shaking the handle. Then there was silence; perhaps he was listening for sounds.

Then I heard a key turn in the lock and the door open. The hall grew brighter; he had turned on the light. Half a minute later he turned off the light and relocked the door and went back up the stairs.

I just stood there, letting the relief take me. Five minutes passed. Probably I should have waited longer, to make sure everyone was settled down, but I didn't have the stomach for it. I ascended the stairs as quietly as possible. The main cabin was dark.

I got to my cabin without encountering anyone. A fan of light spread from Bobbi's cabin, and I heard Cort's voice. I couldn't hear what he was saying, though.

It was only after I sat down heavily on my bed that I noticed I was still clutching the diving mask in my left hand. It would have been awkward explaining it if I had run into George or Cort.

I turned on the light and looked at the mask again. I had not been mistaken. There, in indelible ink, it said "R. Lee."

I got tape from my bag and placed a strip over Lee's name. I wrote "BIGGINS" on the tape. Then I put it in the drawer with my socks and underwear and spare shirt.

I was exhausted but too full of nervous excitement to sleep. I wondered if Bobbi would come in. There was no telling how long Cort would keep her.

I drifted off eventually. Once I woke with a start; it felt as if I had been falling. My skin was tight, and my heart pushed up, as though it alone had not been plummeting down with the rest of me. I lay awake for a while and then fell back to sleep.

16

The next morning Bobbi and I had a fight.

At breakfast she still looked green from seasickness. When Cort asked about fishing, she said she couldn't think of anything she'd like to do less. She announced she was going to sunbathe on the deck. Then she looked at me and asked if I would join her up front by the prow. I didn't think it was the happiest way of arranging a private rendezvous, but I agreed.

I was already covered with sweat by the time she arrived with a big towel and two plastic bottles of sunscreen. Neither of us spoke at first. Bobbi sat down and began to apply sunscreen. It seemed she was covering every square millimeter of exposed surface, using one bottle for her face and the other for the rest of her body.

Her meticulousness got on my nerves. After a long time— she was still anointing herself—I asked if I could borrow some sunscreen.

"Didn't you bring your own?" she asked peevishly.

"I didn't think of it."

She shook a bottle. "It's almost gone. I only have enough for myself."

"Oh," I said, waving my hands in a big false apology. "Please keep it then. By all means, I wouldn't want you to run any risk."

"You really should get your own," she said, pushing a bottle over toward me. "Sponging off other people is so tacky."

"Oh, I wouldn't want to be tacky," I said, pushing the bottle back toward her.

That more or less set the tone for our conversation. We bickered a little longer over sunscreen. Then I said, "Thanks for leaving me in the lurch last night."

She was studying her foot, where the splinter had gone in. "What's that?" she asked sharply.

"I just voiced my appreciation for your leaving me to do all the work last night."

She gave me a withering look. "I have a very bad headache." She spoke slowly and distinctly, as though determined to keep her temper in the face of great provocation. "My foot is throbbing, and I got very little sleep last night because of your screwing up. I really am not in the mood to hear your whining. Frankly I'd much rather be by myself, but I wanted to know if you did what you were supposed to do. Did you find the drugs?"

The remarkable thing about people who shock you by their egocentrism is that they are able to keep on doing it. No matter how many times you tell yourself not to be shocked, you still are.

"No," I said after a few seconds, as coolly as I could. "I did not find any drugs. What do you mean, my screwing up?"

"Please keep your voice down." She glanced up at the steering area. "You may not care if George hears, but I do."

"What do you mean, my screwing up?" I repeated in a fierce whisper.

She raised herself on an elbow. "You told Cort you weren't gay. Now he's jealous and suspicious, and he doesn't trust me. I had to stay up half the night, calming him down. Finally I promised to go off for a little romantic lunch together, just me and him. Otherwise he would never have left my cabin . . ." She shook her head. "At least we're going ashore. I'll be able to eat something."

She gave a short, unfriendly laugh. "It's strange. You get all sort of squeamish and liberal whenever I say 'fag' or 'queer' or something that doesn't mean anything, it's just a word, but here we are in a—a situation where my life is on the line and you aren't even willing to play along. I wonder why that is. Are you so unsure of your masculinity that—"

"Oh, for chrissakes, Bobbi. What TV show is that from?"

My voice had risen. Bobbi looked in George's direction. But he had deserted his post; we were not observed.

Neither of us spoke for a minute. The tension abated slightly.

"How did you wind up with Cort?" I asked. "I thought you were just going to give the key back to Macho."

"Yeah, well, good old Macho ran off and told Cort about my borrowing the keys." Her eyebrows lifted sardonically. "He's too gutless to do anything by himself. Like a certain other party I could name."

I didn't rise to the bait.

"So?" I prompted.

"So I chatted with him. There I was, entertaining murderers and drug dealers, and you were off playing hide-and-seek. If anyone should have been scared, it was me. I was sure you were going to blunder in like the Pillsbury Doughboy. So you didn't find anything?" she concluded dismissively.

"I found some things," I replied.

After a while, with obvious reluctance, she asked for details.

I told her about the scuba equipment and the wreckage and, after a moment's pause, Lee's diving mask. I also described George's visit. I spoke dispassionately, almost as if I were giving an inventory.

Maybe my tone was wrong. Or maybe Bobbi was just in too foul a mood to admit that I had accomplished anything.

"Well, what do you think?" I asked after I had finished and she had said nothing.

"I think you didn't find any drugs or anything to do with drugs and you left before you finished. I guess that means I'll have to figure out a way to get in there again and search it for real. Of course, it'll be twice as hard to do now."

"If I had stayed any longer, George would have found me."

"Yeah," she drawled. "That would have been terrible. The Foreign Service would probably never recover from the loss."

She stretched her arms. "Now, if you don't mind, I think I'll take a nap. I didn't get much sleep last night, and I've got a heavy social obligation in front of me." She put goggles over her eyes.

I left a minute later.

A little after one we docked at a small harbor. Bobbi and Cort went ashore for lunch. Half an hour later I realized there was no reason to stay aboard; I wrote a note saying I had to get back home early and went ashore. A man by the pier knew someone who could drive me into Wellington.

At home I turned on the air conditioning and got a beer. I lay back on the couch and felt comfortable for the first time since I had gone aboard that damn boat.

Bobbi's behavior, I decided, was the result of physical discomfort and fear. She wasn't like me. She didn't sweat visibly and turn red in the face, but that did not mean she was fearless. When she was scared, she became rude and defensive and irrational. And then she stayed that way for a while because she resented having been frightened. She had been afraid in front of the open door to the engine room and perhaps even more afraid all the time she spent talking to Cort. That was why she had acted as she had.

I wasn't mad anymore, but I did feel a turning point had been reached. I was sure we would never sleep together again. More to the point, I did not really want to. That streak of reckless egoism in her that I had found fascinating no longer seemed attractive. She was too good at getting me into dangerous situations. No doubt she would argue it was all for my own good, affording broadening experiences. But I didn't really think it would have been for my good if George had found me the night before.

In the future, I decided, I would transmit information to Bobbi and take her reports, but that was all. With any luck, the case would not run much longer. I had had my fill of the secret life.

The phone rang just after I stepped out of the shower. It was Bobbi, as bubbly and friendly as ever. Apparently a lunch on terra firma had vast restorative powers.

She wanted to know when would be a good time to stop by the consulate tomorrow. She made it clear she had something to tell me and I shouldn't report to Ben first. I got her off the line as quickly as I could, before she started dilating on the joys of espionage. Telephone security was not on her mind.

I doubted her news would amount to much. Still, despite everything, I was glad we were no longer enemies.

For an hour I was at peace with the world. Then I glanced at the *Bugle*.

CORT HERO TO AMERICANS was the headline. The story had the *Bugle*'s usual misspellings and deviant syntax, but its thrust was perfectly clear.

> Thomas Cort, "unionist" and "senator" from Beverley but known to every decent person as a cold-blooded and vicius killer, has stamped by the U.S. Government with official approval. This evil man, implied in very

many crimes too numerous to mention, is listed as "Hero" and "Rugged Individualist" in secret confidential U.S. Consular Documents, obtained by this Newspaper.

These very same papers reveal our late revered President and leading light of the 3rd World Movements in the most scandalous and false light. The late Sir Harry is named a "bastard in law and fact" in these odorious papers from "The United States Consulate of Navidad."

It went on for another twelve paragraphs. All the spiciest passages in Cort's autobiography, the first chapter of which I had sent to Bobbi a week ago, were well represented.

There were six more references to "official" U.S. consulate documents. When I put the chapter in an envelope, I had noticed that two or three sheets of paper felt different from the others. Somehow my official stationery must have got mixed up with my private stock. The letterhead would have been on the reverse side from the printing—I couldn't have failed to notice it otherwise—but the *Bugle* made no reference to that.

I wondered how the chapter had come into the possession of the *Bugle*. There was no telling, of course.

The phone's ring was jarring even though I half expected it.

"I've been trying to get you since last night," said Janine, Rollo's secretary. "The ambassador wants to see you. It's about something in the paper."

"I know," I replied.

17

In a way, my interview with Rollo was more like my idea of diplomacy than anything I had done since joining the Foreign Service. We discussed a problem in foreign relations and how to resolve it. It was a drawback, certainly, that my ignominious return to Washington was one of the solutions considered, but the experience was extremely interesting.

I lied about a few things. Not about editing Cort's autobiography or the accidental use of consular stationary. Rollo had to know about those. But I didn't disclose the nature of my relationship with Bobbi.

He had clearly been hoping I would say the whole story was a fabrication by the *Bugle*. When I said it wasn't, he briefly became petulant.

"I don't see why you couldn't just have marked up her manuscript," he said. "Leaving aside the potential for exactly the kind of embarrassment that has resulted, it must have been a good deal of work for you, typing it all over again."

"Well, yes . . ."

"So why did you do it?"

He looked as if he had spent a life as a prosecuting attorney rather than as a doctor.

"There wasn't any manuscript."

He scowled. "I don't understand. You said she asked you to look over her draft."

"Yes, that's what she asked," I replied slowly. "There wasn't a draft, though. Not really. There was a page or two that was supposed to be the beginning, and after that it was just notes. I had to write it myself."

The notes had been amusing. Apart from some elementary biographical facts about Cort they were mostly restaurant reviews. Bobbi had described in detail every place the two of them had gone. At the bottom of the page on Jojo's Fish-House (appetizers too salty, sauces gelatinous) was a jotting in different-colored ink. "Asked cook about cocaine. No dice. Says George smokes ganga, lots. Think he does, too." I burned that page.

Rollo looked at me for a while. "Why, Jim?" he finally asked.

"Pardon me?"

"You're not stupid. Yet on this occasion you went to considerable trouble to do something that could pose a serious embarrassment to the U.S. government. Last night I went to a party at which the minister of foreign affairs was present. I spent the evening avoiding him. His wife, you may not know, happens to be one of Sir Harry's daughters."

He cast his eyes up to the ceiling. "I simply would like to know why you felt impelled to write this thing."

"I never thought my authorship would become public. I'm very sorry, sir."

He looked at me sharply. "Does Miss Lyons have some sort of hold on you?"

For a vertiginous second I wondered what his reaction would

be if I said Bobbi was a spy for the CIA, I was her case officer and lover, and I had written the chapter to solidify her position with Cort.

"No."

"Are you . . ." He paused for a second. "Normally I would not ask this, but in the circumstances I feel I must. Are you romantically involved with her?"

"No."

His eyes seemed to soften. "Jim . . . if it is a question of a lady's honor . . . I assure you what you tell me would not pass beyond these walls."

The words did not quite sound ridiculous. Rollo was, after all, an ambassador, a nineteenth-century role if ever there was one.

"Bobbi is just a friend," I said after a few seconds. "When we—when we worked together in New York, in publishing, I used to help her out the same way pretty often."

"I see," he replied dryly. "In those days you were not an official representative of the United States government. Now, however, when you embarrass yourself, you also embarrass your country."

We were in his living room. He poured himself a glass of ice water.

"I could send you back home," he said after a minute. "For health reasons or whatever, officially. Unofficially I would offer an apology. Do you think that's what I should do?"

My throat was dry. "Is there an alternative?"

He compressed his lips for a second. "I suppose I could tell the minister that a friend of the consul asked to borrow some stationery, and unfortunately she took official paper rather than the personal stock she was supposed to. In other words, Bobbi wrote it. Is that your idea?"

"Yes," I said.

"That would make you look quite careless."

He looked out the window briefly. "Of course, there is another problem with it," he added flippantly. "It's not true."

It could not have been more than five seconds before he resumed speaking. They were a long five seconds, though. "Well, things have not yet reached the stage where a diplomat can't tell a lie in a good cause. That is the story we shall use. I shall regret Miss Lyons's deplorable lack of political judgment, but since she is not a member of the embassy and since Navidad shares with the United States a profound respect for unfettered free expression"—his eyes sparkled with amusement—"I shall not have to apologize overmuch. And of course there is the question of how the _Bu_ came into possession of unpublished papers. Presumably they are Miss Lyons's private property. Did the newspaper steal them? Is there a crime here? That may be a tack worth taking."

As I was going out the door, Rollo took me by the arm. In a not unfriendly way he said that doctors could bury their mistakes, but diplomats had to be more careful. I promised I would be.

Cort tagged along with Bobbi the next day.

"This bozo insisted on coming," she said cheerily. "He wants to apologize."

"That's right, Mr. Biggins," Cort said. He was beaming. "I was a bastard. Saying I wanted to throw you overboard, all that. I'm ashamed of myself."

I muttered something.

"No, it was very bad of me. I was host. I should have been nice. Instead I was a bastard." He laughed. "It is the boat's fault. I am not happy on it. I am head of the Fishermen's League; of course, I must have a boat. But I am not happy on it. I do not trust it."

Bobbi nodded, as though Cort were a student reciting a lesson. It all seemed cozy and friendly and slightly distasteful.

Then Cort laughed again. "I read the _Bugle_ yesterday," he

said. "That was a good story. Angry, aren't they? Did you give them the chapter?"

"Pardon me?"

"You gave them the chapter?"

He was smiling broadly, obviously delighted. For a moment I had trouble finding words. "No," I finally got out. "I have no idea how they got it."

"I thought you sent it to them, so they'd see the embassy markings and know I was your friend. Show them what's what, like."

I shook my head. "I don't know how they got it. Do you have any idea?"

He shrugged. "Who knows? You did a good job, though. Wrote my life just like it was."

"Actually Bobbi's the author. I just checked spellings—"

Cort smiled and shook his head. "You wrote it."

I took a breath. "For diplomatic reasons, it's best that Bobbi is the author—"

Bobbi broke in. "You do what Jim says, Thomas Cort. It's the least you can do after scaring him to death the other day." She pointed to the door. "Now vamoose. You made your apology. Jim and I have things to talk about that don't concern you."

He protested briefly but left. He tried to kiss her as he was going, but she playfully pushed him away. There was something eerie about the whole performance, as though it had been lifted out of some 1950s sitcom.

Bobbi sat down and smiled. "I came to apologize, too, Jim."

I laughed a little sharply.

"No, I mean it," she said. "I was nasty to you on the boat. You were doing your best, and I gave you a hard time."

Belatedly I remembered about bugs. We moved out to the patio.

"Was that why you came, Bobbi? Or did you want to say anything else?"

"A bunch of things," she replied. But then she fell silent. She picked up a leaf and slowly tore pieces off it. Then she looked up and stared at me for quite a long time.

"I guess I better say the hardest one first. Jim, I think you're really wonderful—I mean it—but I don't think we should see each other anymore."

I had heard the same thing on other occasions—not in exactly those words but close enough. One thing remained the same. The worst time was the three or four seconds between the moment you knew what was coming and the moment it was actually said.

Of course, I had already decided I didn't want to continue with Bobbi. Presumably I should have felt different. Perhaps I did; I don't really know. There was still a sweaty, airless instant in which I seemed to plunge downward.

"All right."

"I think you're a great person, Jim. But I don't think we're suited for each other. I mean, we got together 'cause we've been doing this exciting secret stuff, and I think that kind of intoxicated us—"

"All right," I repeated. "I see your point, Bobbi. You're right. We're not really suited."

"But ve vill still be friends, *mein Führer*? I vant it. Oh, zo much I vant it. I haf vays, you know, of making you friendly."

She extended a sandaled foot and stroked my ankle.

"You know, you're totally shameless," I said.

She grinned. After a moment she rested her chin in the palm of her hand and looked steadily at me, smiling.

I smiled back, briefly. But then a bubble broke, and annoyance seeped out. I had been outmaneuvered again. The previous night, thinking over Rollo's warning, I had decided I couldn't be her case officer any longer. The risks were too great. But if I said that now, she'd think I was reacting to the breakup. And maybe I would be. I didn't know anymore.

She was still looking at me. I could feel myself turning red.

She let out a sigh, as though she had been holding her breath. "I think we should call it quits with the spy get-togethers, too."

"*What?*"

She nodded, agreeing with herself. "I just think I should report directly to Ben from now on. It'll be simpler. And you won't have to mess up your career with all this undercover stuff."

It took me a while to speak. "I thought it was supposed to be safer if you met me."

She cocked her head to one side. "Oh, Jim, I just said that because I couldn't stand Ben. I mean, I still think he's putrid, but I can manage. Anyway, Ben's safer than you, the way things are."

"What do you mean?"

She grinned. "Well, it's because of Bobbi-Jim cover story number two. What I told Cort at lunch yesterday. Cover story number one—you're queer—was dead. OK. What I told him yesterday was that you were a forlorn admirer of mine, real sweet but like completely and utterly not my type. In other words, you're No Threat. I laid it on pretty thick."

She tossed her head. "Anyway, he bought it. I think he even felt kind of sorry for you. But he's not going to keep on believing it if I keep on seeing you. So, everything considered, grotto Ben is the safer bet. No one—not even Cort—could think I'm interested in him."

I got up and walked around the patio.

I was free. I could return to being a simple consul again. It might not be the most exciting life in the world, but it had its moments. It would be a great mistake to regret getting what I wanted. I told myself that several times. Then I breathed deeply and sat down.

"Anyway," Bobbi said, "this whole thing is about over."

"What do you mean? Did you find something out?"

"Yeah. Cort's not smuggling drugs." She waved a hand. "Ta-da."

I didn't say anything for a second or two. "What exactly did you learn?"

She smiled at me. "I'm reporting to Ben now, Jim."

"Bobbi. Come on."

She let her head fall back and stared up into the sky. Her throat was lovely, shadows sculpting hollows in it. I would miss her.

Then she lowered her head and looked at me. "I'll tell you this one time, Jim, but that's it. I don't want you pestering me, and I don't want you running to Ben and talking about me. If that gets out, it's—" She drew a finger across her neck. Then she settled back with a prim set to her lips.

Not for the first time I thought that while there were a million good reasons for not liking Bobbi, one of the best was the sanctimoniousness with which she preached rules of behavior that she herself flouted whenever she felt like it.

"I fail to see how Cort would learn about conversations I might or might not have with Ben," I said.

"Yeah, well, I bet you failed to see how the *Bugle* would be printing that story either. But they sure did."

She sniffed triumphantly. "Don't get offended. I said I'd tell you, and I will. It was at lunch yesterday. We got pretty friendly. We had a couple of bottles of wine. I mean, Cort had a couple of bottles, and I had a sip or two. Anyway, I figured, what the hell, why not just ask him? What's this big mystery about the boat? I said. Why does it go out on these midnight jaunts, and why is the engine room locked and everything?"

I was surprised, perhaps more so than I should have been. There was no reason for Bobbi to confine her recklessness to her dealings with me.

She smiled smugly. "You know, you and Ben think I'm dumb, but I'm not. I mean, he's not going to shoot me right there in the restaurant. Besides, I didn't say anything about drugs. I just asked what was going on. He could always make up some story."

I thought about it. Maybe Bobbi was right. It was, in any case, a fresh approach to espionage: Go up to your target and ask him what he's doing.

"So what's he up to?"

She cocked her head to the side. "He's building a hotel. I mean, that's what he's planning to do."

She smiled benignly, as though she weren't in the least let down by what she was saying.

"And the scuba gear?" I asked finally.

"That's part of it. He gave me a tour of the engine room after we went back. He's actually got a whatchamacallit, a compressor, to fill the air tanks. You didn't see it. He offered to take me down on a dive—have George take me down, I mean—but I told him no thanks. That stuff gives me the creeps."

I chewed it over briefly. "I don't see it, Bobbi. Why is he keeping it secret and what does the scuba stuff have to do with a hotel?"

Her head was motionless, but her eyes moved. Half a minute passed. "OK, I'll tell you. But this is secret, you understand?"

I gave a helpless shrug.

"You understand?" she repeated.

"Bobbi, I was under the impression that everything we talk about is secret."

"Right. But this isn't just Ben's little games. This is big business; money is at stake."

She looked at me urgently. I grimaced, then nodded solemnly.

"There's this like reef Cort's discovered," she said after a few seconds. "Well, he didn't discover it—people knew it was there, but no one had really looked at it. Apparently it's fantastic.

I mean, from a fish point of view. Cort says it's like the Great Barrier Reef in Antarctica."

"Australia."

"Wherever." She waved it away. "There's zillions and zillions of fish, and they're all real exotic. Anyway, it's like paradise for divers, but it hasn't been developed at all. So what he plans to do is build a hotel that'll cater to scuba freaks. But first he's got to scope out the reef and take pictures and everything, so he'll be able to get financing. And he can't let anyone know what he's doing while he's doing it."

I raised my eyebrows. "Why not?"

"Jim—it's business!"

"That's what I don't understand, Bobbi. If it's a legitimate enterprise, why does he have to be secretive?"

Her face took on a pitying expression. "Oh, Jim, you're so naïve sometimes. Do you think these people here give a damn about its being a 'legitimate enterprise'? If they find out, they'll steal the project before you could blink. Because it's worth a lot of money, for one thing, and because they hate Cort, for another. He's put a lot of work into it, and he doesn't want to lose it. You know, it's not like this reef is on land he owns; it's out in the ocean."

Neither of us spoke for a while.

"Eventually he's going to have to announce the project," I said mildly. "You can't build a hotel—you certainly can't run one—in secret."

"Of course," Bobbi agreed. "The thing is, it all depends on the timing. If people find out early, the government can steal the project easy. They just set up some commission to study this precious natural resource, and then the commission says it should be developed by Joe Schmo, who happens to be the president's brother-in-law. Cort's out in the cold. But if he can keep it quiet until he gets everything lined up, until he has some big-money guys from New York behind him and everything is all arranged, then they won't be able to do that. Cort'll announce the hotel and say it means a thousand jobs and a new septic treatment plant or whatever. No way the government would dare trash that. Plus he could always grease a few palms if he had to, which obviously he would. He explained it all over lunch."

She settled back in her chair, looking very pleased with herself.

"When we met Cort, he mentioned the project," I said. "It didn't seem like he was trying to keep it secret."

"Oh, he was. You remember, he didn't want to talk about it."

"I remember. Still——"

"It was Niso," Bobbi said bitterly. "Cort told me about him, too. He's trying to blackmail him."

"What?" I spoke loudly, startled. "Who's trying to black-mail who?"

"Niso's blackmailing Cort. Trying to, I mean."

She bent forward. The top button of her shirt was undone. I barely saw the soft darkening of the top of a nipple.

"Look, here's what happened. Somehow Niso found out Cort was checking out the reef. So he goes to Cort and says, 'Deal me in. I want a piece.' At first Cort laughs, but then Niso talks to a couple of people about this hotel Cort is planning with Cuban aid. He doesn't mention the reef or scuba diving—he's careful about that—but still it's a threat. Like if Cort doesn't play along, the whole thing'll get blown. So Cort plays along."

Disgusted by the tale she was telling, she was shaking her head.

"How do you know this, Bobbi?"

"Cort told me. Besides, it's what spies do. I'm sure Ben would do exactly the same——"

She saw my expression and broke off with a shrug.

"What do the Cubans get out of this?" I inquired curtly.

Bobbi laughed. "The Cubans? The Cubans get zilch. But Niso gets a lot of money, so he can retire in the style to which he would like to be accustomed. That is, he does if it all works out. It's tricky. Cort doesn't have money now. I mean, he's comfortable by the standards here, but he doesn't have any real money. If the hotel gets built, then he'll be rich. But how will Niso collect then? He has to have a share or something, but it's tricky. So there's a lot of tension."

I chewed it over for a few seconds.

"I guess this ends the investigation," I said after a few seconds. "We're interested in drugs, not hotels. . . . I wonder what Cort was doing with Lee."

"Who?"

"The American kid we went to the Hook to ask about. I told you I found his face mask on Cort's boat. You didn't ask about that, did you?"

She grimaced. "How was I going to ask about that? Probably George or someone just found the face mask lying around and brought it back."

A breeze shifted the branches overhead.

"Niso may be smuggling drugs," Bobbi volunteered.

"What?"

"Niso tried to get Cort to do some stuff along that line, but he refused. He thinks maybe Niso got someone else. It's like Niso's doing anything he can think of to make a buck."

Her brow furrowed. "Anyway, that's why I said things aren't completely over. Cort would love for Niso to wind up in jail. He'll tell me if he learns anything. And I'll tell Ben. Not you, *mon vieux.*"

She got up and stretched. "I should be moving along," she added, her voice light now, no longer conspiratorial.

I didn't move or say anything. I felt rooted to my chair.

Bobbi's news somehow was fascinating and weightless at the same time. I suppose that was because I knew there would be no sequel. Not for me, anyway. Perhaps Ben would tell me the outcome, but I wouldn't be having any more secret tête-à-têtes with Bobbi. I certainly wouldn't see her on my bed again, naked and laughing as she dialed a telephone number.

She put her hands on my shoulders and squeezed. "Cheer up, amigo. You look like your favorite gerbil died. I thought you'd congratulate me."

"Congratulate?"

"Yeah." She kneaded my shoulders. "For all I found out. And for acting like an adult and moral person."

"You found out things, but where does the other stuff come in?"

She laughed. "I could have made up some story and collected my ten thou from Brother Ben. But instead I settled for the boring truth. That's pretty adult and moral, isn't it?"

"I guess so."

"You know, I know people in New York," she said meditatively. "Money people. Maybe I'll put Cort in touch with them. I mean, I was thinking last night. This spy stuff isn't like a long-term career option. And I'm a lousy journalist. I mean, I'll kill you if you ever say that to anyone 'cause I may always change my mind, in which case I'm a great journalist, but right now I'm thinking I'll bag the writing. But one thing I *am* good at is people. I could help Cort a lot with this hotel. If I did, I'd be positioned pretty well for getting more work like that. Plus I might make a little spare change."

She looked at me expectantly.

"I agree that writing is perhaps not your forte."

She chuckled. "Well, kiddo, I better be going. Now remember, you're not a spy anymore. Don't go talking me over with Ben for old times' sake. I mean that."

She frowned sternly, then bent forward and kissed me. Then she left.

In writing an account such as this it is difficult to calculate the impressions one leaves. It is best therefore to be explicit. On that day, and for a little over a week thereafter, I still thought of Bobbi as on my side. I assumed she might have shaded the truth in a few particulars; it never occurred to me that she might be lying about everything.

18

I learned what Cort and Niso were really doing because of a man's death.

Eight days after I saw Bobbi, Winston Mannion went to a bar in East Wellington. Greely's was cheap and dirty and apparently the sort of place Mannion liked; he went there often. That night he struck up a conversation with a young woman. Captain Drabney told me her name, but I do not recall it. After a while the woman's boyfriend came in. Words were exchanged. Mannion hit his opponent over the eye with a brass ashtray. The injury was superficial. The knife wound to Mannion's chest was not. He died on the way to the hospital.

The death was reported on the morning radio broadcast, but I missed it. Consequently I was unprepared for the sudden appearance of Jossie Leeds, just after twelve-thirty. She came in like a Greek Fury, trailing Sammy behind her.

"My husband's dead, and he said for me to tell you what he saw, but I think maybe you're why he got killed."

Those were her first words. Most noncitizens treat the American consul with great deference. Jossie Leeds did not.

Sammy told me her name. I had no trouble remembering her; she was Mannion's common-law wife. I had stopped by her house the week before, trying to locate him. She hadn't been home, and the neighbors denied any knowledge of his whereabouts. I had been hoping Mannion could tell me why Lee's face mask was on Cort's boat.

Sammy left the room, and I got her to sit down. Her face held anger and something else. After a while I saw it was fear.

Jossie was sure the bar fight had been staged, that Cort was responsible for Mannion's death. What she wasn't sure about was my role in the affair. She thought I might be working with Cort; she had seen the story in the *Bugle* about Cort's biography.

My protestations of innocence did not carry much weight with her. I think what did matter was that Mannion had told her to try to sell his story to me if he was killed. That furnished an incentive to believe I wasn't guilty. It would have been hard to deal with the man who helped arrange her husband's death.

I don't know if Mannion's fear of Cort was well founded. Perhaps it was paranoia, and the bar fight was exactly what it seemed to be. But Jossie certainly believed Cort was behind it.

Even after she decided to talk, I did not hear the story immediately. We had to dicker over price. Her first figure was ten thousand dollars. I laughed. Then we were stuck for a while at a thousand; she may actually have believed she had a shot at that. We settled on three hundred dollars. Then we waited while Sammy went to the embassy and cashed a check for me and brought back the money. Only after she had put the cash in her purse did she begin to speak.

Mannion and Lee met by chance at the Hi-Life Club. Jossie had been with Mannion that night; according to her, Lee was a likable young kid who was bumming around the islands.

But he had had some money. Jossie said he had made it by selling exotic shells he harvested from a restricted marine park off Saba. He had been diving at night without a companion, so it had been dangerous as well as illegal. From Jossie's account, it seemed the danger had been as much an attraction as the money. It had been an adventure.

I asked if Lee had had anything to do with drugs. She looked shocked. "He wouldn't even smoke ganja," she said. "He knew lots of boys who got killed or in jail 'cause of drugs."

Lee hired Mannion to drive him to different beaches; he was hoping to find more salable shells. But Navidad wasn't Saba: He didn't find good shells, and in any case he didn't have a potential purchaser lined up. Mannion knew of a couple of fences, but they weren't interested in shells.

But the diving did lead to another interest, one that proved fatal. At the shop where Lee rented his gear he heard gossip. Someone named Cort had been renting equipment. Then he stopped renting, but the people in the dive shop heard that he had purchased his own gear. Why would he do that? No one thought Cort had suddenly become a scuba enthusiast. He had to be up to something.

Lee got interested. At first Mannion found his questions amusing. Then he got worried. It dawned on him that Lee was seriously thinking of spying on Cort. Mannion told Lee that would be very dangerous. Lee became more interested.

"Why did Mannion stay with him if he was so scared?"

"He was getting paid, wasn't he? Besides, Winnie never did anything smart. If it didn't make sense to do something, he'd go ahead and do it. I've seen him like that a hundred times. He'd get all scared and clumsy, but he'd go right ahead. . . ."

She dabbed her eyes with a bright yellow handkerchief.

"Ricky"—that was how she referred to Lee—"was all excited about the Hook. He had read books in school about places like it, he kept saying. I don't know—I don't think those books could have been very good. The way he thought, it was like something in a movie. Romantic, you know? Like they were all slaves who had run off to be free and were doing everything for themselves, not taking shit from anybody. Winnie kept telling him it wasn't like that, that they were real poor and bastards, too. Ricky wouldn't listen. He was real smart, going to college, but he didn't know anything about things here."

As she talked, I got a picture of the two men. Jossie had mentioned movies; it wasn't hard to imagine a movie being made about such a twosome: the näive college kid and the cynical small-time crook. Lee hadn't had much money; probably the main reason he hired Mannion was that he was intrigued by the islander's personality.

Of course, in a movie they wouldn't end up dead.

"Did Lee learn that Cort was interested in a reef?" I asked.

"A reef?"

She shook her head in bewilderment.

"I understand that . . ." But I had given no promise to keep Cort's projects confidential. "I understand that Cort is considering building a hotel, one that will cater to divers. There's supposed to be a reef with . . . exceptional fish life somewhere around here."

When Bobbi had talked, it had sounded reasonable enough. But now, as I listened to myself, it sounded like a fairy tale.

Jossie laughed. "You've been hearing some funny stories."

"That's not what he found?"

"A reef?" She laughed some more.

"Did he discover that Cort was involved in drug trafficking?" I asked eventually.

She looked at me as though I were crazy. "No. It's nothing about drugs. You got drugs on the brain."

"Well, then . . ."

"Cort was going after a wreck," she said finally. "That was one of the things they guessed, at that diving place."

"A wreck," I repeated tonelessly.

"Yeah. You know, sunken treasure. That was what Ricky was thinking it might be, and he was right. He saw it. I mean, he saw the wreck. I don't know about the treasure. Don't know if there was any."

Lee and Mannion visited Beverley. No one was particularly eager to talk to a pair of outsiders, but they did see Cort's boat, and they learned he had been taking it out at night in recent weeks.

Then they drove to a place just outside the Hook called Jack's Creek. They found someone there who would rent them a boat. Lee was spending the money he had made on Saba as if there was no tomorrow, but evidently he had decided this was his chance to have an adventure. In a week or two he would return home and go back to school and eventually graduate and get a job; if he wanted to look for pirate gold, now was the time.

They rested and the next evening set out in their rented boat. The drive from Beverley to Jack's Creek had been fast and easy; sailing back in the dark was long and hard. It was also very stupid, in Mannion's opinion. But Lee was running the show.

Just before they reached Beverley, they spotted Cort's boat heading toward them. They managed to avoid being seen. They trailed Cort's boat, and after a while it stopped. Two divers went over the side. Lee announced that he would put on his gear and go after them.

"Winnie said it was like he was crazy, he was so excited. They'd been drinking rum and eating sandwiches, and Lee had told Winnie he couldn't go diving if he did that, but now all of a sudden he was saying it didn't matter."

They argued in whispers. Finally Lee quieted down. A little

later the divers returned to Cort's boat, and it moved off toward Beverley. Lee and Mannion returned to Jack's Creek.

The next day they went out again. This time the trip did not seem so hard; it was light, of course, and that made a big difference. When they got to the spot where Cort's men had dived, Lee donned his equipment and went into the water.

Without question he was extremely lucky to find it on the first dive. There had been no way to mark the exact spot where Cort's boat had been, and the wreck was 235 feet down. In one sense it was a disappointment. It wasn't a Spanish galleon. It was a boat of this century, not too big. It was encrusted with growths, but Lee didn't know if that meant it had been submerged for five years or fifty.

"Was he able to see a name on the boat?"

I asked the question more or less at random. Jossie took something out of her bag.

"He brought this back up. Winnie kept it."

She put a corroded metal object about the size of a quart container of milk on my desk. It was a figurine of a man on a base. The man's arms were raised in what looked like an awkward position; the hands were missing.

Suddenly I realized what it was. If the hands hadn't been broken off, the figure would be holding a golf club. It was a trophy.

I picked it up to look at the base. Someone had made a partially successful effort to remove the encrustations. The Spanish was not very difficult.

Eduardo Malmierca had taken second place in the 1957 golf competition of the Havana Merchants' Association, senior division.

For a while I simply held the trophy in my hands. I didn't remember everything Ben had told me, but I did remember Malmierca had gone missing in a boat. And he had been rich.

I looked up at her. "Can I keep it?"

Of course, that was the wrong thing to say. I should just

have said, "I'll keep this." It cost me forty-seven dollars. The way we arrived at the figure was simple. It was all the cash I had on me.

The name Malmierca meant nothing to Lee or Mannion. But Lee was still very excited by his discoveries.

Mannion was more scared than excited. All the way back to Jack's Creek they argued. Mannion's position was that they had found out what Cort was up to—what they had aimed to do—and now they should forget about it. Even if the wreck did hold something valuable, retrieving it was impossible. Salvage at that depth, by Lee's own testimony, was extraordinarily difficult, a job for experts. Anyway, if they made an attempt, Cort's men were bound to discover them.

Lee acknowledged everything Mannion said but refused to let it drop. Never before in his life had he come close to anything half this exciting. He couldn't simply walk away from it.

They drove back to Wellington still arguing. When Mannion saw Jossie that night, he told her that it would be crazy to keep spying on Cort, that he wouldn't help Lee anymore. She agreed but sensed that Mannion himself was wavering: He was talking in order to persuade himself.

By this time Lee had five hundred dollars left. He offered it all to Mannion if he would go out with him one more time. Lee wanted to wait for Cort's boat and then dive down and surreptitiously observe the divers. Mannion thought it was a dangerous plan that would accomplish nothing, but he wanted the money. He agreed.

They went out early and hid close to shore. When Cort's boat appeared, Lee slipped over the side. Mannion had brought along a bottle of whiskey, but he was too scared to drink.

He had also brought binoculars. After a while he noticed a commotion on Cort's boat. Then a limp body was hauled aboard. He began to feel sick. It could be one of Cort's men, but he didn't think it was. Then two divers climbed aboard, and he lost what little hope he had. Cort's boat moved off immediately in the direction of Beverley.

Mannion then did something as uncharacteristic as it was courageous: He followed Cort's boat.

Two or three miles shy of Beverley Cort's boat stopped. A minute later a dinghy headed into shore. Mannion beached his own craft a few hundred yards away and watched.

Four men got out of the dinghy. Two waited by it, and two walked off toward town. An hour went by. Then a truck appeared. The two men who had waited—one was Cort, Mannion was sure—pulled a body out of the dinghy and laid it on the road. The truck drove over it. Then they put the body in the truck, and it drove off. Cort and the other man returned to the boat, which then continued on to Beverley. Mannion went back to Jack's Creek and then drove to Wellington, where he told Jossie everything.

"Why didn't he go to the police?" I asked, once it was clear Jossie had finished her story.

"The police?" She shook her head as though the idea were too ridiculous to bear examination. "Even if he was friendly with the police, he wouldn't have. He was afraid if he talked, Cort would find out and kill him." Her eyes bore in on me. "Which he did."

I ignored it. "You went to the police."

"Yeah." She shrugged.

"Why did you do that?"

She looked down at her lap. I realized—I should have seen it earlier—that one of the emotions she was feeling was guilt. She thought her visit to the police had led to Mannion's death.

"He was driving me crazy," she said finally. "He kept talking about Ricky and Cort. But he also kept going on about that boat, the one that was sunk, wondering what was on it, saying it must be worth a lot. I could see he was working himself up to go after it. And then he'd be dead, too. I thought if I told the cops, maybe that would get the whole thing over."

"But you didn't tell them. I mean, you didn't tell them what you've told me. You just said Cort had murdered Lee."

"Well, that's the main thing, isn't it?" she replied angrily. "I sure wasn't going to say more than that; my neck was already stuck out far enough. Winnie went crazy when I told him. Said we were done for. He made me swear not to tell any more. He went to stay with a cousin 'cause he knew the police would be asking for him."

Sammy entered, and I had to talk to him for a minute.

"You got the CIA here?" Jossie asked when he left. Her tone was confidential and slightly aggressive at the same time.

"Pardon me?"

"You got CIA here?"

"I'm not sure I— Why are you asking?"

"Winnie figured the CIA could get Cort." She stared at me. "Take him out."

The last three words sounded like something she had memorized from a movie.

When I finally found words, they tasted pompous in my mouth. "There aren't any CIA here. In any case, the CIA doesn't do things like that."

She seemed to think I had not understood her. "I mean, like, they could kill him."

"I understood what you said, Ms. Leeds. The CIA doesn't kill people."

"They oughta kill Cort," she replied with quiet intensity.

I shrugged. "Well, I'm sure the world would be a far nicer place if only the CIA killed everyone they ought to, but—"

She looked baffled. "You going to tell the police what I told you?" she asked after a few seconds.

I hesitated. "It is the policy of the U.S. government to cooperate with local authorities," I finally said. "However, there are features of this case that . . . require consideration. I cannot say what exactly we shall do at present."

I had a twinge of guilt. As a bureaucrat I had really arrived. But I didn't see what else I could say. At a minimum I had to talk to Ben and Bobbi before doing anything.

I walked her to the door. As I opened it, a thought struck. "Do you know anything about Lee's passport?" I asked.

"What?"

"Richard Lee had a U.S. passport. It didn't turn up among his effects. I doubt he would have taken it diving. So perhaps Mannion kept it, and I thought you might——"

"I don't know about that," she interrupted. "I haven't seen any passport. I never saw any passport."

She left. I already thought her story was basically true, but now I was convinced. She was a terrible liar.

I called Drabney. There had been no progress in locating the consulate bomber. After finding that out, I mentioned Mannion. Drabney gave me the details of his death that the police had learned. It was clear they regarded it as a barroom fight that had got out of hand. I didn't say anything about what Jossie Leeds had told me.

I met Ben at the club. I hadn't seen him in the past week, partly out of respect for Bobbi's wishes and partly chance.

"Glad to be out of it?" he asked when he arrived. I was sitting by the pool, on my second gin and tonic.

"I guess so."

I tried to marshal my thoughts. Ben spoke before I did.

"Bobbi's funny," he said. "Don't get me wrong. She's deplorable, but she's weird, too."

"Why do you say so?"

He stretched lazily. "Oh, everything. She does this complete reversal on Cort. Before he was a total crook; now she gives him a clean bill of health. Says she's checked out the boat and there's nothing, repeat, nothing, there. The mysterious midnight voyages are fishing trips. He likes to fish at night, what's wrong with that?"

He threw his head back in histrionic exasperation. Suddenly I felt cold.

"She's even stranger about Niso," he continued after a few seconds. "She says he's smuggling drugs but no one will ever be able to prove it, so I should just bump him off. I pointed out that doing that would eliminate the need for her, since she was hired precisely to find evidence that Niso was smuggling drugs. She didn't blink. Said she was hired to spy on Cort, not Niso, and she was getting tired of the spy business anyway."

"Oh."

"She kept saying what a great thing it would be if Niso had a slightly fatal accident. I didn't realize she was so bloodthirsty. Finally I told her I had bagged my limit of foreign agents this year. Then she started asking me about diamonds. Diamond brokers, I mean."

I looked at him. "Why is she interested?"

"Because she's an idiot," he replied complacently. "She has this wacky idea that she should buy diamonds with the money we're paying her. I guess she saw a movie where a spy carried around diamonds. We're paying her by deposit in a bank in the Bahamas. Apparently writing a check to transfer the money is not exotic enough. No. She thinks she should buy diamonds and sew them into the lining of her bikini, I guess."

I wondered if Malmierca had had diamonds aboard his boat.

"Did you have anything particular you wanted to ask?"

I should have told him everything then. But my throat was dry. The gin had done nothing. And I wanted to talk to Bobbi first. Maybe she would have an explanation.

I didn't think she would, but I had to give her a chance.

"I—I was wondering how you were getting along with Bobbi."

"About what you would expect. Ours is a relationship founded on a solid basis of mutual lack of respect." He shrugged. "With any luck, it won't last much longer."

It turned out he was right about that.

19

Before Bobbi went to work for Cort, we agreed on two code messages. If I phoned to say that a letter from her mother had arrived in the pouch, it meant danger, and she should duck and run. The second was a request to see some snapshots. Bobbi could ask it of me, or I of her, and in either case it meant a meeting was necessary. The message simply conveyed urgency; the actual arrangements were to be made openly over the phone. I had expected more messages for more contingencies, but Ben said it was best to keep things simple.

When I called that night, I got Macho. I left a message saying I had her tickets for the Marine Ball and I wanted to see the snapshots.

I called again when she didn't respond by noon the next day. This time I got the cook. He said Bobbi had gone out. I left the same message.

I called a third time in the early evening. I had now put off telling Ben what I knew for a full day. I was getting nervous.

Macho answered, but this time Bobbi finally came to the phone.

"Hi," she said. "I've been superbusy. Cort wants to go to the Bahamas, just the two of us, and there's a million things to get squared away first."

She wasn't unfriendly, just distant and unconcerned.

I told her about the snapshots. "What snapshots?" she asked blankly.

I said something.

"Oh, yeah. I don't know, Jim. We're real busy. I'll drop 'em off when we get back from Nassau."

"No, Bobbi. I need them now. Right away."

I could hear myself holding my breath. I forced myself to relax.

"After I get back," she said, announcing a decision. "That'll be plenty soon enough."

Somehow I had never envisioned this situation. I felt desperate.

"OK?" she said cheerily. It sounded as if she were about to hang up.

"No, it's not OK." I took a breath. "If you do that," I continued, "I'll be sunk. You know, like a boat that's gone down underwater? Like that? I'll be sunk. I need the pictures now."

She didn't say anything for a while.

"Bobbi?"

She sighed. "OK, if you're going to act that way, I'll stop by tomorrow. I'll come by your house around noon. Does that make you happy?"

I would rather have seen her that night, but tomorrow was acceptable.

"It'll do."

We hung up, and I cursed her for several minutes. Alluding to sunken boats over the telephone was criminally stupid, but she had given me no choice. I decided it was her neck, not mine, and I didn't really give a damn.

At eleven-thirty the next day I returned home from the consulate. It had not been a good morning; I had been too nervous to concentrate.

By twelve-thirty she had not appeared. I called the consulate, figuring she might have forgot we had agreed to meet at my house. But she wasn't there.

I waited thirty minutes before calling Cort's house. At that point I assumed she was either very late, which would not be out of character, or had simply decided not to come. I was mad.

Cort himself answered. He said Bobbi had left at ten with Macho driving her. She should have arrived in Wellington by eleven-thirty.

"Do you know if she was planning to do some shopping?" I asked.

"I don't think so." He sounded worried. "She wanted to get back as soon as possible. We are leaving for a vacation, you know. She still has packing to do."

"Maybe they had a flat tire," I said.

I heard Cort breathing between his teeth.

"Will you call me, Mr. Biggins, as soon as she arrives?"

"Sure," I said.

The doorbell rang. "Hold on a minute," I said. "This may be her."

But it wasn't. It was the guard who had been stationed at my house since the consulate bombing.

"A man went by on a motorcycle just now. He went by this morning, and yesterday twice," the guard said. "Probably it is nothing, but I should report it. The police can stop him and find out what he is doing."

I picked up the telephone again. "Mr. Biggins?" Cort said.

"Yes."

"Is that Bobbi?"

"No, it wasn't her." The guard was standing by the phone, waiting to use it. "I have to get off now, but I'll call you as soon as she comes."

"Please do," he said. We hung up.

The guard made his call. He was on the phone for a while, first waiting to get someone with authority and then explaining the situation. Then I called Sammy again. Bobbi had not appeared or called the consulate. I told him I would not be back until late or possibly not at all.

At two Cort called. "Has she come?"

He was brusque, obviously controlling his worry.

"No."

"I am going to come to your house. If she has had an accident on the way, I will find out. I am leaving now."

"Are you sure——" I didn't finish the sentence.

"I am leaving now," he repeated, and hung up.

I looked out the door. The guard grinned and pointed to a gray car parked a couple of houses away. "Police," he said. "They just got here."

I went inside and picked up the Trollope novel I was reading. It was not a good time for Victorian ecclesiastical politics, however.

After a while I called the hospital. For once I got someone who could understand a question and answer it. She said no young white woman had been admitted in the past twenty-four hours, as a traffic accident victim or for any other reason. I hung up, feeling a little better.

The phone rang a little later. A woman with a foreign accent asked to speak to Mr. Cort.

"He's not here."

"Oh. Is this the house of the American consul general?"

"Of the consul, yes."

"I called Mr. Cort's house. They said he was at the consul's house."

She sounded as though she suspected me of some kind of deception.

"I'm expecting him. If you give me your name and telephone number, I'll ask him to call when he gets here."

There was a pause. "I will call," the woman said. "When do you expect him?"

"I'm not sure. Maybe a half hour, maybe an hour."

"I will call," she repeated, and hung up.

I got a beer and put on a record. Cort showed up twenty minutes after the telephone call. George was with him.

"Is she here?" he asked the moment I opened the door.

"No."

He stood at the threshold.

"Come in," I said. "Someone called for you."

He walked in. George surveyed the grounds, staring at the unmarked police car.

"You got a bathroom?" George asked.

I pointed, and he walked off.

"Who called?" Cort asked.

"A woman. She didn't give a name. She said she would call back."

Cort sat down heavily in an armchair. He looked tired, and the lines in his face seemed deeper.

"We were going to the Bahamas this afternoon," he said after a minute. He noticed the beer I had left on a side table. "Can I have one of those?"

While I was getting a beer, George returned to the living room. "She's not here," he said to Cort.

For half a second I didn't see why he was repeating what I had said earlier. Then I understood: He had searched the bedrooms. I could feel myself flushing.

Cort gave a weary smile. "I didn't know——maybe you were playing some game. Didn't think so, but——" He shrugged. "Had to make sure."

I wanted to tell him to get the hell out. But ultimatums should be issued only when one has the force to back them up. The subject had been covered during orientation.

I handed him his beer. George went to the door and opened it.

"There's a police car," he said.

Cort looked inquiringly. "You call the police?"

"Yes."

He took a pull of beer.

"Why? You scared of me?" He had an amused expression.

"Nothing to do with you." I was angry and nervous. "You might recall that the U.S. consulate was bombed a while ago. The police are here because of that."

"You got a police car baby-sitting you all the time?"

He sounded incredulous.

"There was a suspicious man on a motorcycle. They're watching for him."

He raised his eyebrows but didn't say anything. I picked up my beer and drank some.

I told him about the hospital. He nodded but did not seem relieved. George got himself a beer without asking and returned to the door to keep watch.

Cort looked old and careworn and more human than he had seemed before. I didn't like him. How could you like someone who acted the way he did? But he did seem to care about Bobbi, care enough so that he was being worn down by it. He finished his beer, and I asked if he wanted another, but he just shook his head tiredly.

The telephone rang. It was the woman who had called before. I handed Cort the phone. "Yes," he said after a second. "I am Cort."

He listened briefly. "Ask," he said. After a couple of seconds he gave a short laugh. "Holes for the nipples," he said. "One side red fuzz, the other black."

He turned toward me. "She wants to know am I really Cort? She asks me to describe a special bra a girl wears. Lucy."

His attention returned to what the woman was saying. After a moment he asked urgently, "She is all right? Not injured?" His face was immobile and grave.

George spoke from the door. "Man on a motorbike. Going slow."

"I must see her," Cort said into the phone.

George looked at Cort, then returned his attention to the street. Cort seemed to hear nothing but what was being said on the telephone.

"No," he said after a while. "First I see her. Or George sees her."

"Bike turned around," George said. "Police car's going after it."

Cort listened to the voice on the telephone, then spoke slowly and decisively. "Tell him I see her or George sees her first. Otherwise he gets nothing. Tell him he will get what he wants, but first we see her. I think . . . yes, it is best if George sees her. That is the only way. Tell him."

He held the phone to his ear, but I didn't think he was hearing anything. Presumably the woman was conferring with someone.

His eyes grew alert. The woman was talking again.

"No, we do not have it with us," he said after a few seconds. "It is not possible. George must see her today, now, and we will trade tonight or tomorrow. That is how it must be."

He listened some more. "That would be stupid," he said. "Tell him what I said."

He looked at me, but I think it was just to have something to rest his eyes on. His gaze wandered around the room.

A minute passed. Apparently the woman was conferring again. Cort glanced at me.

"Is it tapped?" he asked, indicating the phone.

"I don't know."

He shrugged. "It doesn't matter. It goes on tape. By the time someone listens to the tape, everything will be over."

At the time what he said was reassuring. I did not reflect that my standing as a diplomat could be compromised by a tape even better than by a live listener.

He started listening again. After half a minute he spoke. "All right. He will be there."

There was a pause, and then he spoke again. "Alone. Yes, of course, he will be alone. . . . I will tell him. We will leave now. First, though, I must say something. If she is hurt, then I will kill him. Tell him that."

He listened briefly. "No, he can't hide. I will find him. You tell him I will find him. I swear to fucking God I will find him."

His voice rose angrily. I was hanging on every word; I remember thinking he would have sounded more impressive if he had spoken calmly. He almost squeaked.

Maybe he wasn't thinking about elocution. He rose from the chair. "I have to go."

"What happened?" I grabbed his arm. "Is Bobbi OK?"

He didn't answer, and he shook off my grip.

"Motorbike's coming back. Fast now," George said.

Cort must have heard, but the words didn't penetrate. George was standing in the middle of the doorway. "Let's go," Cort said.

George didn't move. Cort looked at him impatiently.

A number of things then happened quickly. A gun appeared in George's hand, and he started shooting. I think he got it from a shoulder holster, but if so, he must have been wearing it under his shirt, next to his skin.

I had been moving toward the door. I was going to insist that Cort tell me what was going on. I took another step even after George started shooting. That was inertia. Then I turned and dived behind a chair. I yelled, "Bomb!"

Cort must have ducked back as soon as I turned. He didn't get as far from the door as I did, though.

I could hear George shooting. He fired five times. I know because his gun was recovered and examined. I would have guessed seven or eight; it seemed he kept on shooting forever. Until the explosion, I mean. The shooting stopped then.

The noise was incredible. Even as I heard it, I was thinking how much louder it was than the bomb at the consulate. It was a ridiculous thing to think about, but it's what was on my mind.

I don't know whether ducking behind the chair was a good idea. The whole house jumped, and the chair fell over me. I hit my head on a coffee table.

Time passed. I don't know if it was a few seconds or a minute or two. Finally I got up into a sitting position.

I wasn't really hurt at all. My head ached, and the skin was scraped, but I didn't even feel stunned. The worst was my ears. They weren't ringing, but there was an ominous lack of connection between me and the rest of the world, as though a bubble surrounded me.

Cort was a few feet from me, lying on his stomach with his eyes closed. As I looked at him one of his pant legs began to turn dark from blood. I looked more closely and saw a large glass sliver sticking right up out of the leg. Then I saw a sliver in his back, above the belt. He moaned and moved his head slightly.

I looked for George. He wasn't in the doorway; he was sitting propped up against the doorjamb of the kitchen. The explosion had thrown him a good twelve feet.

I first thought he was all right. That was because he was sitting up. That thought was gone in half a second.

Except for a few tatters he was naked; his clothes were gone. So was most of his skin and face. His head hung at an unnatural angle.

I made myself get up and go look at him.

His chest looked as if a truck had rolled over it. There was nothing but blood where his neck should have been, and a piece of flowerpot was embedded in his head, right over his left eye. The back of his head, where it rested against the jamb, was a mess of brains and blood and bone.

"Is he dead?"

Cort's eyes were open, and he had lifted his head an inch off the floor.

"Yes," I said. "He's dead."

Cort's eyes closed again, and I heard him panting. Looking at George had induced a wave of nausea. I also felt the same utter tiredness I had experienced after the consulate was bombed, but it did not seem to have the same effect. I was tired, but I did not feel incapacitated. My mind seemed relatively clear.

It is all a matter of practice, I suppose.

I went to the phone.

"What are you doing?"

I found the question extremely annoying. "I am going to call for a doctor," I said impatiently. "Also the police. Also the embassy. And . . . I don't know. There must be other people to call."

I picked up the phone, but there was no dial tone. I kept

trying, but I couldn't get one. The explosion had knocked out the line.

I remembered about Cort's wounds. I got a dishrag from the counter and went over to him.

The glass sliver in his back had fallen out; some blood was oozing, but it did not seem too bad. But the big piece of glass was still sticking out of his leg, and the pant leg was sopping with blood.

Gingerly I took out the sliver. Blood didn't spurt, so I hoped I had done the right thing. I pressed the dishrag to his leg, and it was soon permeated.

"Can you hold this here?" I asked him.

He didn't speak, but he pressed the rag to his leg. I went to the kitchen and got a cloth potholder and a roll of masking tape. I put the potholder over the wound, throwing the dishrag aside, and wrapped the masking tape several times around his leg as tightly as I could. I didn't know whether the tape would hold, since it would soon be soaked with blood, but I couldn't think of anything else.

The whole process must have been extremely painful. Cort grunted several times, but he didn't make any other noises.

I looked him over. There was a big bruise on the side of his head and a large number of smaller bruises and cuts. Nothing looked immediately life-threatening, as best I could tell.

I started to get up when Cort grabbed my arm. "You have to go," he said.

I had no idea what he meant. I thought that he probably didn't mean anything, that he was speaking out of shock.

"I'm going to go next door, to telephone," I said after a few seconds. I spoke slowly and gave a slight emphasis to the word "go."

His grip tightened. "No," he said. "You have to go to Bobbi. She has been kidnapped."

I shouldn't have been surprised, I guess. I had surmised something like that, hearing his side of the telephone conversation. But that was before the bomb.

I shifted my weight and ended up losing my balance and reaching out to support myself. My arm landed on his back. He gasped in pain.

I waited a second or two, until he looked able to answer. "Is she all right? Who kidnapped her?"

He grimaced. I think it was frustration at my slowness, not pain. "Niso. Who else? You have to go now. I told them George would come." His eyes flicked toward George, and then he gave an infinitesimal shrug. "See that she is all right and make arrangements."

"Arrangements?"

"For the trade." He looked impatient. "See what he wants. If I have it, I will give it. Tell him not to ask too much; it was not as good as he said."

He closed his eyes and clenched his teeth. Then all of a sudden he heaved, and he was sitting up, his side propped against a chair. His mouth opened wide, but there was no noise.

"I'll go next door and phone a doctor, and then we'll see about Bobbi," I said slowly. "Maybe we should tell the police . . ."

He had let go of my arm when he raised himself, but now he grabbed it again. "No. No, you can't do that. You must go now."

His eyes flicked over the room. "You think you have to call? The police will be here any second. So will everyone else. If you don't leave now, you won't get away. And then Niso will kill her."

I didn't reply immediately. As much as I cared for Bobbi, it was hard to think about her with the shambles all around me. A dead man lay ten feet away, and an injured one was beside me. And I did not believe Cort. Why would Niso kill Bobbi since she was his ace in the hole?

I started to say that. Cort strengthened his grip on my arm until it was painful.

"No," he said. "You don't understand. Niso is not to be trusted."

I almost laughed. The idea that anyone would ever dream of trusting Niso was ludicrous.

Cort saw my expression. "You don't understand," he repeated. He spoke quickly. "Niso is—he is doing something he has never done before. He is like you."

Had Cort gone crazy? I couldn't imagine what he meant. But he kept talking, even though it was clearly painful.

"He works in his office, he talks to people, he— But now he is doing something he has never done before. He is scared and crazy. He will do anything. And he hates her. You have to go."

I heard a car siren.

"Go where?" I asked.

He told me.

"They will be looking for George."

He shrugged. "They will find you." He drew a breath. "Go."

The gray police car had just pulled up in front of the house. One man was inside, talking on the radio. Another was bending over the guard who had been outside.

"Is he OK?" I asked.

"He is breathing," the policeman said.

"There is a wounded man inside, and a dead one," I said as I walked to my car. "I am getting help."

I thought one of the policemen might try to stop me, but neither did. I drove off.

20

George had been supposed to drive thirty miles and then leave the coast road for a spur that looped into an abandoned pilot greenhouse project. After going on the spur a couple of miles, he was to stop his car, get out, and start walking back toward the coast road. He would be picked up and taken to see Bobbi.

The person who picked him up was exposed, of course, if Cort decided to seize him. But that would presumably doom Bobbi. On that part of the island it would be extremely difficult to tail a vehicle without the driver's being aware of it. Because of the bomb, I started later than George would have. When I got out of the car, I was five minutes over the time limit.

The spur road was dirt. Orange dust rose as I walked along. There were clumps of bushes thick enough for a man to lie concealed. After a while I decided it was pointless to worry about being spied upon from a bush when I was offering myself to be picked up by kidnappers. My head was throbbing where it had hit the coffee table, and pretty soon I had a first-rate headache. I wished I hadn't hit my head, and I wished the sun weren't shining so brightly, and I wished I had brought along a canteen of water and some aspirin. Then I started laughing, thinking of all the things that I could wish were different. I was a little giddy. There was no one in sight.

I didn't have my watch, but I must have walked for more than half an hour, because I made it all the way back to the coast road.

When I had done three quarters of the distance, I made a brief excursion. Something in a little gully off the road was attracting flies. As I pushed aside bushes to find out what it was, I caught a whiff, and my stomach began to weaken.

It was a dead goat. I glimpsed it briefly, started back, and then from some odd compulsion went back and checked again. It remained a goat. There were a lot of flies. The ones by the eyes were the worst.

When I got to the coast road, nobody was in sight. After a minute or two a car went by. Then another. One car slowed; the driver obviously thought I might be in need of assistance. But I waved her on. Niso wouldn't be using a young woman with a baby in a car seat to make the pickup.

I stood there for perhaps a half hour. After a while I began to lose hope. I wondered if they weren't coming because I, not George, had come, or if Niso had simply changed his mind about the rendezvous. If so, what did that mean? Had he called my house again? But he couldn't have, since the telephone was out. I wondered what was happening with Cort. Had he been taken to the hospital? Was he all right? For the first time it occurred to me to ask myself what had happened to the man on the motorcycle, the bomber. I spent a couple of minutes wondering if he could possibly have survived. Then I remembered something I had seen but rejected from consciousness as I was getting in my car. An arm.

It had been lying on the ground, against the curb on the other side of the street. I had looked at it and told myself it was a branch even though I could see quite well it was part of a human body. Charles Tinsley would not do any more bombing.

After that I tried to think about Niso and what he would probably do, but I didn't make a very good job of it. All I could think about was how thirsty I was and how tired and how I didn't know what was going on. I was out of communication standing out there, but I was afraid to leave.

Finally I started back. I hadn't made up my mind to go, but it seemed I might as well get back to the car.

The sun must have dazed me. By the time I heard the motorcycle it was just a few yards away.

The rider was a middle-aged black man, wearing jeans and a nylon Windbreaker and a helmet with the visor flipped back. Later I heard Niso call him Arthur. He had binoculars on a strap around his neck.

He pulled up next to me and stopped. "Hello, Mr. Biggins," he said. "We were expecting someone else."

I explained about George. He lost his skepticism as I talked. No doubt there was a great deal about kidnappers and spies that I did not know, but I had become fairly good at describing the effects of a bomb.

He tossed a bag on the ground beside me. "Take off your clothes and put these on. Take off everything. I will watch."

I made a halfhearted protest. He brushed it aside. "You want to see the girl, don't you? Hurry. We don't have all day."

In the bag were pants, a sweatshirt, and rubber thongs. When I first started to put the pants on, he held up his hand. "No, take off your underwear, too."

The idea that I would have an electronic homing device built into a jockstrap was ridiculous, but there was nothing I could do.

It was embarrassing to strip naked on a dirt road in broad daylight.

I put my clothes into the bag. My contact motioned to the ground. "Leave it," he said. "You can pick it up later."

He blindfolded me with red electrical tape and had me put on the motorcycle helmet. Then he guided me to the bike.

"Put your arms around me, and hold on," he said. "You have ridden before?"

"No."

He grunted. "Lean with me. I won't go fast."

"I can't see," I said, rather unnecessarily.

He laughed. "You don't need to see."

We moved off slowly. I could feel the different surface grade when we got to the coast road. "Lean," he said.

Then we went in circles. I came close to throwing up and falling off. Presumably the object was to ensure that I didn't know which direction he turned on the coast road. He certainly achieved that.

Once we started really moving, though, there was something oddly soothing about the ride. The wind felt good. The effort of keeping my balance required enough attention to stop me from thinking about other things. After a while—more than a half hour and less than an hour—I could tell by the surface that we had turned off the coast road. A little later we stopped.

"We are there," my guide said.

I was escorted inside a house.

"You took your time," said a man's voice. It was, I soon learned, Niso Carreras. His English was very good. Ben had said he had attended an American school as a boy in prerevolution Havana.

The man who had brought me started to explain. Niso interrupted. "You're sure you weren't followed?"

"Yes."

Someone walked toward me. Then Niso's voice sounded much closer. "You are well, Mr. Biggins?"

"I'd like to see," I replied.

There was a pause. "I suppose we can allow that," Niso said. The tape was taken off. It hurt, but I was glad to see again.

Niso looked much as he had in the photograph Ben had shown me. He was slight and neat and fit, rather professorial in appearance. He wore tortoiseshell glasses. His hair was thin, a few long, wispy strands brushed over the bald crown. His eyes sparkled, and there was a birdlike nervous energy to his movements.

The room was small and dingy. There were two chairs against a wall and a small TV resting on a card table. The windows were curtained. A paper bag doing duty as a wastebasket stood next to a door to another room.

"Is Bobbi all right?"

Niso gestured to the door. "She is fine. She has a little scratch on her cheek—nothing, you understand—only I tell you so you will not be surprised. First, though, I want to know why you have come instead of George."

"He's dead."

He raised his eyebrows. "The bomb?"

"Yes. How do you—"

He pointed to a Walkman radio. "I heard five minutes ago. There were no details, though. Is Cort alive?"

"He was hurt, but I don't think too badly."

Niso gave a sigh of relief.

I looked at him, surprised.

He laughed. "If Cort is blown into a million pieces tomorrow, I will drink a toast. But I want him to live until then. He owes me a great deal, and I want him alive to pay it."

He sat down and lit a cigarette.

"Can I see Bobbi now?" I asked.

A thin smile appeared on his face. He tipped the chair back so that he was balancing on the two back legs.

"There is a nice ring of concern there," he said. "I ask myself, is that a consul worried about one of his nationals? Or is it a man worried about his girl friend, or an employer of spies worried about an agent? Or perhaps all three?"

He laughed. I started sweating.

"We are going to have a talk, Mr. Biggins," Niso said after a moment. "You are involved now. Not by my wishes, but you are involved. I think it will be better if I explain things to you. If you understand what this is all about, you will see I am not such an evil man, and we can . . . trust each other? Just enough, I mean, so that we can do our business."

He took a few puffs of his cigarette.

"You like her, don't you?"

I did not reply. He shrugged politely.

"I must say, Bobbi and I never quite hit it off. That air of superiority she has, simply because she is nice-looking: I find it infuriating." His mouth twisted in bitterness.

Then he chuckled. "I'm afraid I used to tease her. Once I bet her she could not name five facts about Castro. Usually she ignored me, but that time . . ."

He shrugged. "Her first fact was that Fidel smoked cigars. Undeniably true." He gave an unpleasant smirk. "Then she said he was a Communist. Right again. Her third fact—I think she was already feeling the pressure of ignorance—was that Castro was a man. I applauded and told her there was no need to go on; such a brilliant revelation counted for at least a dozen facts all by itself. . . ."

Niso paused, savoring the memory. "Cort was there. As were a number of other people. I think she found the moment rather humiliating. She was mad. Actually, mad is not the word for it. She was ready to kill me on the spot." His eyes grew moist with suppressed laughter.

"Still, I never expected her to do what she did," he said. His face was purple. "All I did was have a little joke at her expense. She can be quite vicious, you know."

For a second I said nothing. I was disgusted, but I couldn't leave without hearing him out. "What did she do?" I asked.

His eyebrows lifted momentarily. "She told my superiors I was spying for the CIA. Not a very nice thing to say, was it?"

He shrugged. "Go have your chat. Then we will talk some more."

Bobbi was sitting on a cot, listening to a radio. Macho stared out the only window.

She jumped up as soon as she saw me and ran over.

"Oh, God, Jim. I'm so glad to see you. It's been horrible, just horrible."

I held her. There was a scratch on her cheek, and her eyes were red. It looked as if the sobs would come any second.

"I think we can leave the friends together for a while," Niso said. Macho walked out the door. "Knock when you are done, Mr. Biggins."

He left the room. A bolt clicked from the other side.

"I want to kill him," Bobbi said.

"Niso?"

She gave a forlorn laugh. "I meant Macho, actually. Bastard. He's a traitor, you know. He's working for Niso. I'd like to kill him, too."

The heaves came back.

"Are you OK?"

She laughed sharply.

"I just meant——"

"I'm great," she interrupted. "I've been kidnapped and beat up and I'm afraid they're going to kill me and they won't even let me to the bathroom and—and—"

She started crying.

For a second I felt myself turning away from her. She sounded histrionic; it was as though I were watching Bobbi doing fear. But of course she *was* afraid. It wasn't her fault if she cribbed her lines from some TV movie. She had always relied on borrowed lines and borrowed thoughts.

"I'm sorry, Bobbi. I just wanted to know if you're physically OK."

"Yeah, I'm OK," she said listlessly.

"It looks like you're going to have a black eye," I said after a few seconds.

"It's my own fault. I was dumb. Macho stopped the car, and this guy told me to get out—I'd never seen him before—and I refused." She bit her lip. "I never thought he'd hit me."

Bobbi's admitting that she had behaved stupidly shocked me as much as anything I had seen thus far. I had never seen her self-confidence vanish like that.

"What happened?"

She replied in a flat voice. "I was coming to see you. We left around ten. A little ways outside Wellington Macho took this side road. He said Cort had told him to drop something off. I didn't think anything of it. Then he pulls off next to this parked car, and I see Niso in it and two guys I don't know."

Her voice came to life. "I knew something was wrong. They got out of their car, and then one of the guys opened the door next to me and reached in and grabbed my purse and a bag. They looked through them, but of course there weren't any di—there wasn't anything in them."

She sat on the cot. When she continued, her voice was small, almost inaudible. "Then he told me to get out—not Niso, this other guy—and I said I wouldn't and he got mad and yelled at me and I told him to go away . . . and then he reached in and pulled me out and hit me. Then they blindfolded me and brought me here."

I sat down beside her and put my arm around her shoulder.

"It's OK, Bobbi. It's OK."

The shuddering began again. "They're going to kill me," she said.

"No, Bobbi."

The reassurance didn't seem to work. She started to sob and speak at the same time. "They're going to kill me. I know it. They're going to kill me. Oh, Jim, you've got to do something. Oh, God."

I didn't speak until the shaking had mostly stopped.

"They want to do a trade, Bobbi. They don't want to kill you. They want to ransom you to Cort."

For a second I wondered if it was a mistake to minimize the danger. Then I realized I didn't have to worry about giving her false hopes because if the hopes were false, she'd be dead.

She wiped her eyes with her shirt sleeve. "Do you have any Kleenex?"

"No. I'm sorry."

She shrugged. When she spoke again, she sounded more collected. "They won't give me anything. No Kleenex, no food, not even anything to drink. Not exactly your perfect Caribbean vacation spot, is it? When I said I wanted to go to the bathroom, Macho said there wasn't one. Then he gave me this . . . Tupperware jar I'm supposed to pee into. I told him to leave the room, but he wouldn't."

Anger replaced self-pity. "All I can say is, Macho better get a long way away from this island if he plans on staying alive much longer. When Cort finds out what he's been doing . . ." She shook her head.

"I'm such a fool," Bobbi said eventually. "I never should have come here. Do you know a guy proposed to me, just a couple of weeks before I left New York?"

The memory lit up her face.

"At the Rainbow Room," she said dreamily. "Can you believe that? It was incredibly corny, but sweet, too. This guy at Goldman, Sachs. He's really nice. But I turned him down. I thought he wasn't . . . exciting. Just a classic yuppie. I thought it'd be more fun to be a career girl in the Caribbean. And then I got a chance to be a spy and I thought I was just Miss Total Maximum Cool. I didn't figure I'd wind up here, kidnapped by a crazy Cuban."

She almost smiled. The shuddering had stopped, and her breathing was more even.

I decided it was time to ask a few questions. "You want to tell me what Cort and Niso are doing?"

She seemed absorbed in her thoughts.

"Bobbi. What is Cort really doing?"

She looked away briefly. "I told you," she said impatiently. "He's got this hotel scheme."

I tried another tack. "When they grabbed you out of the car, what were they looking for in your bag?"

She shrugged impatiently. "Who knows? They just—I don't know—they probably just like to look in girls' bags."

"Jesus Christ, Bobbi."

I was disgusted. I knew she was frightened, but that seemed all the more reason for her to be honest for a change.

"Macho is working for Niso?" I asked after a while.

She pursed her lips. "I've only told you that a dozen times."

"This kidnapping," I said, ignoring her tone. "Obviously it had to be organized. Could Macho have overheard us yesterday?"

Her expression changed. "Oh, God, he probably did. When we got here, Niso asked all these questions, and some of them—well, he had to know about the phone call. I figured he had tapped the line. But probably Macho just picked up the extension in the kitchen."

"It wasn't until I said I was sunk, like a boat underwater, that you agreed to come."

Bobbie didn't reply.

"Why was that?" I persisted.

She looked away.

"Why?" I asked again.

"You were being such a pest and you sounded so desperate, I just decided to be nice. That's all. You know, it's really all your fault I was kidnapped. I mean, if I hadn't driven in this morning—"

"Then Niso would have tried something else," I interrupted. "Cort and Niso have been trying to get something up from a Cuban refugee's boat that went down a long time ago, right? Look, Bobbi, I know a fair amount. But I want to know the rest. I think Cort told you what he was doing when you had that lunch with him, when we were on the cruise. I think that's why you wanted to cut me out and deal directly with Ben, because you had made up your mind you were going to keep Cort's secret for him and you figured Ben wanted to fold up the investigation anyway."

She didn't say anything, so I continued. "You didn't tell Ben about the scuba gear aboard Cort's boat. I spoke to him; he thought there was nothing on the boat. I think you did that because you thought it might somehow give him the idea of underwater salvage. It wouldn't, of course, because he was never thinking of that, but you still didn't want to run the risk. Why didn't you tell him, Bobbi?"

She rolled her eyes. "What was the point? I mean, why bother him with irrelevant details—"

I wanted to slap her. She saw my expression and shut up.

After a few seconds I got control of myself. "Look, Bobbi. I'm going to ask a few questions, and I want you to tell me the truth. For a change."

I paused a second. "And try to remember that you're not in the Rainbow Room now. You have to rely on me to get you out of this, and I damn well want to know what's happening."

It was pure bluff, since I would do what I could for her whether or not she was honest. But the words had an effect. She had been frightened quite thoroughly in the preceding hours, and my speech reminded her of that. The air seemed to go out of her.

"OK?"

"OK," she replied.

"You know about the boat Cort's looking for?"

She twisted the small ruby ring on the fourth finger of her right hand. "Yeah."

"When did you find out?"

She took her time replying. Finally she heaved a sigh and looked at me with a weak smile.

"He told me at that lunch." She gave a little laugh. "You were kind of a help actually. He was jealous of you. I think telling me about the boat was his way of . . . well, showing he cared about me, so I'd prefer him to you."

"And cutting me out of the operation?"

"You know, what I told you before was really true. He's jealous, so it just seemed smarter. And then I figured Ben'd be easier to fool. I mean, he thinks I'm so dumb I couldn't ever be connected to anything important."

She shrugged. "I figured if I told him there was nothing going on, he'd buy it. I mean, he's probably got a dozen other agents doing all kinds of stuff that he has to worry about. But you—all you've got to do is stamp visas all day long, so naturally you get hyper about everything to do with Cort and scuba gear and stuff. It just seemed smarter."

She got up from the cot and walked over to the window and stared out.

I didn't speak for a while. "I don't understand," I finally said.

"What?"

"I don't understand why you lied."

She tapped the window nervously. "I didn't really lie. I just didn't tell you everything."

I laughed. "All that hotel garbage?"

She made a face. "I had to say something. You kept asking, so I had to make up something."

"But why didn't you simply tell the truth? For chrissakes, Ben was paying you to tell him what you found out."

She turned back to the window. "He was paying me to find out about drugs. Cort doesn't have anything to do with drugs. I found that out and I told him. The other stuff—well, Cort told me that in confidence."

She was perfectly serious.

"Jesus, Bobbi. Cort was your target. He was the person you were spying on. What he tells you is not to be kept in confidence."

She shook her head. Her mouth assumed a prim expression. "Well, that's not how I saw things. Cort has been very good to me. He's really a pretty good guy when you get to know him. I wasn't going to sell him out to Ben. Who was paying me next to nothing, I might add. I mean, if Cort *had* been doing drugs, of course, that would have been different. I would have told you and Ben everything. I did tell you everything, as long as that's what I thought it was. But then it turned out to be something different, so I had to be different."

"Which is probably why you've been kidnapped," I replied.

For an instant she started to get angry. Then she gulped and almost wavered on her feet. "Oh, Jim, I'm so scared. I'm so scared. Can't you take me home?"

Suddenly I didn't feel very good. She was already scared to death, and I was doing my best to scare her more. I walked over and held her. "I'll do everything I can. I promise."

She started to cry. "Don't worry, Bobbi. I'll get you out of here. I swear it."

Finally she stopped crying. "I know I've been stupid, Jim. I know it." She looked at me. "But I can't do anything about it now. It's spilt milk. I'll be a good girl from here on in, I promise, but you've got to help me."

The crying had puffed up her eyes. She wasn't nearly as pretty as usual.

"I will, Bobbi," I said. "I will."

She sat down on the cot. I doubt she found my words very reassuring. Certainly I didn't.

"How does Niso fit in?"

She was staring at her hands. "What?"

"How did Niso get involved with Cort?"

"Niso was the one who knew about the boat. He knew where it was."

"Oh."

She leaned back against the wall and spoke tiredly. "Cort really did all the work. Niso just sort of had a general idea of where the boat was; Cort had to look around for a long time and spend a lot of money, and then, when he did find it, it was real deep and hard to get to."

"I see."

There was the sound of someone in the other room. I looked at the door, but nothing happened. Apparently we had a little more time to ourselves.

"Why did Niso approach Cort in the first place?"

She smiled. "What else was he going to do? He knew about this wreck that was supposed to have diamonds on it, somewhere off the Hook. He knew it would be hard to find, and he's kind of conspicuous. So he went to Cort and said, You find it and we'll split the take.'"

"How did Niso find out about the wreck?"

She shrugged.

"Come on, Bobbi," I said impatiently.

She looked distraught. "I don't know, Jim. I really don't. Cort never told me. Maybe Niso never told him. I just figured it was something Niso learned somehow, being a spy."

I went to the window and looked out. I no longer trusted my ability to tell when Bobbi was lying, but I couldn't see any reason for her to lie about this.

"Why are you here?" Bobbi asked. "Did Niso call you?"

I told her about Cort's coming to my house and the telephone call. She went white when I told about the bomb, but when I said Cort had not seemed too badly hurt, she relaxed. George's death did not evoke any grief.

"So Cort told you about the boat and everything?" she asked.

"No. Lee—the American who died—discovered some of it. He had someone with him. A guy named Mannion. Mannion's girl friend told me what he knew."

"Oh," she said quietly.

"What do you know about Lee? Did Cort kill him?"

"Oh, no." She looked shocked.

"So what happened?" I asked after a moment.

"It was an accident. Cort told me about it."

I raised my eyebrows and waited.

"Cort never knew who he was until you showed him that photograph in Beverley. He was just some strange guy who showed up dead."

I let out some air. "Lee did not die from being run over, Bobbi. He was out diving. He discovered Cort was going after Malmierca's boat."

She nodded vigorously. "I know, I know. Cort told me all about it. Not that there was much to tell. It was just after Cort finally found the boat. He spent ages looking. Anyway, it was like the second or third time they were checking it out, because it was really deep, almost too deep to work at. He had a couple of divers down looking it over, making sure it was the right boat, and they see this other guy they don't recognize. They're like freaked by it, but they swim toward him to see who he is. He swims away, but he doesn't do it the way he's supposed to; he swims straight up, as fast as he can. Cort said maybe he didn't even know he was going straight up, but it was like the dumbest thing you can do—it's guaranteed to kill you. Anyway, that's what happened. The guy died. He was still alive when they hauled him aboard, but he died a few minutes later. The other divers, Cort's guys, they came up, too, but they did it slow so they wouldn't get the bends."

Bobbi shrugged and rolled her eyes. "So anyway, Cort's got this dead body, and he has to do something with it. I guess he should have just dropped it overboard with weights, but he figured if he made it look like a traffic accident, people wouldn't ask questions and look for him. He was wrong about that, but that's what he did. Then he stayed away from the wreck for a while, just in case Lee was with the cops or something. But nothing happened, so he started working again. The whole thing made Niso real suspicious, though. He wasn't on the boat when it happened, and he thought it was some story Cort had come up with to try to cheat him out of his share. I mean, Niso was already suspicious, but this Lee business just made him crazier."

"Is Cort trying to cheat Niso?"

She pursed her lips and shook her head. "No, of course not. Cort gave him his share a week ago, a whole bunch of diamonds. I mean, it was a lot. But Niso has crazy ideas about how much was on the boat, totally out of line, and besides, Cort had to spend all this money getting the stuff."

"So you decided to give Cort a helping hand by telling the Cubans that Niso was spying for the CIA?" I asked sarcastically.

Her face froze. Then the tears started again. "Oh, Jim, I thought you were supposed to be helping me. But all you do is attack me and attack me and ask questions and—"

The sobs took over.

"I know I haven't been perfect," she said after an age. "But I—I've tried to do my best and I thought you were on my side and—"

The door opened. Bobbi stopped abruptly.

"As you see, Miss Lyons is healthy," Niso said. "It's time we had our talk."

I looked at Bobbi. "Be brave. I'll get you out of here as soon as I can."

Niso bolted the door behind me. He got a Coke from a six-pack on the floor.

"I'm abstaining from alcohol for the duration of this business," he remarked idly. "One must make sacrifices for a desired good."

"When will you let Bobbi go?"

He brought the can to his lips but didn't drink. "I will release her when you give me six million dollars or its equivalent in diamonds."

For a second I didn't reply. "What did you say?"

"Relax, Mr. Biggins." Niso smiled. "When I said 'you,' I merely meant you could serve as courier, since you're already involved. I did not mean that you should furnish the diamonds yourself. Of course, if you feel inclined to do so, I would not object. I just want the diamonds."

He laughed offensively.

"Why don't you sit down?" He waved at the chair next to the table. "I would like to tell you a few things. I think it would help in creating an atmosphere of trust."

I decided I had to say something. Letting Niso just smugly continue had to be wrong. I cleared my throat.

"Yes?"

My throat was dry. I took a breath and began to speak. "I want to say that while I am willing to listen to whatever you have to say, it's ridiculous to speak of an atmosphere of trust while you are holding an American citizen against her will. That is a grave mistake on your part. The best thing you can do—really the only sensible thing—is release Bobbi Lyons immediately. If you do that, then, possibly, you may get out of this mess in one piece."

I stopped rather abruptly. Still, I felt better. I had conveyed what I had to convey.

Niso listened attentively. Then he laughed. "Please excuse me, Mr. Biggins. It is just that . . ."

He started laughing again. Finally he took out a handkerchief and wiped his eyes.

"You reminded me, just now, of a character in one of those cartoons on TV. A pig—not a bad fellow, really, but he gets very mad when the rabbit tricks him. Which the rabbit always does. It was quite a funny cartoon. I don't know why you made me think of him. . . ." He smiled. "I'm afraid I couldn't help myself."

He dabbed his face with the handkerchief again. When he resumed speaking, the false bonhomie was gone. "Mr. Biggins, five days ago I received instructions to return to Havana for consultations." He cocked his head. "Do you know what I did?"

I shook my head.

"I called my ex-wife." Niso smiled. "Luz and I were not happy together, but since our divorce we have been good friends. She is very knowledgeable. Her new husband has a senior position in my department. Luz herself learns a good deal from her secretarial duties. I have frequently found her information helpful."

He sighed. "She told me I was suspected of spying for the Americans. She didn't come out with that immediately, of course. She was nervous and made sure our conversation was idle chatter. But we have an arrangement. An hour after we spoke I called a café. Oddly enough, she happened to be there. She said that three days earlier a boy had delivered a note to the embassy—my embassy—here, the substance of which was that I was a paid agent of Ben Jacoby, the CIA station chief. The note said I met him at a brothel called Annette's and gave certain other details of my movements, although it had nothing that could remotely be called proof."

Niso smiled wanly. "Proof, though, is not really necessary in such cases. The boy who dropped off the note was located and questioned; he claimed that a pretty young white woman with red hair had paid him to deliver the note. Luz asked if I had been mistreating any young redheads."

Niso studied his fingernails. Finally he looked up and stared at me. "Tell me, Mr. Biggins. You know her better than I do. Can she be as amoral as she appears to be? Does she truly believe it is permissible to engineer the destruction of an individual simply because that person has teased her once or twice? Is that possible?"

He looked utterly sincere.

"What do you say, Mr. Biggins?"

I drew a breath. "I have no intention of discussing Bobbi Lyons's morality with the man who has kidnapped her and threatened her with death."

Niso stared briefly. Then he laughed. "Very good, Mr. Biggins. But please, let's not be angry with each other. Bobbi did me an injury, and I responded. That is all it amounts to. I responded the way I did because I thought she might be useful. She is no innocent; even you must see that. But still, I will gladly hand her over unharmed if Cort provides me with the diamonds I am entitled to. Tell him that."

"I see. And if he doesn't?"

"I am not going to retreat, Mr. Biggins."

His voice held a nervous edge of unreasoning finality. "She has burned my bridges for me. I won't go down alone."

Neither of us spoke for a minute. Niso made a production of getting a cigarette lit.

"Some time ago, Mr. Biggins, I realized that I did not want to return to Cuba permanently. I wanted to live—comfortably, of course—in Madrid or the Costa del Sol or Buenos Aires or . . ." He waved a hand. "It doesn't matter. There are any number of places that would do, but Havana is not one of them."

Despite my anger, I felt a tremor of hope. He seemed to be heading in a direction that might allow a way out.

"You could defect," I said.

"Yes." He nodded. "I could defect. The idea is inevitable for one in my position. There is only one problem with it: I have no wish to defect. The idea repels me."

"But you just said—"

"That I wished to live in 'the West.' " You could hear the quotation marks falling into place. "Is that so strange? I have spent most of my career abroad. I have discovered I like it, and I have lost touch with people in Cuba. Perhaps I have also become a little disillusioned about conditions there. All that is true. What it means is that I wish to spend my retirement in a city of my own choosing. It does not mean that I wish to betray everyone I ever worked with. Nor do I wish to become a paid servant of the CIA."

He took a sip of Coke. "I hope I am not boring you, Mr. Biggins."

I found the fake politeness exasperating. I didn't go around comparing people with cartoon pigs. I certainly did not kidnap people. Perhaps it was silly to suddenly be overcome with dislike for someone I already had good reason to hate, but that is what I felt.

"I'm listening," I said. "But I don't have six million dollars, in diamonds or otherwise."

"Please, Mr. Biggins. I already said you are merely to be the courier."

He sniffed disapprovingly. Then he settled back in his chair.

"It is one thing to decide to retire where one wishes; it is another to have the money to do so. My pension would not go far . . ." He grimaced. "Not that it is likely I would get a pension if I chose to live abroad. Anyway, I realized I needed money, but unfortunately I had no idea how to get it. No idea at all. But then an opportunity arose. I doubt you would ever guess where from."

Amusement appeared on his face. As for me, I was thinking how much he must want to talk. He had said he wanted us to trust each other, but I think primarily he wanted to tell his story. It must be lonely, being a spy.

"Last year," he resumed, "I had to spend a few months in Havana. An old lady cleaned my apartment. One day"—he paused for dramatic effect—"she told me about a hidden treasure."

Niso laughed. "She had a son, you see. He drove a truck, carting fruit to the city. He had stolen from his truck, and he was caught. She came to me in hopes I could save him from jail."

"And the treasure?"

Niso blew out a smoke ring. "Teofilo—that was the son's name—had seen it. That was all she knew. If I wanted to know more, I had to talk to him. So I did." He shrugged. "I assumed, naturally, it was a fairy tale, but I had nothing to lose."

He looked away, remembering the interview. His voice grew serious. "I have been a spy for twenty-five years. Sometimes—it is rare, but sometimes—you know immediately you are hearing the real thing. I knew it that day with Teofilo."

He looked back at me. His voice regained its usual tone. "As a young man Teofilo worked for a businessman named Malmierca. When Castro came to power, Malmierca decided to leave. He had already sent his wife and son to Miami. For his class, it was the normal thing to do.

Niso laughed sourly. "He invited Teofilo along. The two of them got Malmierca's yacht ready. When they were ready to go,

Teofilo carried the suitcases aboard. There were also four black satchels, but Malmierca wouldn't let him touch them. Teofilo knew what they were, however; Malmierca had a diamond brokerage, among other businesses. The satchels were for gems."

Niso licked his lips. "They set sail. Some of Malmierca's friends were with them. Everyone except Teofilo drank a good deal. After a while the friends—not very good friends, I think—insisted Malmierca show them the jewels in the safe. They talked as though they just wanted to look, but—" Niso shrugged.

"There was a fight. Malmierca was hit on the head with a bottle and fell into the water. Or perhaps he jumped. He drowned, certainly. The men weren't sure what to do. They couldn't open the safe with the tools on the yacht, and they were afraid to go on to Miami. Malmierca and his boat were known there. They didn't want to return to Cuba. They decided to come here."

"What about—"

"Teofilo? He was very scared. Naturally. He thought he would be killed, too. He did everything the men told him to do and otherwise stayed out of the way."

Niso sighed. "They didn't kill him immediately. Perhaps because they knew nothing about boats and Teofilo did. Still, he was sure they would never let him go ashore alive. He knew what they had done. Navidad was the first land they came near. While they were rounding the Hook, Teofilo started a fire below, next to the oil tank. Then he jumped over the side and swam for shore."

Niso spoke matter-of-factly. In New York a friend whose parents were Holocaust survivors had used the same tone in describing how they had hidden during a search by the Germans. It seemed strange that matters of life and death could be told so simply.

"Did the others live?"

"Teofilo thought not. There was an explosion, and the boat sank quickly. The men were all drunk anyway."

Niso rose and looked out the door.

"So what happened then?" I asked when he turned back.

"Teofilo came back home. He told his mother a little, but no one else; he thought it could only make trouble for him. He only talked to me because he was afraid of jail."

"Did you help him?"

Niso smiled. "Yes. He got six months with a labor battalion in Jagüey Grande. Five years is normal."

He took a sip of Coke. "I made a deal with Cort, Mr. Biggins. I told him about the boat; his part was to bring up the safe. We would each get half. A week ago he sent me thirty-seven diamonds worth—I have a friend who knows gems—about three hundred thousand dollars. He said that was all I would get."

He shook his head. "I had to deal with someone, and I picked Cort. I knew a few things I thought he would want to remain unknown. Perhaps I made a mistake; perhaps he doesn't value his secrets at six million dollars. But I want my share—my full share. If he wants to see Miss Lyons alive, he must give me my half."

Niso spoke calmly, but sweat covered his temples. I felt sick. I was sure he had persuaded himself he had no choice but to kill Bobbi if he didn't get the ransom.

"Cort . . . after the bomb, when he told me to meet you, he said I should tell you it wasn't as good as you thought. He must have meant—"

"He was lying," Niso interrupted. "For two months I studied Malmierca. I learned everything I could about him. He was rich. Very rich. That safe held at least twelve million dollars in diamonds."

We stared at each other. I didn't think argument could reach him. He had fixed on the figure of six million dollars, and so the safe had to hold at least twice that.

Niso brought his fingertips together. "I had a chat with Ms. Lyons after we got here. She was quite forthcoming about her relationship with you and Mr. Jacoby. I made a videotape of her confession. It would be, I think, rather embarrassing to the U.S. Embassy. You might bear that in mind when you talk to Cort."

He cleared his throat. "I do not wish to offer only threats. There is also a—what is the word? Carrot, right." He smiled. "Like the rabbit and pig in the cartoon. You can tell your friend Mr. Jacoby that if everything works out the way it should, then I will prepare some notes on my colleagues. My former colleagues."

He held up a monitory finger, like a schoolteacher. "A few notes. I will submit to no interrogation, and I will use my own good judgment. But what I tell him will be useful. I wish everyone to be pleased and everyone to have an inducement for this affair to end happily."

He nodded cheerfully. He was pretending that what had taken place was no different from a meeting between a couple of businessmen. He and I might be tough negotiators, but still, we had interests in common.

It was sickening.

"It is time for you to go. Be at the bar of the Hotel Randolph tomorrow at five. There will be a telephone call for Mr. Goldsmith. I hope—I hope very much—you will have my property with you."

I was blindfolded again. The trip back seemed quicker. Perhaps that was because I had things to think about.

I was dropped off a couple of miles from my car. Unwrapping the tape was a long and painful job. With the walk to my car and the drive back, it was past nine when I got to Ben Jacoby's house.

He didn't speak for a few seconds. "You're alive," he said finally. "I guess that's good news. I wish I knew."

Ben and I drove to the beach. It was scenic and deserted, and the waves were pounding hard enough to interfere with directional microphones.

I told him everything. Everything of relevance, I mean; I didn't mention the night Bobbi and I had spent together. It didn't seem to matter anymore anyway.

He grunted when Bobbi's lies came out. I was surprised he did not react more. When he did speak, it was not at first about Bobbi. "There was a bit of excitement at the Cuban Embassy today. Working files removed for shipment to Havana, clerks told to take the day off, lots of cable traffic."

"How do you know?"

He raised an eyebrow but didn't answer. "Our friend Mr. Carreras failed to appear at work this morning. Just for the hell of it I drove over to his house. A half hour after I got there a couple of guys came out carrying a box. It was heavy, loaded with papers probably. One of the men I recognized. Colonel Collazos.

A very tough customer. He's responsible for embassy security."

"What does it mean?"

He looked up at the stars. "Obviously, they think it's a defection. We know better. I don't know that it does us any good."

He stared out to sea. Several hundred yards out was a freighter that had turned over in a storm a couple of years ago. The bottom, dimly illuminated by a warning light, was a muddy grayish green. I wondered if anyone had died when it turned over.

"What do you think Niso will do?" I asked.

"You mean, do I think he'll kill her?"

"Yes."

"I don't know." He turned away.

I wanted to ask Ben what we should do, but first I wanted to understand him. I didn't now. I had expected him to be angry. I wouldn't have been surprised by a tantrum or, if he were feeling different, ill-concealed delight over the prospect of getting to act like the Man from U.N.C.L.E. What I hadn't expected was what I was seeing: a reluctance to come to grips with the situation, as though he wished he could wash his hands of it but didn't think he could. Quite.

For a minute I didn't speak. Then I said, "You don't seem surprised . . . that Bobbi lied."

He grunted.

"Did you know already?" I asked.

"We've got things to do, Jim." The words were impatient; the voice was oddly unemphatic. "No, I had no idea she was lying. I believed her right down the line."

He threw a rock and waited to hear the splash. The surf drowned the noise. "That's not quite right," he went on. "I never trusted Bobbi. Not really. I thought she was bad news from the start. But she had Cort eating out of her hand. What was I going to do? I needed an agent. I held my nose, and I hoped. I believed her that much."

He laughed. I began to get mad. It wasn't the right time for Ben's self-pity.

"What are we going to do?" I asked after he finally stopped laughing.

He didn't reply.

"What do we do?" Anger was rising up my throat.

"I guess we, or maybe just you, go to ask Mr. Thomas Cort if he likes Bobbi six million worth."

I could feel my face getting hot. "Of course we'll do that. What if he says no?"

Ben shrugged.

I stared at him, not believing that he wouldn't say something more.

"What if Cort says he won't or can't give that amount?" I repeated as calmly as possible.

He took his time turning toward me. "You said he would give whatever was necessary."

"He said he would. But—"

Ben had a mildly interested expression, as if we were discussing the possibility of objective truth in literary criticism.

"Jesus Christ," I exploded. "Niso wants six million dollars! I don't know if he has it. Or if he does, I don't know if he will give that amount."

Ben nodded. "That's why we have to ask him, isn't it?"

He turned back toward the sea. "What I'm wondering about," he added after a moment, "is what we tell Rollo. And my boss. I never told him about your role in this thing. That was a major violation of procedure. It's the sort of thing people get fired for. . . ."

For the first time that night he sounded truly regretful. He grimaced. "I would greatly like to avoid explaining now, but if this thing blows up in our face . . ." He didn't complete the sentence.

"You mean, Bobbi's getting killed might have an adverse impact on your career?"

"On yours, too, *mon vieux*," he said with a smile. "The shit would really hit the fan if Niso sends that videotape to *The New York Times*. That would be most unfortunate."

I waved my hand. It was simply a gesture of frustration; I had no intention of hitting him. Ben's response was completely unwarranted.

He grabbed my wrist and twisted. It was extremely painful. "Listen, buddy," he said, still twisting my wrist. "You've had a chip on your shoulder since we started talking. I want you to understand one thing: You are not my conscience, and I am in no need of your advice on morality."

He let go.

"That's no so——"

"Shut up," he said.

"I'm sorry about what happened," he went on after a few seconds. "I do not regard it as my fault, but I am sorry. I will do what I can to see that Bobbi gets out of this alive. I will do it not because it is in my interest—although I don't see why its being in my interest is a point against me—but because I'm against people getting killed. Even if they're liars and cheats, which I think is a pretty fair description of Bobby Lyons. Does that make you feel better?"

The waves crashed several times before I replied. "Bobbi got into this mess because she was working for you."

He ignored that. "Your wrist OK?"

"Yes."

Neither of us spoke for a minute.

"About a week and a half ago," he said calmly, "if not earlier, Bobbi stopped working for me and started working for Cort. That's why Niso grabbed her."

"I think he grabbed her because last night——"

Was it only last night that I had spoken to Bobbi on the phone? A good deal had happened since.

"Yes?" Ben said.

"Macho overheard my call to Bobbi. When I kept harping on her bringing the snapshots, I think he thought that was a code word for diamonds. He thought I was in on it and wanted my share. He figured Bobbi would have the stuff in her bag." My wrist gave a twinge, but I bore on. "So it was that neat code message you figured out that got her kidnapped."

A car drove by. Ben watched the headlights approach and recede.

"It's possible," he agreed. "Of course, you would never have made that phone call if she had been reporting honestly and promptly like a good little spy. . . . Jim, she lied—lied repeatedly—and then she topped it off by pulling that crazy stunt with the note to the Cuban Embassy. That was a nice touch, using my name. I mean, she could have just said Niso was spying for the CIA. I guess she felt it would read better if she said Ben Jacoby."

He blew out a long sigh. "Fuck it. I refuse to feel guilty. I refuse."

He looked at me, a weary smile on his face. "It really doesn't matter, does it? I mean, who's responsible. What we do now is what's important. You're worried about what happens if Cort won't pay. What about her parents? Could they give Niso the money?"

My mind seemed to be slowing down. I found it very hard to think about Bobbi's parents.

"Her father's dead," I said.

"Yeah, well, she's got a mother. A stepfather, too?"

"Yes. But Niso said—"

"Niso wants money. Cort is obviously the first choice, but if he can't or won't, what about Mom and Dad? Stepdad, I mean. They're rich, right? Just treat it as a straightforward kidnapping for ransom. Why couldn't they—"

"They're not rich," I broke in.

Ben looked at a loss. Clearly he had made up his mind that Bobbi was well off.

"The way she talks, she obviously moves with a very ritzy crowd—"

"Her stepfather's a lawyer in some small town outside Boston. Middle class. They don't have anything like six million. I'm sure they don't have one million. Bobbi likes to hang out with rich people. She envies them, and she's good at getting them to take her to expensive clubs, but she's never had any money, any real money, herself. That's probably why it's so important to her, if that doesn't sound too Psych 101."

Ben fingered his mustache. "Her parents bought her an apartment in New York. I remember she said that."

I shook my head. "She told me about it. It's the size of your foyer. At the most it couldn't have cost more than one fifty, one seventy-five. And they could only afford that because of an inheritance."

Ben looked away. I stared out at the overturned boat. I wondered if anyone would ever haul it away or if it would just be there forever, a reminder of how things can go badly wrong.

"It's getting late," he finally said. "Let's go see Cort. You talk to him alone. If he sees me, he'll think it's more devious than it is."

"And then what?"

"Then I take you home—my home—and you sleep. I'll see Rollo and tell him you're OK. He's curious. It's not every day one of his junior officers gets bombed and disappears. I'll tell him a little, prepare the ground. Just in case things don't go the way we want them to."

He looked at me, anticipating a protest. I was too worn out to make one.

We had walked up the beach. We turned around and headed

back toward the car. Neither of us spoke as we walked along.

I was tired and depressed. Perhaps that's why it was easy to imagine things going badly. Actually it was hard to imagine things not going badly.

Ben was a few feet away, but I felt alone. Alone and detached from everything.

If Bobbi were killed, what would that mean? It would be terrible, of course, but would it really be terrible for me? I probably had not thought of her more than a couple of times in the year before she had come to Navidad. Since then, of course, I had thought of her every day, practically every hour, and we had slept together once. But it was strangely easy to imagine my life continuing normally if she were dead.

Even while I was obsessed with her, there had been something unreal about the feeling. All that self-dramatizing manipulativeness—how long would it have been before I stopped being entertained by it and simply found it obnoxious? She was too in love with money and too unintellectual—too pretty, for that matter— to be the sort of woman I could imagine spending my life with. Even spending a night with her had almost exceeded my powers of imagination. If she were gone, probably I wouldn't think about her much after the first month or two.

It was late, and I was very tired. Still, I felt rather disgusted with myself.

"How about the CIA?" I asked as we made our way up to the coast road.

Ben didn't pretend to misunderstand. "You mean, would they pay the ransom?" he asked.

"Yes."

He didn't answer until we got to the car. "I can try, if it gets to that. You must have got the lecture, though, about how the U.S. government never pays ransoms or gives in to terrorist demands."

"Yeah, but——"

Ben smiled. "Yeah, I don't totally believe it either. I think they're kind of selective about applying that policy." He whistled. "The problem is, Bobbi hasn't exactly built up the kind of track record that makes people eager to break the rules for her."

We got into Ben's car. It hadn't been checked recently for listening devices. We didn't talk on the way to the hospital.

Cort had been sedated and was sleeping. The doctor sounded dubious at first about my seeing him the next day, but after I repeated several times that it was a matter of the greatest importance—I didn't say "life and death" because I was afraid he would think I was a crank and afraid that if he didn't, he might talk to people—he admitted Cort would be awake, although probably not alert, the next morning. I said I would be there at eight, and he said I would not be admitted until eleven, and we finally compromised on nine. He promised to leave a note for the nurse on duty then.

The doctor refused to discuss Cort's condition until I said I had been with him when the bomb exploded. Then he said that the leg and back wounds were not serious but Cort had lost a lot of blood. He had also broken a knee, and there was concern about internal injuries. And he had suffered a concussion.

"But he's going to live?"

He tugged at his ear briefly. "We must keep him under observation for a few days, but if nothing new appears, then I should say he is probably not in danger." He glanced at a hovering nurse and back at me. "You are his friend?"

It was a perfectly reasonable question. Somehow, though, I had not been expecting it.

"Yes." My pause was just long enough to be awkward.

A smile appeared and vanished quickly. "You should tell him to lose weight," he said. "Heart attacks are not as noisy as bombs, but they kill more people."

Then he turned toward the nurse. "I am sorry, but I have other patients besides Mr. Cort who require my attention."

Ben and I drove to his house in silence. I took a sleeping pill and to my surprise fell asleep a minute after I got into bed. You always dream, I read somewhere, but I don't remember any dreams that night.

Seeing Cort the next morning, I was struck by two things. One was his feet. The other was how weak he seemed.

The bedclothes were in disarray, and his feet were exposed. They looked more like dark, gnarled pieces of driftwood than living matter. The toenails were discolored, and the little toe and the one adjoining it on his left foot were misshapen, as though squashed in some long-ago accident. A couple of times I found myself thoughtlessly staring at them.

The Cort I was used to was exceptionally vital. It was hard to adjust to the change. He had a tube attached to his left arm. His right leg was immobilized. His head was propped up with pillows, and it was clear that the act of turning to look at me was exhausting. I understood that it was temporary, but it was still a shock to see him like that.

He was alert, though. The nurse who escorted me to his

room said in an accusatory voice that he had refused a painkiller after learning that I was coming. Perhaps that was why he looked so worn down.

I put a cassette player on the table next to Cort's bed and turned it on. Ben said it would block eavesdropping.

"You saw him?" Cort asked. His eyes were barely open.

"Yes."

"Is Bobbi all right?"

"Yes."

I didn't want to say the wrong thing, so I said almost nothing. But that was a mistake. Cort's eyes narrowed in annoyance. "Tell me," he said. "It is hard to talk."

I drew a breath. "Niso wants six million dollars from you. He'll take it in diamonds."

I drew another breath and went on. "He says you owe it to him. It is half of what you recovered from Malmierca's boat. He says if he doesn't get it, he'll kill Bobbi."

Cort had let his eyes close again. I studied his face, but there was no perceptible reaction.

"He says he can't go back to Cuba because they suspect him of spying for the CIA," I continued. "He thinks Bobbi is responsible for that. He—maybe he was acting, but I think he will kill her if he doesn't get the money. He doesn't like her."

I stopped speaking. I was upset with myself. People don't usually kill other people simply because they don't like them. I had ended on a false note. I should have said something else, but it seemed too late now.

His feet looked like carved figurines, little statues that were listening and finding my story extremely unlikely.

I tried to think of more arguments. I couldn't think of any. It was up to Cort.

Time passed. Cort's eyes were closed. I wondered if he could possibly have fallen asleep. Finally he stirred.

"Mr. Biggins."

"Yes?"

The words that came were slow and tentative. "If I give the diamonds, do you think——"

He stopped talking, and his eyes closed again. I waited a few seconds before speaking.

"I think he'll let her go," I said. "Anything else would be stupid——"

"No." He moved a hand slightly. He was annoyed again.

His eyes sought the table by his bed. "Water," he said.

I held a glass to his lips. He took several sips and then turned away slightly.

After a minute his eyes found mine. "I am not asking about Niso," he said, pacing himself so he could keep talking. "I know Niso. He will kill her if he does not get the diamonds. If he does, maybe he will not kill her."

His eyes flicked away, an equivalent of a shrug. Then he stared at me intently. "I am asking about Bobbi."

"Yes?"

The words again came slowly. "Will she love me?"

A breeze shifted the curtains so that the squares of light on the bed moved. Cort stared fixedly. I could sense a flush spreading over my face.

"I think . . . I think she . . . I don't know." It was three discrete little emissions of awkwardness.

Cort's expression remained frozen.

"Obviously, if you save her life, she'll feel incredibly grateful," I said hurriedly. His eyes closed.

I was a fool. "Incredibly grateful"—it was a phrase you would put in a thank-you note: "I want you to know how incredibly grateful we are for your taking the trouble to water the plants while we were away."

"When I saw her yesterday—last night, I mean," I told him,

"she was speaking very fondly of you. She obviously thinks very well of you. She lied for you."

That was how rattled I was. I didn't even see my error until Cort spoke. "Lied for me? What do you mean?"

So Bobbi had not told Cort she had been spying on him but had been nice enough to falsify her reports on his behalf. I glanced down, away. The skin between his big toe and the next one was cracked with eczema.

"What I meant," I said finally, "was just that Bobbi used to always tell me everything she was doing—when we were back in New York, I mean—the work she was doing and the people she saw and . . . well, just everything."

Suddenly I worried that he might become jealous.

"I mean, it was just that she used to talk all the time to me. I was like her confessor figure. . . ."

Now I saw myself in a movie. I was wearing a cassock, sitting in the confessional. "Speak, my child." I was a little giddy.

I drew a breath and bore on. "But here you were, looking for this treasure, and she knew about it and she never told me. She never said a word."

His expression hadn't changed while I was speaking. I couldn't tell whether he believed me.

Five minutes passed. His eyes opened several times and closed again. Finally he spoke. "You will see Niso again?"

"He is going to call me. This afternoon."

"I will give him the diamonds."

My ankle itched. I scratched it. I could breathe again.

He turned his head toward the water, and I gave him another sip.

"You will have to do it," he said after licking his lips. "The exchange. You will do it?"

I nodded. Then, not sure he had seen me, I said, "Yes."

Somehow he beckoned. I leaned forward so my ear was close to his lips.

"Mrs. Kelly," he said quietly. "She lives behind the First Moravian Church. In a blue house. Last week I gave her a box. That is the diamonds. All of them. Tell her I sent you; she will give you the box. Give them to Niso."

I started to say that Niso had asked for only half, but he shook his head. His eyes were closed again. I decided not to say anything more. I was afraid if I started talking about halves and wholes, he might change his mind. Who knew what was going on in that battered dark head?

"Tell the nurse I want the shot now," he said after a minute.

He spoke once again when I was at the door. "Good luck."

It took me a while to find the right nurse and give her Cort's request. When I got outside, the parking lot was glaringly bright. I stood for a while, letting my eyes adjust. A man in stained pants and a white T-shirt sat on a chair, a hospital gurney lying on its side beside him. He was using a screwdriver on one of the wheel fixtures. Two nurses were sipping coffee in the shade, discussing a doctor who was engaged to a girl in Trinidad but going out with a nurse here. Everything was ordinary.

As I drove to the embassy, I asked myself why Cort had told me to take all the diamonds. Maybe he hadn't heard me clearly. I tried to remember exactly what I had said. As best as I could recall, I had mentioned the figure of six million only once. I felt bad. It wouldn't be right if Cort gave Niso more than he had to simply because he had misunderstood.

It was just nerves. Cort had been weak but perfectly lucid. There couldn't be any reasonable doubt that he had understood me. There was a straightforward explanation available: The diamonds from the boat—all of them—were worth six million dollars. Niso's calculations were wrong.

The hospital is some distance from the embassy. I took it slow. I felt washed out. There was another emotion, too, but it took me a while to admit it to myself: I had not expected to feel pity for Cort.

Bobbi had never struck me as a great one for disinterested gratitude.

23

Eight hours after I saw Cort I was driving west on the coast road, a briefcase full of diamonds and a .38-caliber revolver on the seat beside me. I had the air conditioning on, but I was sweating.

Ben had gone with me to pick up the diamonds. Mrs. Kelly handed them over without any fuss, but in the car back to the embassy Ben's eyes kept flicking to the rearview mirror. Finally I asked. We were being followed.

There were three vehicles: a light blue Toyota, a green van, and a girl on a motorbike. Ben had noticed the Toyota on his way to work in the morning. He refused to speculate as to who it might be.

The gun was Ben's idea. The point was not to get into a shooting match with Niso; it was simply a precaution against robbers or—more likely—one of Niso's colleagues deciding to hijack the ransom. Carrying a fortune in diamonds makes you worry about things like that.

The diamonds—all 445 of them—were genuine and worth millions. Unfortunately they were worth one or two million less than the six Niso had specified. I felt sick when Ben told me.

"Are you sure?" I had been resting—trying to rest—on a daybed in the ambassador's office. Rollo wasn't there.

"Yeah." Ben grimaced. "You know Phoebe Hughes, the Brit commercial attaché? Her husband's a jeweler. I swore him to secrecy and showed him the goods. He said five tops."

It seemed unfair. I had more or less persuaded myself that I wasn't too scared to meet Niso again, but shortchanging him hadn't been part of the bargain.

"I tried to call Cort," Ben said after a moment. "I figured if he coughed up a bit more—"

"That's all there is," I interrupted bitterly. "I told you."

"Yeah, well . . ." He shrugged. "Anyway, I didn't get him. He took a turn for the worse. The docs are working now, and even if he makes it, he'll be in no condition to talk."

I was shocked. Despite his appearance, I had never doubted Cort would live.

Ben coughed. "Jim, I think we've got to go ahead with it, even if we're a little short. If we stall . . . Niso may just get rid of Bobbi and run. Hell, he'll probably never know there's not six million there. . . ."

I didn't say anything. I suppose I knew Ben was right, but my mind was too frozen to allow words.

"I'll go," he said.

"No."

We had already discussed that. Ben had begun by insisting that he should be the one to go, but it didn't make sense. There was no question that things would go better if people were not nervous, and everyone—especially Niso—would be less nervous if the ransom were carried by the inoffensive and wimpish consul.

Everyone except the inoffensive and wimpish consul, that is.

I saw Rollo briefly in the afternoon. Ben had given him a very partial briefing, sketching Bobbi's career but omitting my role as her case officer. He had cautioned me against saying anything at all. By that point I was too worried to take offense.

"Are you sure you're feeling all right, Jim?" Rollo asked gently.

"I'm fine."

He regarded me skeptically. He clearly believed I had been unhinged by the bombing.

The local authorities were eager to talk to me, but he had told them I was not in condition to be interviewed. "I trust you will sustain that fiction by avoiding conspicuously healthy behavior," he added.

Finally we left the topic of my health. "I must say," he remarked, "I thought Ben was extremely . . . cavalier in his assumption that you should assist Miss Lyons in her troubles. I gather he was . . . employing Bobbi himself."

I probably should have defended Ben's good name, but I just muttered something about Bobbi's being my friend and wanting to help her. A moment later I excused myself. I was happy Rollo had not chewed me out. It wasn't until later that I realized he might have been reluctant to speak harshly to someone about to deliver himself into the hands of kidnappers.

At four Ben and I left for Hotel Randolph, to wait for Niso's call. We took a circuitous route. After fifteen minutes Ben said he was sure we weren't being followed.

At the hotel we went into the bar and got drinks that we didn't touch. After a while Ben began talking about the spy novels of John le Carré. Their worst failing, it appeared, was the irresponsible treatment of American intelligence officers. "They're all amoral bastards or grade A morons," he complained, vastly aggrieved. "How realistic is that?"

I had heard it before, a thousand times. By five I was ready to jump out of my skin. The call came at five-eleven.

We didn't talk long. I told Niso I had the goods and would be carrying a gun. He said the gun was unnecessary but did not object. He told me to follow the coast road west and watch for a white sign with a blue circle. No one should come with me.

I told Ben. He shook my hand and wished me luck. "Give Bobbi my regards," he called as I was pulling out of the parking lot.

The sign was a piece of stiff white paper held up by a pine board. Taped to its back was an envelope. "Drive back two miles to the top of the hill," the message inside read. "Turn left onto the dirt road. Drive as far as you can; then get out and walk. Bring this along."

If there hadn't been a low, weedy hedge, I don't know if I would have spotted the road. As it was, all I saw was a break in the growth that could simply have been a few feet of ground too stony to nurture plants. Not until I turned onto it did I see the ruts left by previous vehicles.

The road went up into the hills, away from the sea. After half a mile I was seeing just one rut, not two. A few hundred yards later I had to stop.

My jeans pockets were too tight to hold the gun. I could carry it in my hand, but that would be awkward. I really didn't want whoever was watching me to focus on the gun anyway. I put it in the briefcase with the diamonds and got out and started walking.

A few minutes later I heard the motorcycle. The rider was Arthur, the one who had escorted me the day before.

He waved when he was twenty yards away. "You have a gun?" he asked.

"Yes."

He nodded. "Well, don't shoot me. I am just the driver."

I started to get on behind him, but he blocked my way. "No, you must change clothes. And put the stuff in this." He tossed me an airline bag.

"This is stupid," I said leadenly.

He shrugged his shoulders. "You must do it."

I changed clothes first. Arthur was suspicious of the cloth containers that held the diamonds, but I let him look at them, and he decided they did not conceal a transmitter. The gun he looked at closely but said nothing when I put it in the bag. It wouldn't be very accessible there, but I had no intention of sticking it under my belt. This time he made no attempt to blindfold me.

"It will be bumpy," he said. "Hold on tight."

We headed northeast. I tried to envision the map of Navidad. I couldn't think of any towns we were aiming for. As best I remembered, there were just some spice plantations in the region.

After a while we started to go faster. "Don't want to do this when it's dark," he shouted. It was still light, but the sun was down.

It was a rough ride, and soon I was aching all over. There was no way a car could follow us. A motorcycle could trail us, but any bike that stayed far enough back not to be spotted would almost certainly lose us.

After we had been going for three quarters of an hour, it was dark. The hills were flattening out; we were near the north coast. A half-moon cast a faint radiance.

We hit a rock and tipped over. We were going slowly; neither of us was hurt, although some rocks gouged into my leg.

"Turn on the light," I said.

"No. We are almost there."

Five minutes later he turned toward a house that had a light in the window. It was only the second house we had seen; the other had been dark.

We got off the bike. My leg was sore, and my muscles ached.

I took the gun out of the bag and held it in my right hand, pointing at the ground. As we approached the house, the door opened. Niso stood there.

"Hello, Mr. Biggins," he called out. "Did you have a pleasant journey?"

My throat was dry. In any case, the question didn't merit a reply.

"Do you have the merchandise?" he asked. He lingered over the word "merchandise," making a joke out of it.

I lifted the bag. "Where's Bobbi?"

"Inside," he said. "She's eager to see you."

The house was much more comfortable than the place I had visited before. The room we entered was large, with wicker furniture scattered around and a bar with stools at one side. There were a couple of museum posters on the walls and a hanging tapestry. On a low side table a TV was switched on.

"The house belongs to a countryman of yours," Niso murmured. "I'm afraid he doesn't know we're borrowing it."

Besides Niso and myself there were four people in the room. Two men and two women. The men were standing on opposite sides of the room, and each had a gun.

The woman at the table I had not seen before. She was white, and she looked fairly tall. That was all I could tell about her. The light was bad, and she was wearing a hat with a wide brim. I couldn't make out her face.

Bobbi was perched on a stool at the bar, staring at me. She looked as though she had been fixed rigidly in that position from the moment Niso opened the door.

"Jim," she said. Her voice was small, almost inaudible.

"Hi, Bobbi." I looked around, but no one was moving. "I'm very glad to see you."

It felt strange holding a gun in one hand and a bag of diamonds in another and making ordinary conversation.

Bobbi seemed frozen on the stool. I walked over and put my arm around her.

She burrowed her head into my shoulder. "I'm so glad you're here," she whispered.

Her movement was furtive. When I tried to look at her, she ducked her head down.

I looked again. Her face was badly bruised. The previous day she had had a scratch and the beginning of a black eye, but this was far worse. She had been thoroughly beaten. Her nose was swollen, and her eyes and her mouth were puffy. There were marks on her neck, too.

"What happened?"

She gave an indecipherable shake of her head.

"Bobbi, what—"

I turned angrily, but Niso spoke first. "She attacked Macho. The poor fellow had to defend himself," he said lightly. I felt Bobbi stiffen.

Niso laughed. "You see, she tried to seduce him. She promised to sleep with him if he helped her escape. He told me, and I said he should insist on being paid in advance."

"Bastard," Bobbi said under her breath.

Niso gave no indication of hearing her. He pursed his lips judiciously. "It was good advice, but I never thought Macho would act on it. I'm afraid I underestimated him."

He smiled at one of the gunmen, who grinned back. "Your friend went along at first, but after a while she changed her mind. Macho was . . . insistent. She scratched his face. Badly."

"Dirty fucking bastard," Bobbi said.

That time he heard her. He shrugged. "Obviously neither side acted in good faith."

He smiled broadly. For a fraction of a second I was on the verge of shooting him.

The rage passed. The gun weighed heavily in my hand, and I felt drained. If I had shot Niso, I would have been dead a moment later. It was frightening to realize I could come so close to doing something completely irrational. When he lent me the gun, Ben certainly hadn't meant for me to try anything like that.

And I probably wouldn't even have hit him. Not unless I was lucky.

For several seconds no one spoke. I think even Niso realized he had gone too far. The woman at the table broke the silence.

"We are—we are sad she is . . . hurt," she said. She had a strong accent. I had heard her before, when she called my house and asked for Cort.

"We are very sad. But you see, she is owing not to do that, with the man. She is wrong to do that. He is wrong, too, but—"

For some reason I believed her—believed, I mean, that she regretted Bobbi's injuries. Perhaps it was her difficulties with English. Awkwardness suggests sincerity. Or perhaps she really was sincere.

"You bring the diamonds?" she asked eagerly. After a moment I nodded.

"I look at them now," she continued. "I look; then we all go. You, she go, we all go. . . ."

There was something pacifying about her focus on business. I was still trembling, but I began to hope that we could do what we had to do and then it would be over.

I walked over to the table and gave the woman the bag. Then I went back and put my arm around Bobbi again.

Niso took a chair at the table. One of the gunmen started to approach, but Niso motioned him to stay where he was.

The woman withdrew the cloth holders from the bag. She looked carefully inside the bag and felt also, to make sure no gems had come loose. The cloth holders she put on her left. To her right was a medium-sized metal suitcase. In front of her was a small but strong lamp, shining on a piece of black cloth. She had a jeweler's loupe, too.

"I start now," she announced. And then, for an hour, she looked at the diamonds. After she checked a batch, she would put them in the suitcase. Presumably there was some holder in there. I couldn't see from where I was.

The first four or five stones she examined at length. After that she began to speed up. Every two or three minutes she would look up to give her eyes a rest. She kept her face turned away from me.

She worked steadily and quietly. Niso, by contrast, could barely contain himself. He had nothing to do, and he was so excited he could not stay seated. He fidgeted and looked around constantly and kept whispering to the woman, although she clearly did not want to be distracted.

A few minutes after she started a smile appeared on his face. She must have told him that the diamonds she had examined so far were real and valuable.

I stood next to Bobbi. We didn't talk. Anything louder than a whisper would have been audible to the others, but in any case neither of us wanted to talk while we were still there. Every few minutes Bobbi shivered. Other than that she was virtually motionless.

The woman had been working for about fifteen minutes when Niso got up and walked toward us. Bobbi became rigid. But he was just coming to the bar; he filled a glass with water and took it back to the woman.

I remembered how thirsty I was. I went behind the bar to get myself a glass of water. After I drank I happened to glance at one of the gunmen. He gave a monitory wave of his gun. I felt a chill, realizing he had thought I might be about to try something.

A few minutes later Niso got up again. This time he went out the front door. The woman continued working, and neither of the gunmen moved.

He returned after five minutes.

"Did you talk to the police?" he asked. I think, odd as it seems, he just wanted to talk. He couldn't seriously have expected me to admit it if I had.

"No."

He nodded. "Macho is listening on the radio. He has heard nothing."

He went back and sat down next to the woman. They exchanged whispers.

A little later he got up again. He came over and stood in front of me. "They are very beautiful, aren't they?" he asked. His eyes gleamed.

I had the bizarre sense that he wanted me to congratulate him on his good fortune.

"I didn't look at them that closely."

"No?"

He sounded amazed. "They are beautiful," he repeated.

I remembered a Saturday in high school. A friend had come over to spend the day in my house. She desperately wanted to go to Stanford but had convinced herself she would not get in. That afternoon her mother called to say an acceptance letter had come in the mail.

Niso looked like her. The diamonds could have resembled grape pits; what he was seeing was a dream come true.

He looked at the table and then turned to look at Bobbi. When he spoke, though, it was to me. "I am surprised Cort values her so highly."

His voice was devoid of the malice it usually held; he was merely stating his opinion. Bobbi was holding my arm, and her grip tightened.

"If you didn't think he valued her, why did you——"

"It was worth a try, no?" He laughed. "It worked." He laughed again.

He went back to the table and stared over the woman's shoulder. After a few seconds she gave a nervous shake, and he walked back to me.

"Mr. Biggins, I hope you will be careful in the coming months. Especially the next few weeks."

"Is this some kind of threat?"

"A threat?"

He was confused for a second; then he laughed. "Oh, no, Mr. Biggins, you misunderstand me. I am not threatening you. I regard you as a friend. You have helped make me rich. No, it is Cort I am warning you against."

He lit a cigarette. "Cort doesn't like people to know about his affairs. You now know a great deal. More than that. You have taken millions in diamonds from him that he would rather not have parted with."

He waved a supercilious finger. "Oh, yes, you have only been a messenger. But will he believe that? He is a suspicious man. Perhaps he thinks you have kept some for yourself. Perhaps he suspects you of making love to Miss Lyons. Will he forgive that?"

Bobbi's fingernails bit into my arm.

"I'm sure Cort doesn't suspect me of anything," I said. "He has no reason to."

Niso smiled. "This man Mannion, the one who told you about our treasure hunt?"

I didn't bother to say it had been Mannion's girl friend, not Mannion himself, who told me. "What about him?"

"He was murdered."

I felt a tightness in my chest. "He died in a bar fight," I said, a little brusquely.

"Yes," Niso said. "If I wanted to murder a man like Mannion,

I would arrange it to look like a bar fight. It would not be hard."

Niso shook his head. "Be careful, Mr. Biggins. I say this from self-interest. If something happens to you, Mr. Jacoby or others may decide to trouble me. It would not be a great trouble—I would be innocent—but I would rather avoid it."

Niso took a few steps, then turned. "We will leave as soon as we are done. You can walk to the road. It is half a mile. I am sure you will find someone there to give you a ride."

Bobbi's fingers tightened again on my arm. It hurt, she was gripping me so tightly. But I understood: Finally she felt hope, and she wanted to hold on to it with all her strength.

"You said you would have information for Mr. Jacoby," I said after a moment.

For a second his face wore an ambiguous expression.

"Oh, yes," Niso said. "Let me get it."

He extracted a manila envelope from a briefcase.

"I rather enjoyed doing this," he said, gazing at the envelope. "It is—you might say it is memoirs of my former colleagues. Personal details, bits of history, their inclinations and aversions. Old girl friends and old embarrassments."

"It doesn't sound like much."

"No, I suppose not. Let me explain." He drew a breath. "I do not intend to hide. My former employers will find me if they wish to. So I must take precautions."

He removed his glasses briefly to massage the bridge of his nose. "There are things I know—current operations—they wish to keep secret. They will know that acting against me will result in the disclosure of those operations, so they will not act against me. Just as you will not act against me or my associates"—he waved at the gunmen—"because you will not want Miss Lyons's colorful career to become public."

Niso smiled.

"But you could still tell Ben," I said. "He's not going to call Havana to tell them what you say—"

"No," Niso broke in firmly. "If I disclose operations, he—his superiors—will take action. They would have no choice. And however subtle their actions may be—not that your government is famed for its subtlety—it will be known. That is obvious. Everything I could possibly compromise will be watched with the closest attention. So you see, I have no choice but to act in a strictly honorable fashion."

He nodded to himself. "Your friend Mr. Jacoby understands all this. He will be happy with what he is getting."

I must have looked skeptical.

"Oh, he will be, I assure you." Niso smiled. "It is gossip, and there is nothing spies like better than gossip about their opponents."

That was the high-water mark of my relations with Niso. He was happy with the world, and I was a significant part of the world.

We stayed friends about fifteen minutes. Then his friend whispered something. Niso picked up the cloth containers and felt them. Only two still held gems. He came over again.

"Did you leave anything behind?"

"No."

"You brought all that Cort gave you?"

"Yes."

Bobbi was no longer gripping me. Her fingers hovered like talons just above my forearm. Niso considered for a second. "Are some larger? The ones in the last holder?"

"I don't know," I said.

After a few seconds he went back to the table without saying another word.

Bobbi was rigid. She stayed that way for a minute. Then she

spoke her first words in three quarters of an hour. "What's happening, Jim? Is something the matter?"

"No, Bobbi. I don't know. I'm sure——"

"What's the matter?"

Her eyes were frantic. I took my time replying. "I think Niso's afraid the diamonds might not be . . . quite worth six million dollars."

"Oh, no. No." She shook her head. "No, no, that can't be. Jim? You brought everything, didn't you? Everything?"

"Of course, Bobbi. Of course I did."

"So it's gotta be six million, right?"

We were whispering, but Bobbi's voice went up slightly at her last utterance. One of the gunmen looked at us.

I didn't reply immediately. I spoke quietly when I did. "It's millions, Bobbi. Millions and millions. I'm sure of that."

Bobbi held her breath. Finally she let it out. "Oh, no. Oh, God. Oh, Christ."

Bitterness entered her voice. "Jim, how could you do this? I can't take it anymore. I just can't take it. You don't know what it's been like."

I tried to take her hand, but she shook me off.

"I'm sure it'll work out," I said. "I brought the diamonds. If it's not six million, it's damn close. It's all there was. All."

She didn't reply. I didn't add anything. For fifty minutes there had been an invisible link between us, but now it was gone. I was her enemy as much as Niso.

Ten minutes passed. The woman finished and closed the metal suitcase. She and Niso spoke inaudibly, and then he walked over to us.

"You did not bring the agreed amount," he said coldly.

I didn't reply.

"At most, these are worth five million. Where are the rest, Mr. Biggins?"

I tried to think how to put it. Finally I said simply, "That's all there is."

I had taken too much time. I sounded nervous, false.

"I think you kept some for yourself," Niso said. "I think you decided to make yourself rich."

"No."

"It is a mistake to cheat me."

"I'm not. I'm not cheating you."

Our eyes locked. I could sense Bobbi holding her breath next to me. For a second I thought she was going to faint.

Then the door opened, and Macho walked in. He had a bandage on his nose. Bobbi shuddered.

Macho and Niso conferred briefly, and Macho went back out. When Niso turned back, he looked worried.

"Who did you talk to?" he asked angrily. "Who did you tell where you were going?"

"No one. I didn't know where I was going until I got here."

Niso stared at me. Bobbi's nails dug into my flesh.

"Who did you tell?" he repeated.

"Just Ben Jacoby. I already told you that. What's the matter?"

He glanced at the gunmen. Over the past hour they had relaxed, but now they were alert. There was fear in their faces, and that scared me.

"What's the matter?" I repeated.

"A car turned off the coast road," Niso said, speaking slowly, as much for the others' benefit as my own. "Macho said it must have parked. He can't see it now, but it didn't go away." He paused. "There is a house down there, but it is boarded up."

He looked away for a couple of seconds. "You did not bring the agreed amount, Mr. Biggins. I am going to leave. I will take Bobbi with me. If you want her, you must give me the rest of the diamonds. I will call you—"

"No," I put an arm around Bobbi and lifted the gun slightly.

I nodded at the suitcase. "That's five million dollars there. You're rich. You wanted to be rich, and you are."

I drew a breath. "I don't know anything about the car. I talked to no one except Ben Jacoby. And Cort, of course. I've kept our part of the bargain. That isn't half of the diamonds. That's all of them. That's all there are. Your guess about what Malmierca had was wrong. I'm sorry, but he didn't have as much as you thought."

Niso hadn't interrupted yet. I drew another breath and went on. "Cort may not live. He can't talk, and there aren't any more diamonds anyway."

"I want the ones you took, Mr. Biggins."

"I didn't take any. I'm not like you. I'm not a thief."

I looked at the woman, trying to recruit her. "Leave with what you have. Do that and you're rich and no one will be after you. Take Bobbi and everyone will be after you. It's not worth it, not for something that doesn't even exist."

Probably it was imagination, but it seemed to me I could feel Bobbi's pulse through my shirtsleeve.

Niso's friend said something to him in Spanish. He replied curtly, and she spoke at greater length. It was too fast for me to follow, but I thought she was urging him to do what I said.

Macho reentered and gave a shrug. Obviously he hadn't been able to see anything more. "Arthur's watching," he said.

The woman spoke again, and this time I thought I did understand her. She was saying the plane was too small to hold Bobbi.

Niso shook his head impatiently, but the woman insisted she was right. Niso frowned. He stood for a minute, lost in thought.

"Get everything ready to go," he said to Macho. "I am going to talk to the pilot."

He turned to me. "Put that away," he said, nodding disdainfully at my gun. "These men will kill you if you try anything. Don't be stupid."

I let it fall to my side. I had never had any intention of using it.

Niso got the suitcase with the diamonds and tucked his arm firmly around it. Obviously he had no intention of letting it out of his sight. "Come with me," he said to one of the gunmen.

He opened the door and turned. I think he was going to say something to the woman, but before he could, there was a loud, metallic noise, and it looked oddly as though he had taken a little hop directly back. Then he was on the floor, and so was the gunman who had been going out with him.

I don't know how many shots were fired. I didn't hear a single one; the metallic noise had to be a bullet striking the suitcase. But both men had been hit; that was clear from the way they fell. The gunman twitched several times as he lay there, and somewhere along the line—I think it was the third or fourth twitch—I realized it was bullets plowing into him. He was dead, or he would be in a few seconds.

Niso had fallen out of the line of fire. Despite being wounded, he was the first to recover from the shock of the attack. "Lights," he yelled. "Turn off the lights."

Macho extinguished the overhead light. Then he drew a gun and fired through the door. I think he was shooting blindly; at least I didn't see anything, and I didn't see how he could.

The other gunman—the one who hadn't been going out with Niso—fired a second or two after Macho. He, however, had a target he could see quite clearly.

I have no idea why he shot me. Well, that is not strictly true: I have an idea why he did it. What I mean to say is, he had no right to shoot me. I hadn't raised my gun or made any sort of motion at all.

I think he did it because he had seen me as the enemy, the threat for an hour. When things went sour, pulling the trigger was automatic. I suppose it's possible he actually believed I was in league with whoever was outside. It wasn't a very sensible notion, but shooting me wasn't very sensible in the first place.

The bullets took me in the back and felt like a big shove. I was standing and then there was a terrible blow and I was on the floor.

I remember Bobbi yelling, "Stop it, stop it." Maybe that is why he fired only twice. But a couple of seconds later he walked over. I couldn't see his hand, but I had the distinct belief that he was pointing the gun at my head. I wasn't really scared. I must have been already in shock.

Niso's friend shouted, "No, don't." A second or two later I heard him walking away.

I had fallen so that I was facing Niso. It was odd. I had only a vague understanding of what had happened to me, and it seemed rather boring. Niso, though, was fascinating. I could see a discrete dark area at his hip where blood stained his pants. It was growing very slowly. I remember concluding that the bullet must not have struck an artery. I couldn't see other wounds, but I told myself with a fine diplomatic caution that it would be wrong to assume that he had not been hit someplace else as well.

"The lamp," he gasped. "Turn it off."

A moment later the room became completely dark. Almost as though it were a response to that, although I don't think it could have been, there was the sound of gunfire outside. This time it was something like a machine-gun burst. It was over in a couple of seconds, and I heard the tail end of a shriek.

I continued to watch Niso. I was impressed with the way he had thought of the lights even though he had been wounded.

He levered himself up slightly. "Arthur?" he asked. I could see Macho nod. "He had the M-16."

Then it seemed as though everyone were just waiting. That was all right with me. I felt detached, ready to float away. I had another feeling, too, one that is a little embarrassing to admit. I was relieved. I had been doing the best I could, but now I was hurt and couldn't do any more. If something bad happened to Bobbi, it wouldn't be my fault.

It might have been an appropriate attitude if I had been relieved of an onerous bureaucratic responsibility. It wasn't a very practical response to a serious wound.

Bobbi crouched and ran her hands over me. I thought she was petting me, as if I were a cat. I was annoyed in a theoretical sort of way. Then I realized she was searching for my gun. She found it under my leg. No one saw her. It was dark, and everyone's attention was focused outside.

I wanted to tell Bobbi not to do anything, but it seemed like too much effort. When she got the gun, she just held it anyway.

I don't know how much time passed. Probably not more than a minute. Then there were footsteps running up toward the house. I could see Niso biting his lip, watching Macho.

"It's me, Arthur," a voice whispered outside the door. "They're gone."

A second later he hurried through the door. He almost tripped over the body lying there.

"Oh, shit," he said. "Is he dead?"

"Yes," Niso replied. "Who were they? What happened?"

Arthur reached out and tentatively touched the dead man's head. He drew his hand back and looked at it. I suppose there was blood on it, but I couldn't see.

"Two," he said. "There were two of them. By the ravine. Fucking pilot was testing the engine, and I didn't hear them. I only saw them when they shot."

He touched the head again. "He's dead," he said.

"Yes," Niso agreed. "Did you kill them?"

"I got one. The gun jammed. The other one—I would have got him, too, but the gun jammed. He picked up the other and ran off."

"You didn't go after them?" Macho asked.

"With a jammed gun?" Arthur asked angrily. "They hear me coming, they shoot me dead."

He swung the rifle pugnaciously. Then he noticed me. "The American get hit?"

"Donny shot him," the woman said.

"Why?" He just sounded curious. "Is he dead?" he added after a second.

"He's alive," Bobbi said hastily. "If he doesn't get to a hospital soon . . ."

Now I think she spoke so the man wouldn't look me over and discover she had my gun. I didn't think of that at the time; I was just distantly pleased that she seemed in control of herself.

"He set us up," the gunman—Donny—said urgently. "He was gonna shoot us from behind while his friends—"

"Shut up," Niso said. "Could you see them?" he asked Arthur. "What did they look like?"

"It was dark. I just saw bodies."

Niso grabbed a chair and got himself erect. He was careful to stay out of line of the door.

The woman asked in Spanish if his wound hurt. I had no trouble understanding her. That seems a little odd to me now, but the gunshots hadn't affected my comprehension. I just wasn't able to care about most things.

Niso shook his head. He didn't want to think about his wound now. He took a few breaths, gathering his strength. "I want to know who they were. Could anyone have followed you here?" he asked Arthur.

He shook his head. "No. No fucking way. Not unless he has a radio up his ass," he added, jerking a thumb at me.

Niso hobbled to the window. There was nothing to see, of course.

"A blue Toyota," I said. "Followed Ben Jacoby this morning. Other cars, too." I took a breath. It wasn't easy to talk.

Bobbi tensed. I wondered idly why. In speaking I hadn't thought whether I was doing us good or harm; that sort of calculation was beyond me. I was simply the good student, trying to solve the problem posed by the teacher.

Niso turned and stared at me. "Did they follow you when you met Arthur?"

"No," Arthur injected urgently. "I was watching with glasses. There was no one."

Niso made a shushing motion. He repeated the question.

"No," I said. "They stopped this morning. No one followed—"

It hurt too much to keep talking. Fortunately Niso didn't seem to have any more questions.

"¿Sabes quien es?" the woman asked. (Do you know who it is?)

Niso gave an indeterminate nod. He looked out the window again. After a few seconds he turned and picked up the suitcase with the diamonds.

"We have to go," he said. "If anyone heard, the police may come. Or others. We must go now."

He took a few wobbly steps, and Arthur came to his aid. "We'll go together. Donny, you go first. Run fast."

Donny looked scared. "Maybe they're still out there."

Niso shook his head. "I think there were only two. They're gone—you heard Arthur. Anyway, we have to go."

The woman spoke rapidly in Spanish. There was a gust of pain from my back. I thought she might be talking about Bobbi and me, but I didn't know what she was saying.

"OK," Niso replied when she was done. It was almost as though he couldn't be bothered. "She can stay."

Then I understood. He was letting Bobbi go. It seemed odd that in the end it apparently mattered so little.

Niso took a gun from somewhere under his jacket. "Take this, Macho. Watch from the window. If anyone shoots at us, get them. When we're halfway to the plane, come on. We'll get there together."

Macho nodded and stationed himself by the window. The woman picked up a bag and a jacket. She tried to take the metal suitcase from Niso, but he wouldn't let her.

They paused for a moment at the door. Niso was breathing heavily. I thought he had forgotten about Bobbi and me, but he turned to us for a second. "Adios," he said.

Donny ran out. He was hunched over, going as fast as he could. Nothing happened. A moment later Niso and Arthur headed out, Niso with his arm wrapped around Arthur. The woman followed them.

I half expected gunshots, but there was only the anticlimactic sound of their footsteps. After a few seconds there wasn't even that.

Macho stared intently through the window. He had a pistol in each hand. After a minute he stuck the one in his left hand into his belt. He turned, the bandage on his nose gleaming whitely. The gun in his right hand wagged casually at us.

That was when Bobbi shot him.

She fired three times. I think all three bullets hit; at least I remember him jerking several times.

She ran over to him. "He's dead," she said after a second.

Then she ran to the door and peered out. "Damn," she muttered. "I can't see a thing."

She kept looking, though. I wondered if Niso or his men would come back. They must have heard the shots.

Time passed. I could hear the noise of a propeller. After what seemed like a very long time it got louder.

"It's taking off," Bobbi said in a low, hopeful voice. "I can just see it."

A little later I spoke my last words before losing consciousness. "Why'd you shoot—"

"Jesus Christ, Jim." She sounded distracted; her eyes kept scanning the landscape. "He was going to kill us. Couldn't you see? He was aiming right at me."

Her left foot tapped nervously. "I'm glad he's dead," she added. I thought perhaps she sounded a little overemphatic.

Or perhaps not. I wasn't noticing things too well then. A little later I closed my eyes. Now that Niso was gone I could start thinking about myself again. There seemed to be a great many things to consider. I recall worrying about what I should say to Rollo and wondering whether I should get someone from AFSA— the Foreign Service union—to represent me. That raised the thorny question of what I should tell the AFSA person. Had I paid my dues? Maybe it was an automatic deduction. I couldn't remember. Then I realized my throat was dry, and I wished Bobbi would get some ice cream for me. Soft ice cream would be best, but where could she get it? I knew vaguely these weren't the most vital matters, but that didn't keep me from thinking about them. I was very tired.

A little later I drifted off.

The remainder of the night I know about from Ben. He quizzed Bobbi intensively before putting her on a plane the following morning.

She kept watch by the door for five or ten minutes after the plane took off. Eventually she decided Niso and the others were gone. I was unconscious. The telephone was dead. She decided to walk down to the coast road and flag a car.

There's no question that in doing so she saved my life. One

of the bullets had deflected off a bone without causing major damage, but the other had penetrated a lung. I would have died if I had got to the hospital much later than I did.

Leaving the house required courage. She had no way of knowing if anyone was waiting out in the dark. It wasn't clear that Niso's entire party had left in the plane, and there was also the matter of whoever had shot Niso. Still, I doubt it was a purely self-sacrificing decision. The idea of spending a night in a remote house with the corpses of two of her kidnappers—and with a friend who might become a corpse at any moment—would not have appealed to Bobbi. She had never liked inactivity anyway.

Before she left, she fired a couple of shots into the woodwork with Macho's gun, keeping his finger on the trigger. "For ambiance," she told Ben. She took Macho's second gun with her and got down to the road with nothing worse than a bruise from the gun grinding into her when she tripped.

She waited a few minutes without seeing a car, then struck out toward the east. A minute later she waved down a beer delivery van. They went back up to the house, put me in the back, and then drove like hell for the hospital.

She promised the driver two hundred dollars if he made it in thirty minutes. I guess he did; she had him drive to Ben Jacoby's house to collect.

I was medevacked to Washington two days later. An infection slowed down the healing: I spent nearly four weeks in the hospital.

Rollo sent notes that were chatty and upbeat and completely lacking in positive information. At some point it became clear that I would not be going back to Navidad. No one knew exactly how much the authorities there knew or guessed, but having me stay away was a good way of avoiding awkward questions.

There never was an official request for my version of what happened. At first I was in no condition to offer it. Later everyone was content to go along with the account prepared by the deputy chief of mission, Linda Wolf. No doubt Linda got instructions from Rollo.

The story was that Bobbi had been kidnapped by disgruntled ex-colleagues of Cort. They got in touch with me, and I agreed to convey money from Cort. My decision was seen as unwise but understandable in view of my close friendship with the kidnap victim and the fact that I was still undoubtedly shaken as a result of the bombing. At the meeting the kidnappers argued violently among themselves and killed two of their number, besides wounding me. They then fled.

Neither espionage nor diamonds were mentioned. Miss Lyons was said to suspect that her assailants had been in touch with a Cuban diplomat she knew. While declining to endorse or reject Bobbi's suspicions, the report noted that this diplomat had recently disappeared.

Ben told me this version during one of his visits. He had left the island the same day I did. That was two days before the *Bugle* ran a story suggesting he had bombed the American consul's house ("when the CIA plugs a leak, they use dynamite") and assassinated or kidnapped—the article wasn't sure which—two Cuban diplomats. Crazy as it was, I'm sure Rollo was glad he had already sent Ben home.

Niso Carreras was one of the vanished Cuban diplomats. The other was Colonel Pedro Collazos, head of embassy security. Ben's main piece of news was that it had been Collazos who shot Niso.

When I mentioned the blue Toyota, I suppose Niso knew it was Collazos. Ben had, of course, suspected the Cubans might be following him, hoping he would lead them to Niso. He hadn't been sure, however, and then apparently the surveillance was dropped. In fact, they had put a small plane up in the air once they realized their vehicles had been spotted. When I went off to a suspicious rendezvous in the hills, the focus shifted to me. There was a moon that night; Ben thought with good binoculars the motorcycle could have been seen all the way to the house.

"How did you find out?" I asked.

"The guy in the plane was broadcasting *en clair*. They weren't even using random-grid map coordinates. They must have thrown it all together at the last minute. Total chaos."

Ben rolled his eyes. "One of our communicators was fiddling

with a receiver and heard it. Fortunately he knew a little Spanish. If he had told me right away . . ." Ben sighed. "Well, he had no idea what it was all about. He passed it along the next day as a piece of interesting gossip."

Ben shrugged. "It was a crazy stunt for them to pull. But defectors make people nervous. And Collazos is a wild man. Shooting people is definitely his idea of how to solve a problem. Lucky for Niso he's not that good a shot."

Collazos had taken a plane for Havana the next day, looking fit. Ben didn't know who it was that Arthur had shot.

I learned all this on Ben's first visit. He tried to be cheerful for my sake, but he was in a glum mood. He was clearly worried about the impact of *l'affaire Bobbi* on his future.

Two weeks later he was happier. He had seen Niso in Barcelona and purchased—he never told me for how much—the gossip Niso was supposed to have given me as part of our bargain. Even better, there were signs that Niso was sufficiently angry about being shot that he would divulge more significant material. Ben's star was on the rise.

I wished him well. At that point I was feeling some career anxiety myself. I'm sure the personnel officer was telling the truth about the difficulty of finding a post in mid-cycle, and he certainly seemed sincere when he said there was no question of punishment involved. Still, overseeing the warehouse and embassy motor pool in Bamako, Mali, is not a plum by most people's standards.

In certain respects my new post is not unlike Navidad. There are no beaches, of course, and English does not take you far. It is hot, though, and the people are poor. There is not much of what you would call café society. The embassy is a very small world, and the United States is very far away.

My job is not very taxing. I spend most of my time signing customs declarations. In the morning and again in the afternoon I take a stroll through the garage, checking if the mechanics are busy. Usually they are, although I do not know enough about cars to know what they are doing. Stealing parts that command a good price on the black market possibly.

I have a good deal of time to read. At the moment I am halfway through Nixon's *Six Crises*. Captain Drabney sent it to me, along with a get-well card, when I was in the hospital.

The mail pouch is a major source of excitement. Ben writes frequently, although some of his missives are just pages torn out of the *Village Voice* or *The Nation* with furious marginalia scribbled in. Sarah wrote that she's trying to persuade him to leave his spleen to science.

A few days ago I received a letter from Bobbi. She called once when I was in the hospital, but I was asleep, and she didn't call back.

Dear Jim,

Glad to hear you're fit as a fiddle again. There *are* fiddles that bulge around the middle, aren't there?

I'm OK. I went to London for a week. Do you know Brown's Hotel? Pure blast from the past, but I was in the mood for sedate. It was just Mom and me and some credit cards getting the workout of their pathetic little plastic lives.

After we got back, I scouted New York. There was a job at *Mademoiselle* I could have had, but that stuff doesn't do it for me anymore. Plus the pay was seriously peanuts. I mean, spying is bad, but publishing is the pits.

As the postmark will doubtless have told your finely tuned brain, I'm back where the island breezes blow and the muggers talk with a cute accent. Yeah, I think I'm crazy, too, but at least Niso's not here, and Cort made me an offer I couldn't refuse. He's paying me five times what I got before. He's also proposed marriage a few dozen times. I've refused a few hundred times. Even so, I worry that in some weak moment I'll cave in. There's this idiot voice in my head that keeps saying, "At least he's not your standard lawyer or doctor."

Which is true, but on the other hand—well, you know what's on the other hand. I've got nothing against salt-and-pepper combos, but Cort is no Sidney Poitier.

You know what, though? The bastard's rich. Turns out he didn't give Niso all the stuff, just a stash he had put aside in case Niso got tough. The other half—the much larger half—he had stashed somewhere else.

I was ready to shoot him when he told me. After what I went through, I mean. I didn't talk to him for two days. Finally, though, he gave me this horrible gaudy necklace, and I broke down. He also made me president of the Windways Island Resort Corp. I was VP before.

Yes, that's my job, and yes, we are actually building a hotel. If it's good enough for a cover story, it's good enough for real, right? We used a few diamonds for seed money, and I talked it up with my investment banker friends in NYC. This time Bobbi is telling you the honest-to-God Truth with a capital *T* and that rhymes with Me.

Another thing he told me—you can believe it or not—was that when he hired me way back in the first place, it wasn't because he was overcome by my beauty and charm and intelligence; it was because you had spooked him with your questions about Lee, and he thought he could use me to keep track of what you were up to. I'm reporting this to show how modest and de-mure the new Bobbi is. Basically I think he made it all up because I had rejected him twenty or thirty times that morning and he was tired of being such a spineless worm.

Gotta go. Give Ben my disregards. For you, hugs and kisses from . . .

Your friend in crime,
BOBBI

P.S. It was Cort who leaked your bio sketch to the *Bugle*. It was sort of nasty, but he just did it 'cause he was jealous and thought it might get you kicked out. He's sorry now. The accompanying gift is his amends and thanks. Please note the atrocious taste. Marry *him*???

A small box held gold cuff links inset with very large diamonds. Bobbi is right, I'm afraid. They look like cheap costume jewelry.

I'll wear them to the Quatorze Juillet at the French Embassy. It is the event of the Bamako social season.